"The man y[ou're lookin]g for is named Adams."

"Adams," Mack Bolan repeated. It was the third name that Giorgio had given him. "Here's your money. I'm leaving now. I hope none of your boys do anything stupid."

The Executioner had taken less than a dozen steps when a gunner on the catwalk shouted, "I see him, Boom! Don't worry. I'll nail the bastard."

His boss's reply not to shoot was smothered by the thunder of a high-caliber rifle. Bolan juked to the right, spotted a lanky figure overhead and drilled the shooter with a burst of 9 mm slugs. It was the signal for guns to open up all over the warehouse.

The warrior took out the light with his next round. Jumping to his feet in a momentary lull, he bolted for the door, figuring he was in the clear.

A few yards were all that remained when Bolan glanced into the gloom and spotted a gunner with an Uzi. The man had the weapon trained on him, had him dead to rights. Even as the Executioner weaved to make himself harder to hit, the Uzi erupted.

DON PENDLETON's
MACK BOLAN®
SHOCK TACTIC

A GOLD EAGLE BOOK FROM
WORLDWIDE®

TORONTO • NEW YORK • LONDON
AMSTERDAM • PARIS • SYDNEY • HAMBURG
STOCKHOLM • ATHENS • TOKYO • MILAN
MADRID • WARSAW • BUDAPEST • AUCKLAND

First edition October 1995

ISBN 0-373-61444-6

Special thanks and acknowledgment to
David Robbins for his contribution to this work.

SHOCK TACTIC

Printed in U.S.A.

A fanatic is one who can't change his mind and won't change the subject.
—Sir Winston Churchill

I can't change a terrorist's mind or deter him from his chosen path of destruction. But when he interferes with the rights and well-being of others, I'll administer a jolt of reality that will bring him to his knees.
—Mack Bolan

CHAPTER ONE

It was just another typical Wednesday night at the Willamette Heights National Guard Armory in Portland, Oregon. Only three of the weekend warriors were on hand. Sergeant Gabe Simms and his two buddies showed up every Wednesday, since it was the one night of the week they had the indoor range all to themselves.

Simms made sure the outer door was locked, then turned and led the way across the main bay past a vintage World War II tank, which the Guardsmen rolled out twice a year to use in local parades.

"I can't wait to try out this new baby," Simms said eagerly, patting his duffel bag. "From what I hear, it's got the stopping power to drop a charging bull elephant."

Private Tony Arnetti snickered. "Then it sure should come in handy. The last I heard, Oregon is overrun with rampaging elephants."

"Yeah," Private Lucius Fry added. "Just be careful, Gabe. You don't want to kill off too many of those big tuskers. Next thing you know, the EPA will declare them an endangered species like the spotted owl and no one will be able to hunt them."

"Smart asses," Simms said jokingly. He opened the door to the narrow flight of concrete steps that would take them down to the firing range. "This is what I get for hanging out with a pair of idiots who don't appreciate real firepower."

"Now hold on, Sarge," Arnetti said. "I like a large-caliber gun as much as the next guy. Hell, I carry a .44 Magnum, don't I?" He paused and winked at Fry. "We just happen to think that a damned Wildey .475 Magnum is going a little overboard."

Fry snapped his fingers. "Hey, I've got an idea. Maybe Gabe would like to have a shooting contest. His new pistol against the tank."

"No way, man. The poor tank wouldn't stand a chance."

Simms ignored the ribbing of his two best friends and switched on the lights. Walking over to the counter, he set down the duffel, worked the zipper and took out the expensive carrying case he had special-ordered for his new weapon. Cradling it as if it were priceless, he gently put down the case and worked the combination tumblers.

"Look at this guy," Fry quipped. "You'd think he was carrying a million bucks in there."

Arnetti nodded. "He hasn't had that pistol two hours and already he's treating it better than he does his old lady."

"Up yours," Simms said. He raised the lid and sucked in his breath at the sight of the gleaming stainless-steel beauty nestled in the soft padding. "For your information, if my wife was this pretty I'd treat her the same way."

Fry clapped the sergeant on the shoulder. "You're a mighty brave man, Gabe, when Ruth isn't around to hear. I'd like to see you tell her that to her face."

Arnetti clucked in disapproval. "What, and have him take a rolling pin upside the head? He'd be in the hospital for a month."

"Keep it up," Simms said as he reverently lifted the .475 Magnum pistol in both hands, "and neither of you jerks will get to take a turn." His grin was vindictive. "Of course, I doubt either of you have ever handled a real man's gun before."

A target hung at the end of the nearest firing line. Simms walked over, slapped a magazine into the pistol and hefted the weapon. "I tell you, I feel like a kid at Christmas." Donning ear protectors, he practiced sighting down the incredibly long barrel. "Beautiful. Just beautiful," he murmured.

"I think he's in love," Arnetti said. From a pocket he took a small red plastic container that held two earplugs, which he inserted into his ears. "What about you?" he asked Fry. "Or do you want your eardrums ruptured?"

Fry simply stuck his fingers in his ears. "Ready when you are, Gabe," he called out.

Simms nodded. Firming his grip on the pistol, he sighted on the black silhouette, right where the heart would be. Then he squeezed the trigger. The boom was near deafening in the narrow confines of the range. The

Wildey kicked, but not nearly as much as he had thought it would. A gaping hole marked the exact spot where he had aimed. Smirking, Simms raised the barrel to his lips and kissed it.

"Oh, yuck," Arnetti said, grimacing. "This man is downright perverted. Next thing you know, he'll be sleeping with it."

"If I could, I would," Simms retorted. He pivoted to leer at his jealous buddies and stiffened on seeing a newcomer framed in the doorway. "Captain Fogarty!" he blurted. "This is a surprise."

The privates snapped to attention as the officer strolled over, his neatly manicured hands clasped behind his narrow back. "Gentlemen, at ease," Fogarty said, oozing the oily charm that had made him the bane of the unit.

Simms removed the headpiece. "What brings you here, sir? I can't recall ever seeing you on a weeknight before."

Fogarty's slick smile disappeared, replaced with a frown. "Are you implying that I don't do my job properly, Sergeant?"

"Never, sir," Simms answered quickly so as not to offend. If there was one thing he knew about Edward Claire Fogarty, it was that the man was as touchy as a nest of stirred-up hornets. "I merely meant—"

"I know what you meant," Fogarty said curtly. With a visible effort he controlled his temper and mustered a pale imitation of a friendly smile. "Actually you have a point. I don't come in near as often as I should during the week." His frown deepened. "I'd forgotten all about your weekly macho sessions."

"Macho sessions?" Simms repeated, barely able to hide his disgust. "We're the Guard, sir. Sure, we're not expected to be as combat ready as Marines, but we should keep our eye in." Reluctantly he added, "Would you like to try your hand?"

To the sergeant's relief, Fogarty shook his head. "I have paperwork to do. You men enjoy yourselves. And don't worry about disturbing me. Make as much noise as you want." Nodding at each of them, he sauntered to the steps and left.

None of the Guardsmen spoke until they were sure the officer was out of earshot. Arnetti broke the silence. "Frigging weird! What the hell was that all about?"

"Beats me, son," Fry said. "That comment about noise makes no sense. He knows the range is sound-proofed."

"Maybe he doesn't," Arnetti replied. "There's a reason everyone calls him 'Rocks for Brains' behind his back."

Simms shrugged. "Who cares about him? We came to have some fun, and I don't intend to let that stuck-up jackass spoil it. So let's get to shooting."

For the next half hour the three men took turns with the Wildey. Then Tony Arnetti produced his Astra Model 44 and took up a position at the head of another line. "Want to shoot for points?" he asked Fry. "Loser buys the beer when we're done."

"In a minute. Nature calls."

Arnetti faced the target, loaded six rounds in the cylinder and banged off the shots. After reloading he waited a while for Fry to return. "Where the heck is he?" he muttered, impatient to win the beer.

A few more minutes passed by. Simms continued to practice with his new weapon. At last Arnetti walked over and tapped him on the shoulder. When the sergeant turned, he commented, "Just to let you know. Lucky went upstairs and should have been back by now. I figure that rat Fogarty collared him to do some work, so I'm going up to see."

"We'll both go. We're not on duty. Fogarty has no business forcing us to work after duty hours unless it's on something really important."

Both soldiers deposited their guns on the counter. Arnetti took the lead. Halfway up the flight he cupped a hand to his mouth and hollered, "Lucky! What's keeping you? Afraid to lose?"

There was no answer. At the top of the stairs Arnetti paused to scan the bay. Fry was nowhere in sight. On the opposite side a lamp burned in the captain's closed office. The bathroom door was also shut.

"I'll go check on him," Arnetti volunteered.

"Hurry it up," Simms said, annoyed at having to break off their practice session. Placing both hands on his hips, he idly surveyed the enormous bay. To his surprise, he noticed the outer door hung wide open. "I know I locked that," he said to himself. Heading toward the front, he muttered, "Stupid officers. If it wasn't for noncoms like me, the military would fall to pieces in no time.''

Simms had gone only ten feet when he glanced around and saw Arnetti frozen in midstride, gaping at the bathroom door. Puzzled, he halted and was about to ask why, when from the rear of the armory, where the munitions were stored, there came a loud thud.

The sergeant's puzzlement grew. No one was supposed to be back in the arms depot. The captain was in his office filling out forms in triplicate, and the two privates were across the bay. Deciding to investigate, he hastened over to Arnetti. ''Tony, did you hear that noise?''

The young soldier pointed at the bottom of the door. Simms looked and felt his blood run cold. Seeping across the concrete was a red pool. Taking a stride, he yanked on the handle and could hardly credit his eyes when he saw Fry prone on the floor, his throat slit from ear to ear. ''God Almighty!'' he blurted.

''I'll get the captain!'' Arnetti said, recovering his wits. He dashed to the office door and threw it open without knocking. A tall intruder loomed before him, a man garbed in olive green *ninja*-style clothing. Arnetti blinked in surprise. There was a distinct click, and the intruder's hand swept toward him, holding the five-inch blade of a sleek knife. At the last possible moment Arnetti jerked aside.

Gabe Simms was equally flabbergasted, but he recovered quickly and charged to his friend's aid. He was too late. The intruder shifted, reversed his grip on the hilt and sank the blade deep into Arnetti's chest. The private went rigid, clutched feebly at the man's arm, then collapsed.

Simms would have torn into the killer had he not seen two similarly dressed individuals appear abruptly in the doorway to the arms depot. A fourth materialized at the front entrance.

The sergeant knew his life was on the line. He needed a means of defending himself, and the first thing he thought of was the Wildey. Bolting toward the stairs, he tried to figure out who the intruders were but had too little information to go on.

Simms figured that he couldn't count on help from Fogarty. The captain, he assumed, had to have been the first to be slain. He was the only one left. And since the armory was situated well off Leif Ericson Drive, he doubted whether any of the people who lived nearby had noticed anything out of the ordinary and phoned the police.

He made it to the head of the stairs a good ten feet ahead of his pursuers. He took the steps on the fly, dreading that at any moment he would feel a searing sensation in his back, but he reached the firing range unharmed and darted to the counter. The .475 Magnum pistol was fully loaded. All he had to do was scoop it up and whirl in a two-handed crouch, ready for action. Only no one was there.

Simms stepped warily to the left so he could see up the steps to the top. The intruders hadn't followed him. So now he had a decision to make. He could stay put and hope they left, or he could confront them and stop them from doing whatever they were up to. It really wasn't much of a choice, not as long as he wore a Guard uniform.

Keeping his back to the right-hand wall, Simms crept back up to the bay. He heard an odd scraping noise, as if a crate were being dragged across the floor. Someone whispered and was answered. Taking a deep breath, he steeled himself, then sprang into the open, the Wildey leveled, his every nerve primed.

One of the intruders stood by the front door, waiting for a second man who was indeed dragging a crate toward him.

Simms covered them both and bellowed, "Hold it right there! Hands over your heads!"

Neither intruder moved. Simms took a few steps to put himself in a better position to take them both. He had never shot anyone before, but he wouldn't hesitate to drop the pair if they balked at obeying his orders. He owed them for Tony and Lucky.

Too late, Simms thought to glance at the tank. A green-garbed figure was already in midair, a gleaming knife in each hand. Simms threw himself backward and narrowly missed having his neck ripped open. Shifting, he tried to bring his pistol to bear, but the man was faster. A blade struck the barrel and knocked the pistol aside just as Simms stroked the trigger.

The attacker closed in, arms flailing. Simms took a blow to the chin that dazed him. Another smashed his wrist and he almost lost his grip on his pistol. Desperately he kicked out, hoping to shatter the man's knee, but the intruder danced aside, coiled and lunged. Simms was caught flat-footed. The tip of the blade sheared into his chest, glanced off a rib and tore into his vital organs. He attempted valiantly to raise the Wildey a final time, but it was too heavy. He collapsed to the floor.

The green-garbed intruder stood over the fallen Guardsman and uttered a short, wicked laugh. "Traitor to humanity!" he said, then kicked the corpse a few times for the sheer thrill of it.

Another man near the door beckoned and whispered, "Enough! Let's get out of here!"

"Yeah, yeah," the killer grumbled.

Moments later the four men in green were gone, leaving the Willamette Heights National Guard Armory as deathly quiet as a tomb.

CHAPTER TWO

Mack Bolan, a.k.a. the Executioner, had a special dislike for traitors. In his opinion, anyone who would sell out his country was beneath contempt. There was no justification for betraying hearth and flag.

So when Hal Brognola, director of the Sensitive Operations Group at Stony Man Farm, offered him a case the FBI had pending that involved a suspected traitor linked to the deaths of three Oregon National Guard members, there was no way he could turn down his friend.

A second reason was equally as important. The Feds suspected there might be a link between the theft of ordinance at the armory where the Guardsmen died and an upcoming visit to Portland by the President.

The warrior now sat in a parked Jeep a block from the home of Edward Claire Fogarty on a chilly Friday night. He was about to pour coffee from a thermos when the front door of the officer's modest house opened and out stepped his mark.

Bolan had seen photos and recognized the man immediately. As bait went, Fogarty was unremarkable—a thin, balding, bowlegged specimen whose sole claim to distinction was the silver bars he had allegedly disgraced—allegedly, because there was no proof of a link

between the theft at the armory and the hefty sum that
had been deposited in Fogarty's savings account just
one day before the hardware was taken. But because
several of the bills had been traced to a bank robbery
committed by a fanatical organization, the FBI was
suspicious.

Brognola's plan had been simple—send in Bolan,
then goad Fogarty into doing something stupid with a
well-timed phone call. At four that afternoon Fogarty
had answered his telephone on the third ring and heard
an anonymous female voice say "Be careful. They know
what you did." Simple, but effective.

Bolan wondered what was going through the man's
mind. Fogarty hadn't made any calls after the woman
hung up, as the warrior well knew since the man's house
had been bugged and Bolan had a portable receiver in
the Jeep. Five hours had gone by, and the warrior was
almost convinced that their rabbit would never flush
when Fogarty appeared. The Executioner capped the
thermos, stuffed it under the seat and bent low to the
right in case the man drove in his direction.

Luck was with the warrior. The National Guard captain squealed out of his driveway and turned east. Bolan gunned the Jeep, slowly pulled out and followed at
a discreet distance. Traffic was light until Fogarty
turned north onto Union Avenue.

Bolan narrowed the gap a little. He could ill afford to
lose his quarry and kept his gaze locked on the sedan's
taillights. If Brognola's hunch was right, the captain
would lead them to much bigger fish, human piranhas

the FBI had been after for quite some time without success.

A series of turns brought them to Interstate 5. Soon Bolan was cruising north toward Washington. Was it possible, he reflected, that Fogarty was fleeing to Canada? He decided that wasn't the case, since the man hadn't withdrawn the ten thousand dollars first, and he couldn't see Fogarty skipping the country without his blood money.

They came eventually to the bridge over the Columbia River. Bolan settled into place two cars behind the sedan. The captain made the task easier by sticking to the speed limit. For about fifteen minutes they bore steadily northward, at which point Fogarty took the Salmon Creek exit.

The Executioner had to fall farther back or risk detection. Salmon Creek was a small town, the traffic sparse. His quarry turned eastward and in due course came to a rural road that wound into dense woodland. There was no other traffic, forcing Bolan to widen the distance to a quarter of a mile.

Several miles later Fogarty made a turn onto a dirt road. Dust choked the air, making it hard for Bolan to see more than twenty yards. He held the speedometer to under twenty miles per hour and rolled down the window so he could listen for the sound of the sedan's engine.

The road twisted and turned, a serpentine ribbon winding steadily deeper into forest. A myriad sparkling stars dotted the firmament. Twice owls hooted close at hand, and once a coyote yipped in the distance.

Bolan's gut instinct told him to switch off the headlights and rely on his parking lights alone. He had to cut his speed even more, but he also reduced the odds of being seen. The road angled up a grade. At the crest, the big man braked to survey the countryside.

Several hundred yards below, the sedan threaded through tall pines and firs. As Bolan watched, the glare of headlights bathed a fair-size cabin. Fogarty pulled in beside two other vehicles and parked.

Instantly Bolan shut off the Jeep's engine. He slid out of the vehicle and removed his gray windbreaker. Thanks to the black skinsuit he wore underneath, he blended into the dark as if part of it. It took only a few moments for him to take an M-16 from under a blanket covering the rear seat and head out at a dogtrot.

The Executioner was rigged for war. In addition to the M-16, a 9 mm Beretta rode in a shoulder holster under his left arm. On his right hip was a .44 Desert Eagle. He had a throwing knife strapped to his wrist, a Ka-bar fighting knife nestled in a sheath low on his right leg and the hidden pockets of his skinsuit were packed with more lethal tools of his clandestine trade.

Fine particles of dust still hung in the air. Bolan breathed shallowly as he moved along the edge of the road, alert for booby traps and electronic surveillance devices. The first was a very real possibility, the latter unlikely since there were no power lines to the cabin, and surveillance devices would use up a generator's fuel that much sooner. Still, it never paid to be careless.

Soon Bolan reached the vehicles. In addition to the sedan, there was a brown Jeep with temporary plates and a small foreign pickup sporting outsize tires. Gliding past the vehicles, the warrior gained a corner of the cabin and squatted in the deep shadows to listen. Muted voices rose inside. Sidestepping to a cracked window, he cocked an ear.

"You can see why I came. What am I going to do? If they're on to me, I don't dare draw my money out. They might be waiting for me to do just that so they can arrest me."

That had to be Fogarty, Bolan mused. The high-pitched, whiny voice matched his physique.

A deeper voice growled, "I don't believe this. I really don't believe this."

"What's not to believe, Hunter? I wouldn't lie to you. A woman did call. She said exactly what I told you. It shows the Feds are on to us. We have to act fast or it will be too late," Fogarty responded.

The man named Hunter snorted in contempt. "You really do take the cake. You know that, chump?"

"Now see here—" Fogarty began indignantly.

Bolan heard a sharp crack, as of a flat hand striking a cheek, then the crash of a chair as someone was knocked to the floor. Reasoning that everyone in the cabin would have their attention fixed on Fogarty and Hunter, he raised an eye to the windowsill and studied the layout inside.

In addition to Fogarty, four men occupied the single room. One lounged near the front door, two others sat at a table. All were armed. The captain was on his back, a hand pressed to his scarlet cheek, the overturned chair beside him. Rearing above it was a tall, powerfully built man with crew-cut blond hair who wore a blue muscle shirt that highlighted his bodybuilder physique. Hunter, Bolan guessed.

"You'll do the listening, not me," the blond powerhouse growled, his fists poised to strike. "You're the one who broke our agreement. Jase told you not to show your face here ever again once you got your greedy mitts on the ten grand. You should have listened to him."

"But I came here to warn you! Weren't you listening to a word I said? I think the Feds are after us."

Hunter straightened, his features as hard as granite. "Wrong. The Feds might be on to *you,* but they're not on to us. At least they weren't. We covered our tracks too damn good."

It would have been easy for Bolan to take the whole bunch then and there, but he held off. So far nothing had been said to confirm the link the Feds suspected. There had been a clue, but nothing concrete, nothing Brognola would accept as proof positive.

Fogarty had risen to his knees. Quite clearly he was scared to death and trying hard not to let his fright show. "I don't see why you have to manhandle me, mister," he blustered. "We're on the same side. I helped you out in a big way, didn't I? And this is how you return the favor?"

Hunter wore a scowl of utter disgust. "You miserable little worm. We're not on the same side, as you call it, and we never will be. You sold out the men under you for money. That makes you scum in my book."

"Oh?" Fogarty said, standing. Anger lent him courage. "For your information, I didn't expect them to be there that night. Hardly anyone ever is on weeknights." He jabbed a bony finger at the bigger man. "You were the one who jumped the gun. The plan was for me to let you in so you could take the crate and get out with a minimum of fuss. Hell, if things had gone right, the theft wouldn't have been noticed for weeks, until inventory time. By then you would have been long gone."

Hunter folded his arms across his broad chest and made no reply.

"The plan still would have worked," Fogarty railed on, "if you had kept a low profile. There was no reason for you to kill Fry. If you'd let him do his thing and go on back down to the range, your men could have snuck out without anyone being the wiser. But no! You had to get carried away."

"Are you through?" Hunter asked in a tone that a wiser man than the captain would have heeded.

"No, I'm not," Fogarty replied. "I won't stand still for being blamed for your incompetence. What was that silly business with the green uniforms? It seems to me that you must have watched too many martial-arts movies when you were a kid. Either that or you just like to dress up and pretend you're a real man like—''

Whatever else he was going to say was strangled off by the iron clamp Hunter applied to his throat. Fogarty struggled, punching at his captor's corded arm to no avail. Hunter had the air of a pit bull with a poodle in its jaws.

"Let me tell you something," the big man declared. "I wear that uniform with pride. I'm ready to give my life in the service of the whole frigging planet, which is more than can be said for an ignorant, spineless, fascist flunky like you." Hunter gave Fogarty a violent shake. "All you serve is one measly country, which just happens to be the worst polluter on the globe!"

Bolan had waited long enough. No mention had been made of the big fish he was after, but it was obvious the link existed. He shifted while reaching for a CS grenade and saw the dark eyes of the lanky man near the front door dart toward the window. There was no time to duck from sight.

"Look! There!" the man shouted, and brought a slung Uzi into play by whipping it up and firing a short burst.

Rounds chewed into the wood above Bolan's head as he dropped. The window shattered in a spectacular spray of stinging slivers. Palming the M-7 A-3, the warrior yanked on the pin, twisted and hurled the grenade through the opening. He moved to the corner and crouched, ready to cut loose when the men broke from the cabin.

The chemical agent in the grenade was so potent that a few whiffs were enough to induce a fit of coughing and vomiting, to say nothing of making it hard to breathe and searing the armpits and other moist areas of the body with burning pain.

Bolan expected the men to come barreling out at any moment. There was only the one door. A glance showed a vile cloud spewing from the broken window. No one was trying to climb out, which was just as well with so many jagged fingers of glass waiting to slash them to ribbons.

Critical seconds went by. At a loss to explain why the occupants didn't appear, Bolan started to slide around to the front. Then the crack of a twig to his rear galvanized him. He dropped into a crouch and whirled.

Advancing through the pale cloud was the lanky gunner with the Uzi. He swatted at the chemical smoke to disperse it and spotted the warrior.

Some men would have been startled by the Uzi-bearer's unexpected advent. They would have thrown their lives away by wondering what he was doing there when he was supposed to still be inside. But not Mack Bolan. He had seen too much combat, been in too many similar situations. So finely honed were his reflexes that as soon as he set eyes on the man, he stroked the trigger of the M-16.

Traveling at over three thousand feet per second, the 5.56 mm hailstorm struck the gunner before his brain had quite registered the warrior's presence. He was stitched from his groin to his throat, his body hurled backward, as if by an unseen catapult, to crumple in a miserable lifeless heap.

The metallic chatter of the M-16 still rang in Bolan's ears when he turned and dived. None too soon. Fireflies blossomed in the darkness behind the cabin. He hit the ground and scrambled on his hands and knees as the patch of earth he had just vacated was chewed to bits by a swarm of lead.

Bolan recognized the telltale tinny burp of an Ingram M-10 or an M-11, with a MAC suppressor, and one or two other subguns. The hardware was more sophisticated than he had been led to expect and put the mission in a whole new light.

Rising but staying bent at the waist, Bolan sprinted to the far corner of the cabin and flew past it into the trees. No gunfire greeted his appearance, which told him the killers weren't true pros. Professionals would have covered both ends of the cabin, not just one. Circling wide to the left, he probed the night for the four men who were left.

The sound of running feet alerted Bolan that he was concentrating on the wrong area. Annoyed at himself for not taking into account his quarry would rather flee than fight, he raced through the brush toward the vehicles.

The warrior was still a good twenty yards from them when the pickup and the brown Jeep roared to life. Their headlights popped on, one right after the other, illuminating Bolan as if it were broad daylight. Tucking the stock of his rifle to his shoulder, the Executioner aimed at the brilliant circles of light. The Jeep's exploded first, then the pickup's.

Bolan elevated the M-16 to go for the windshields. He thought the two vehicles would back up and speed off, but the driver of the pickup had other ideas. It leapt forward, engine roaring, and rushed toward Bolan like a charging bull, its huge tires flinging clods of dirt high into the air.

The warrior held his ground and fired a half-dozen rounds into the windshield, which splintered and cracked but stayed intact. It didn't deter the driver, who sloughed the vehicle to make it harder to hit, then streaked straight as an arrow for the big man. Bolan threw himself out of harm's way, firing in midair, his shots lodging into the pickup's body but doing no major damage.

Rolling as he landed, the warrior got up on one knee. His magazine was almost empty, so he expertly slid it out and slapped in a new one. He heard the Jeep speeding away up the dirt road, but there was nothing he could do. The truck had made a tight U-turn and was thundering back toward him.

Again the stock molded to Bolan's shoulder. The tinted windshield prevented his seeing the driver, so he fixed a hasty bead on the approximate spot where the man's chest should be, and fired. This time the glass dissolved, cascading onto the hood and into the cab. Bolan glimpsed a dark silhouette crouched low over the wheel. He tried to compensate, but the pickup was almost on him. Rising, he bolted to the right.

The vehicle veered sharply, its bumper rushing at the warrior like a chrome battering ram. Only a last-second leap enabled Bolan to save himself. Spinning, he drilled the rear window and the cab with a sustained burst, but to no effect.

Looping around, the pickup roared toward the big man in black a third time. The only visible part of the driver was the crown of his head, above the steering wheel. Bolan snapped off a few shots while rapidly retreating. He was going to use the same tactic as before, which was to wait until the truck was so close he could clearly see its shattered headlights, then jump safely aside.

Fate intervened. The Executioner had backpedaled a dozen feet and was girding himself for the jump when he inadvertently stepped into a rut. His left heel made contact and he slipped. Throwing his arms out, he succeeded in keeping his balance. But the distraction had proved costly, allowing the pickup to bear down on him.

The driver smiled grimly, thinking he had his target dead to rights.

Death was imminent. The vehicle's grille was mere yards away. Whether Bolan threw himself to the right or the left was irrelevant. No matter which he did, the pickup would smash into him with all the force of a runaway train.

So Bolan did neither. He dropped straight down onto his back, flattening just as the truck reached him. Thanks to the oversize tires, the undercarriage was a good three feet above the ground. Then the vehicle was above him, and the heat of the engine seared his face like that of a blast furnace. But the Executioner had the M-16 in his left hand, aligned with the length of his leg, while his right held the Desert Eagle. He banged off two shots, shooting up into the floor directly under the driver's seat. The prospect of a ricochet didn't worry him. The cartridges had enough penetrating power behind them to punch through both the metal and the seat. A strangled yelp confirmed he had scored, or else had a near miss.

Then the pickup zoomed past and Bolan rose. He shoved the Desert Eagle back into its holster and brought the M-16 into play.

The driver had apparently had enough. He angled to the left, heading toward the road.

By that time the Jeep was well out of range. Bolan wondered if the pickup driver had deliberately delayed him so the other vehicle could get away. It would prove costly. The warrior flicked the M-203 grenade launcher's safety to the forward position, waited for the monster pickup to put enough distance between them so he wouldn't be hit by stray shrapnel and let the grenade fly.

To be on the safe side, Bolan hugged the grass. The explosion lit up the forest. Metal screeched as if alive, and flames shot into the sky. The pickup became airborne. Resembling a blazing meteorite, it sailed its own length, smashed into the earth and tumbled end over end, casting debris and flames in all directions. When it came to rest, it was a burning wreck, the driver a charred husk.

Bolan knew better than to leap erect and expose himself to possible unfriendly fire. Snaking into the trees, he eased into a squat in the shelter of a towering pine, his shoulder propped on the trunk. In the distance the Jeep vanished around a bend. The only sound was the loud crackle of the flames consuming the pickup.

Had any of the hardmen been left behind? That was the big question Bolan had to answer. Fogarty's sedan, he noticed, was right where it had been. The captain had either fled in the Jeep or he was hiding nearby.

The warrior commenced a sweep in a grid pattern. It took ten minutes, but finally he assured himself that he was alone. Catfooting to the side of the cabin, he peered in the broken window. A pair of feet were visible under the table.

Moving to the door, Bolan leaned on the jamb and swept his fingers over the ground until he located a suitable rock. He chucked it inside, listened to it clatter and entered in a combat crouch, the M-16 tucked to his waist.

The precaution proved unnecessary. Fogarty lay on his side, his neck bent at an unnatural angle, his throat horribly mangled. Only someone enormously strong could have snapped his spine and pulped the soft flesh of his throat at the same time. The warrior made a mental note to be extra wary of the blond bodybuilder when he encountered him again.

Bolan rummaged through the traitor's pockets and found a small notebook. Evidently Fogarty had been the meticulous type. Listed were medical appointments, dental appointments, meetings with his supervisors and others. On page twenty-three Bolan came across the link he had been looking for. Noted were a date, a time and three simple words that were bound to interest Hal Brognola and set the government's law-enforcement wheels into motion in a massive manhunt: Creed. Green Rage.

CHAPTER THREE

"This stinks, Striker," Hal Brognola stated while pacing back and forth in the office he had been temporarily allotted in the Federal Building in Portland. "It confirms the meager Intel we have."

"That Green Rage has graduated from a mere nuisance to a major threat?" Bolan said.

"Exactly." The big Fed faced the picture window and stared out over the downtown Portland skyline. "Apparently Jason Creed himself approached Fogarty. It took only two meetings and that worm was willing to turn Judas."

Bolan stretched out his legs and steepled his fingers. "I know a little about this Creed. Give me an update."

Brognola moved to the large desk that dominated the room and flipped open a manila folder. "Jason Muncy Creed, age thirty-eight, height six feet six inches, with an ego to match his size. Born in Indiana, raised in California. His father worked in Silicon Valley. Creed must have inherited some of his dad's smarts because he was a whiz at science and did so well on his SATs that he was able to get into Berkeley. That's when the trouble began. He took up with the woman who headed the San Francisco chapter of the Nature Brigade. You've heard of them?"

"Sort of like Greenpeace, only prone to violence."

"You've got that right. They believe humankind is raping and pillaging the planet, and they've set themselves up as the saviors of Earth. Members have been arrested for spiking trees, sabotaging lumber and mining equipment, vandalizing corporations they brand as polluters. All the usual stuff." Brognola took a seat. "Creed was arrested three times in connection with their activities."

"Is he still a card-carrying member?"

"No. Creed and the Nature Brigade went their separate ways quite a while ago. Believe it or not, the Nature Brigade's methods weren't violent enough to suit Creed." Brognola slowly shook his head. "The lunatic has declared war on the human race in the name of protecting the environment."

"Another fanatic."

"Which doesn't make him any less dangerous," Brognola said. "He founded his own organization, Green Rage, two years ago. Shortly after that he went underground and hasn't been seen or heard from since, except for the crimes his little band of crazies commits." He ran his finger down a list. "Bank robberies, kidnapping, murder, extortion, the illegal use of explosives—you name it, Creed's bunch have done it."

"They rob banks to finance their activities?"

"And kidnap children of corporate execs. Six months ago they snatched the five-year-old daughter of Miles Wilson, CEO of ChemTex, from her day-care center. Creed phoned Wilson and promised to release the girl in exchange for half a million in cash. Wilson agreed and wouldn't let the FBI or the police interfere.'' The big Fed closed his eyes and wearily rubbed the lids. ''Green Rage got the money. About a week later Wilson's daughter was found in a trash Dumpster.''

Bolan frowned. ''I remember hearing it on the news.'' Standing, he walked to the window and gazed down at the people filing along the sidewalk. Among them were a few children. Once, in another lifetime or so it seemed, Bolan had dreamed of one day having kids of his own. Circumstances had decreed otherwise, but he still saw children as the treasures they were, and it filled him with revulsion that a man like Creed had coldly murdered that innocent little girl.

''Nailing Green Rage is one of our top priorities,'' Brognola went on, ''but so far they've stayed two steps ahead of every agency after them.'' He slapped the file shut. ''Recently we heard through the grapevine that they had something big planned. Then they hit that armory and stole four M-72 missile launchers.''

''Maybe they intend to take out an armored car,'' Bolan suggested.

Brognola leaned back in his chair. ''If that was all I thought they were going to do, I wouldn't be personally involved.''

''What do you mean?''

''In two days Portland is hosting a major 'Timber Summit.' With so much of U.S. timberland ruled off-limits by the courts, a conference has been called to chart a new course for the country in the coming century. Unless new markets are found, we stand to see the cost of all wood-related products go through the roof. The cost of housing alone will triple. Our economy would be crippled.''

''So you think Green Rage will try to disrupt the conference?''

''Or worse. Representatives from American timber concerns and their counterparts from several leading timber-producing countries will be on hand. So will the man who called for this summit in the first place.''

With a sinking feeling in his gut, Bolan said, ''Who did, as if I can't guess.''

''The President.''

''Damn.''

''My sentiments exactly. It can't be a coincidence that Green Rage struck when and where they did. They hate timber companies. Creed once said that the planet would be better off if all the people were gone so the trees could grow unmolested.''

''Too bad one never fell on him.''

The big Fed was in no mood for levity. ''Green Rage is going to hit the conference. I'd stake my life on it. Security will be tight, but you know as well as I do that it won't be airtight. If Creed is determined enough, he'll find a way to wreak havoc.''

Bolan returned to his chair. ''Count me in on the long haul for this one. What do you want me to do?''

''That's just it. There's nothing you can do until we get another lead. There's nothing anyone can do. Unless we get a lucky break, the first inkling we might have of Creed's plan is when the President of these United States is blown to kingdom come.''

GARTH HUNTER WAS in a foul mood. Usually killing someone with his bare hands gave him a feeling of intense satisfaction. But not this time. Since leaving the cabin he hadn't stopped mentally cursing Fogarty for being the biggest jackass ever born. If he had it to do again, he would take more time in killing the bastard, maybe castrate him first.

The Jeep came to an intersection and Hunter braked. He looked both ways, then proceeded at the speed limit. Traffic was light on the outskirts of Portland at that time of night, just as he had anticipated.

For the past five hours Hunter had been lying low in a grove northwest of the city. Convinced that he had shaken pursuit and that the Feds had no idea where he was, he had taken it on himself to go in search of new wheels.

"I don't think this is such a bright idea," complained the burly man in the passenger seat.

"I agree," the scarecrow in the back chimed in.

Hunter glanced at each of them in turn. The man on his right, Ely Welch, had been with the movement for less than a year. Pete Slater, the human string bean, was a relative newcomer. Both of them, he suspected, had joined Green Rage more for the money Creed lavished on them than out of any sense of outrage over the atrocities being committed against the environment.

"We need new wheels," Hunter reiterated. "The Feds might have a make on this one. So keep your eyes peeled for another four-wheel drive."

"What's with you and four-wheel drives?" Slater asked. "Why can't we snatch a nice Caddy or a Rolls for once? Hell, anything with air-conditioning and padded seats would be nice."

"Spoken like a true New Yorker," Hunter snapped. "All you can think of is how to make life easier on yourself." He gestured at the city. "But this isn't New York. You're in the Pacific Northwest now, mister, where there are more rural roads than there are highways and city streets combined. If we need to make a fast getaway, we can't very well head into the mountains in a Caddy, now, can we?"

That silenced them, but for only a minute. Welch cleared his throat and remarked, "Shouldn't we contact Creed? He'll want to know what happened."

"Yeah," Slater said. "We have to tell him about Tim. Those stinking Feds must have used a bazooka on his pickup, the way it lit up the sky like that."

"Bazooka, my butt," Hunter said. "And for your information, there was only one guy."

"Bull," Slater disagreed. "I'd guess there were five or six, minimum. The Feds wouldn't be stupid enough to send in just one man to take us out, even if it was a Green Beret."

It took all of Hunter's self-control to keep him from smashing Slater in the mouth. For far too long he had put up with the man's constant whining and not-so-subtle digs at his background. "I wasn't a Green Beret," he said lamely. "I was a Marine."

"You still dress and act like one," Welch stated. "I'm surprised you ever quit the service. Why didn't you put in your twenty and retire with a fat pension?"

"I didn't have a choice," Hunter said, and let it go at that. As far as he was concerned, his past was none of their business.

"So what about Creed?" Slater prompted. "Do we call him or not?"

"Not."

"Mind giving me a reason?"

"Once an envio squad is in the field, there is to be no contact between squad members and home base," Hunter stated, repeating their orders verbatim. "We're committed to the assignment we were given. There's no turning back."

"I'm not talking about backing out on the job we were given to do," Slater said, then fluttered his lips in exasperation. "Ah, what's the use? Trying to get through to you is like talking to a brick wall. It must be all that brainwashing the Marines put you through."

Hunter's last vestige of restraint snapped. Burying the brake pedal, he spun and seized hold of Slate's shirt.

"I've had about all I'm going to take from you," Hunter warned. "Orders or no orders, President or no President, the next time you give me lip I'm going to rip your lungs out with my bare hands."

"Is that a fact, Mr. High and Mighty?" Slater said, a sly smile curling his lips. "I'd think twice, if I were you. And I'd let go of me right this second unless you're fond of looking like a sieve."

Something pricked Hunter's abdomen, and he glanced down to see a doubled-edged boot knife pointed at his gut. One wrong move and Slater would bury it in him.

Welch had backed up against the door in case they started swinging. "Enough is enough, fellas. We're all supposed to be on the same side, aren't we? Why do you always have to be at each other's throats?"

"Because the Marine here thinks he can lord it over us anytime he pleases," Slater said. "Haven't you noticed how he looks down his nose at us? He treats us as if we're not good enough to be in Green Rage, and I, for one, am sick and tired of his rotten attitude."

Hunter was so mad his temples pounded. As always, his blood lust nearly got the better of him. He would have torn into Slater despite the knife if not for the fact that killing Slater would drastically cut the odds of their mission being a success. They had already lost one man. He choked down his pride and anger and slowly eased back into his seat.

"That's better," Welch said, patting Hunter's arm. "Look, I know Creed put you in charge of this squad, but that's no cause for you—" Suddenly he glanced to the right and gave a small gasp of alarm. "No! Not now! What do we do?"

"Of all the lousy luck," Slater declared.

Hunter looked and wanted to kick himself for being stupid enough to stop in the middle of the street. A police car cruised slowly toward them. He could see two officers in the front seat, one talking into a mike, no doubt running a make on the Jeep's license.

"What do we do?" Welch repeated anxiously. "They have us dead to rights."

"It'll take a minute for the dispatcher to get back to them with any wants or warrants," Hunter said calmly. "So we play it cool, act innocent. And take them out when they let down their guard."

"With the Uzi and the Ingram?" Welch asked. "We'll wake up everyone for a mile around. This place will be swarming with cops in no time."

"Then we do it quietly," Hunter said, pleased that he was staying so levelheaded in the midst of the crisis. It was a source of deep pride for him that his hair-trigger temper never muddied his thinking in combat. When push came to shove, when he was faced with a life-or-death situation, he always kept his wits about him and did what had to be done. "I'll take the driver. Slater, slip out the far door and nail the other cop on my cue."

Shifting into Park, Hunter plastered a smile on his face, threw the door open and climbed out just as the officer behind the wheel did the same. "Evening, sir," he said pleasantly. "Thanks for stopping. Maybe you can help us."

"What seems to be the problem?" the young officer responded, his right hand resting on his hip within inches of his pistol.

"I wish I knew," Hunter said. "We were driving along when it suddenly quit moving on us. I think it could be the transmission, but I'm no mechanic."

"May I see your license?" the patrolman requested. "I'm sorry to bother you, but we've had a report of a prowler in this area."

"Yeah. No problem." Hunter pulled out his wallet, making a show of twisting sideways so the cop could see that he was unarmed. He wasn't fooled by the prowler routine. It was the oldest scam in the book, one cops used to check a person's ID when they had no legal cause to do so. The officer in the patrol car was holding the mike in his lap, apparently waiting for a reply from the dispatcher.

"Fred Mitchell," the officer said, reading the phony license aloud. "You live on the east side of the city, I see."

"Yes, sir," Hunter lied, glad that Creed was able to obtain forged documents only an expert could tell were fake. "My buddies and I are on our way home from a friend's. Wouldn't you know it, my Jeep would pick tonight to conk out on me. Murphy's Law, I guess."

"I guess," the officer said, handing back the wallet.

"Is there anything you can do to help us, Officer Hardy?" Hunter said, leaning forward as he read the cop's nameplate. "We tried pushing the thing, but it wouldn't budge, even in neutral. Without a tow truck, there's no way we can move it."

Hardy pivoted and pointed. "There's a pay phone about four blocks from here on the south side of the street, in the parking lot of a hardware store. You can't miss it."

"Thanks, sir," Hunter said. He had been observing the other cop on the sly, so he was ready when the man tossed the mike down and leapt out of the cruiser as if the seat were on fire.

"Hardy! The Feds have—"

Everything happened at once. Slater materialized behind the second officer, clamped a hand over his mouth and stabbed him in the side repeatedly. Hardy clawed for his service piece, but Hunter was faster. A finely timed karate chop across the young officer's throat staggered him. A second blow, to the kidneys, slammed the officer against the patrol car and caused the pistol to fall from his nerveless fingers.

Hunter struck several more times, using his precise knowledge of human anatomy to land blows where they would be the most painful. Hardy arched his back, crying out. Gripping the officer's jaw in both brawny hands, Hunter jammed his right knee against the man's spine and heaved backward.

Hardy frantically tried to throw himself to either side but could not. He clutched at Hunter's thick fingers, seeking to pry them loose, but he might as well have been trying to pry concrete apart. His movements became more desperate, and he gurgled deep in his throat.

Every sinew on Hunter's superbly developed body stood out in stark relief. Gritting his teeth, he exerted more and more pressure until there was a loud snap and the lawman went as limp as a wet rag. Letting the body slump over, Hunter stared at the palms of his hands. That exquisite tingling he loved so much was back, running up his arms and down his spine to the heels of his feet. He savored the sensation, knowing the glow wouldn't last long.

Welch had climbed from the Jeep. "Dear Lord! Cops! We just wasted two cops! We must be crazy."

"What's the matter?" Hunter responded. "You've killed before. Remember that bank guard? And the lumberjack who had the flat tire?"

"That was different," Welch said. "Cops are special. Kill one, and the others never rest until they've nailed you." He looked in both directions. "Let's get out of here before someone sees us."

"First things first," Hunter said. Stooping, he slipped his arms around Hardy and stuffed the body in the back seat. Slater did the same with the other policeman. The radio was quiet but wouldn't be for long. Once the dispatcher realized that Hardy and his partner were taking too long to check in, backups would be sent.

"Slater, you go with Welch. Follow me in the Jeep," Hunter directed. Sliding into the police car, he executed a U-turn and drove the four blocks to the hardware store. It was closed. Wheeling to the rear, he parked in the deepest shadows he could find. As he began to climb out, the speaker squawked with static, then a female voice spoke urgently.

"Unit Fourteen, please respond."

"Not in this life, bimbo," Hunter quipped as he hurried to the Jeep. Welch slid over so he could drive.

Speed was essential. Hunter bore south for several miles before turning eastward again. He never stayed on the same street for more than a few blocks and kept an eye on the rearview mirror. Once, several minutes after they left the hardware store, he thought he heard sirens wailing in the distance.

Welch also heard. "Soon they'll have every cop in the city looking for this Jeep."

"But then we won't have it," Hunter assured him. They were soon in the heart of the city, where more people were abroad. With the police swarming to the northwest suburbs, it seemed the smart thing to do.

The Jeep turned onto a lively neon-lit avenue lined with nightclubs and taverns. Hunter drove past each slowly, checking the parking lots. They had traveled about a half mile when he saw a truck he fancied, a model noted for its off-road capability. Turning into the lot, he parked a few rows from his choice and switched off the ignition. "That beauty there," he said, pointing.

"Want me to hot-wire it?" Welch asked, reaching for the handle.

Hunter was about to say yes when the door to the club opened and out strolled two attractive young women. He watched them, admiring their figures and reflecting on the last time he had enjoyed female companionship. It had been much too long. The brunette and redhead made straight for the truck. Giggling and joking, they hopped inside, and in moments the vehicle was heading out of the lot.

"Christmas just came early, boys," Hunter told the other two, and he set off to shadow the women.

Welch put a hand on the dash. "You can't be thinking what I think you are, not with every boy in blue in Portland after us. Not with what we have to do in two days."

"Relax. Creed thought of everything. By the time the police sort it all out, we'll be underground again. Having a little fun won't interfere with our schedule."

"For once I agree with him," Slater said, his eyes alight with wicked desire. "Let's treat ourselves. We're entitled. Three days from now we might not be alive."

"That's encouraging," Welch grumbled.

Hunter chose to ignore the pessimist. He trailed the truck to the northeast, past Maywood Park and halfway to Troutdale. "We'll have to move fast once they stop. Slater, you take the brunette. I'm partial to redheads."

"What do we do with the bodies after we're done?"

"We're not far from the Columbia, so we'll dump them in the river and hope the current carries them out to sea. With any luck, no one will ever find them."

Welch shifted, averting his gaze. "Count me out. I don't want any part of this."

"Why not?"

"I don't think Creed would like it, is all."

Hunter laughed. "Trust me. He won't care one bit. If we were about to chop down a pair of redwoods, it would be a different story. Trees are everything to him. If he could, I swear he'd make love to them.''

''That's sick.''

''But true,'' Hunter said, and grinned when the truck turned into a parking lot beside a rooming house. ''Get set. It's time to do what comes naturally.''

CHAPTER FOUR

The large brownstone appeared no different from any of the other run-down buildings in that section of Portland, but Mack Bolan knew better. Wearing a trench coat with the collar turned up, his hands plunged into his pockets, he made another circuit of the block.

A frontal system had brought heavy rain to the city. Bolan was grateful for the downpour, since it gave him an excuse for having his chin tucked low to hide his features from prying eyes.

As the warrior passed the truck for the second time, he confirmed the license-plate number matched that of the reported stolen vehicle. Not that he needed to. His local contact had verified it more than an hour earlier. But Bolan had learned the hard way never to take anything for granted. He had survived as long as he had because he always checked and rechecked the Intel he received before he committed himself to a course of action.

The Portland police hadn't been very happy when the FBI had intervened and claimed jurisdiction. Technically, kidnapping did fall under the province of the FBI, so Brognola had a shaky legal leg to stand on. But the chief of police had raked the big Fed over verbal coals.

Bolan couldn't blame the man. Portland's finest had lost two of their own. Then, adding insult to injury, the people responsible for the deaths of the officers had abducted two young women out for a night on the town.

Fingerprints found in the patrol car and in the Jeep abandoned at the rooming house where the women lived established the link. The prints also enabled the FBI to identify two of the suspects.

One was the blond guy. Garth Hunter, it turned out, was a former Marine who had been dishonorably discharged after serving time for beating a superior so badly that the sergeant had been in traction for six months. If not for the noncom's admission that he had provoked the fight, Hunter would have stayed in prison until he rotted.

The psychological profile on Hunter supplied by Marine psychologists hadn't helped much. Their evaluation branded Hunter a "deeply disturbed individual with delusions of persecution and a compulsion to destroy."

Then there was Peter Allen Slater. He had spent a third of his adult life behind bars for various crimes. At the moment he was in violation of his last parole and could be picked up on sight by any law officer. Where and how Slater fit into the scheme of things, the FBI had no idea. The man was as political as a brick, and until he joined Green Rage the only interest he had shown in ecology was when he cultivated a small garden at a prison farm.

Bolan raised his head as he approached a narrow alley that flanked the brownstone. Brognola had ordered the local team to pull back and had withdrawn his own people so as not to accidentally spook their quarry, and to give Bolan a clear playing field.

Pausing at the alley mouth, the warrior pretended to wipe something off the bottom of his shoe by rubbing it on the curb. When he had established the alley was empty, he rushed into it. At the first window he ducked low. Beyond it was a fire escape. He had to leap to catch the bottom rung, then pulled himself hand over hand until his feet secured purchase.

Moving as silently as the creaking metal allowed, Bolan climbed to the first door and tried the knob. It was locked. The second door proved to be the same. He made his way to the roof, checked to be sure the coast was clear, then clambered up and over to the top of the opposite fire escape.

The rain slackened to a drizzle. A clock on a bank down the street told him the time was one o'clock. In less than twenty-four hours the Timber Summit would convene.

Brognola had alerted the President to the threat posed by the eco-terrorists. The chief executive had let the big Fed know that he had every confidence in the Secret Service and Stony Man, and that he was going to attend no matter what.

Bolan hoped that confidence was justified. Slipping a hand under his coat, he drew the Beretta. From an inner coat pocket he pulled a suppressor and fitted it to the barrel. Then he tried another doorknob.

The door was locked. The big man took two strides back, leveled the pistol and fired all the rounds in the clip into the jamb. The wood splintered and cracked. He replaced the spent clip with a fresh one, grabbed the knob and yanked hard.

A gust of warm air fanned Bolan as the door flew open. He smelled a musty scent that brought to mind age and decay. Cautiously stepping inside, he crouched in the gloom to let his eyes adjust. A faint rustling sound came from below, but no other noise.

Once Bolan could distinguish shapes, he moved on. The floor was littered with broken furniture, old magazines and dust. He swatted a cobweb aside and stepped over a brass lamp. From the look of things, no one had been there in ages.

A door opened onto a narrow hall. The warrior listened for a while before resuming the hunt. No tracks marred the layer of dust underfoot. He began to think that he was wasting his time, that the FBI and police had gotten themselves all worked up over nothing. It could be that Hunter and company had simply abandoned the truck next to the building and gone elsewhere in yet another vehicle.

But if so, Bolan mused, what had happened to the two young women? A rickety flight of stairs was the only means of reaching the lower floors. He gingerly applied his weight to the highest step to see if it would creak. When it didn't, he went down slowly.

The warrior stopped shy of the bottom to scan a corridor. He could see that it was empty, but clearly etched in the dust were footprints, dozens of them, coming and going in both directions.

Adopting a two-handed grip, Bolan crept to the nearest door, which hung slightly ajar. He braced himself, then poked the door with his foot. It swung inward to reveal a room in the same condition as the one on the floor above. There were a few footprints, those of someone who had entered, walked in a small circle as if searching for something and gone back out again.

The next door was closed. The knob rattled when Bolan tried it, and one of the hinges squeaked when he pushed. Here there were more footprints but no sign of the eco-terrorists or their captives.

As Bolan went on, he heard a low creaking sound coming from the room ahead. Most of the footprints led to the door. Hoping he had struck pay dirt at last, he curled his finger to the Beretta's trigger, rammed his shoulder into the top panel of the door and burst inside expecting the worst. He found it. Both women lay on the floor, dead.

A sweep of the first floor verified the Green Rage members were long gone. Blankets had been spread on the floor of a large room near the entrance. Piled in a corner were recently emptied cans of stew, baked beans and peaches. Scattered about were the torn clothes of the women. The warrior turned away from the mess and waited for Brognola's arrival.

Bolan stuck the Beretta in its holster before opening the front door. Stray rays of sunshine peeked through the clouds. He gave a brusque wave, then stood aside as the local FBI squad rushed in. Brognola was the last to enter, his expression an accurate reflection of Bolan's mood.

"I was hoping this time we would nail them," the big Fed commented. "Any sign of the women?"

"Upstairs."

"Dead?"

"Yeah."

Brognola sighed and motioned for Bolan to follow him outdoors. "Sometimes this job can be a real bitch."

Bolan said nothing. The FBI agents were cordoning off the brownstone. Already a team was going over the truck with the proverbial fine-tooth comb.

"While you were in there, I received word on the terrorist killed out at the cabin," Brognola continued. "There wasn't much of him left, but we've been able to make a tentative identification based on his dental records." Out came a notepad. "His name was Timothy Carl Branson, aged twenty-seven. He had served time for armed robbery and manslaughter and was just released four months ago."

"Another former convict?"

"There does seem to be a trend here," Brognola agreed. "Ex-cons, a dishonorably discharged Marine. Apparently Jason Creed has tapped into a whole new source of recruits for his organization. It sets me to wondering if he has expanded his original agenda or if he's paying all this new talent to carry out his old one.''

"Either way, he's twice the menace he was before," Bolan noted.

"True. Which means we have to work twice as hard to bring him down." Brognola turned and scrutinized the brownstone. "I don't need to be a fortune-teller to know that we're not going to find the missing missile launchers in there. And no matter how hard I try, the President won't agree to postpone the summit or cancel his appearance. I'm back to square one, and I can use your help tomorrow, Striker."

"Say the word."

"I'd like to assign you to summit security under your old cover of Mike Belasko. You're free to rove as you see fit, or you can pick one spot and rely on a sniper rifle. Whichever you prefer."

"Something tells me I'd better rove."

"Let's just keep our fingers crossed that this time luck favors us instead of them." Brognola glanced up as light drops splattered onto his head and shoulders. The sky was clouding over again, and more heavy rain threatened. "Perfect. I'd say this weather about sums up the state of affairs here. If only we knew where to find Creed!"

"We'll find him eventually," Bolan vowed.

"Sure we will. But how much damage will he do in the meantime?"

HUNDREDS OF MILES to the southwest, the subject of their conversation stood on the balcony of his luxury condominium and contentedly gazed out over the sprawling city of Phoenix, Arizona. Buildings and roads shimmered in the blistering afternoon heat. In the distance the Phoenix Mountains framed the horizon.

Jason Creed adjusted the green towel he wore around his waist and went back inside. He locked the sliding door, then padded to the master bedroom. A raven-haired beauty emerged from the bathroom, wearing a towel that matched Creed's.

"Mmm, that was nice," Julie Constantine said. "There's nothing like a cold shower to start the day."

Creed walked to the closet and let his towel drop. "You're a bad influence on me, woman. Usually I'm up at the crack of dawn. Sleeping in until noon is not my idea of being productive."

The woman smiled impishly. "Is that what we were doing? Sleeping?"

"You know what I mean." Creed put on a pair of lightweight slacks and a blue cotton shirt and admired himself in the full-length mirror. His imposing build, combined with his rugged, tanned features, lent him the look of a professional athlete. Which suited him just fine. He had gone to great lengths to ensure his cover was flawless, even to the point of dying his hair black and shaving off the beard and mustache he had worn since his days at Berkeley.

"So what's on the schedule for today, lover?" Constantine asked. "Golf? Swimming? A party, perhaps? Or do we have more business to attend to?"

Creed looked at her, glad yet again that fate had conspired to pair them up. She was the ideal mate for a man like him. Under her beauty-queen exterior lurked a heart as cold as ice, a brain as calculating as a computer. And she was as devoted to the cause of protecting the environment as he.

"Personally I hope we can go swimming," the woman stated before he could answer. "You make me look like an albino. I have a lot of catching up to do." She casually discarded her towel and opened a dresser drawer.

"Swimming it is, then," Creed said. "You might as well enjoy yourself while you can. In a few days we set the wheels in motion for the greatest acts of eco-terrorism the world has ever seen."

In the process of dressing, Constantine asked, "When do you expect to hear from the Neanderthal?"

"In two days, provided Hunter's squad isn't caught or killed. He's to join us, while the rest of his people will give support to Envio Squad Two."

Constantine froze in the act of donning her bra. "Must he come with us? You know I don't like that man. There's something about him." She shuddered. "Have you ever looked into his eyes? *Really* looked? No wonder the Marines kicked him out. When he was a kid, I bet he got his kicks by plucking the wings from insects or choking chickens."

Creed moved to the draperies and peeked out. Years of being a fugitive had ingrained in him the habit of constant watchfulness. "Granted, he has a taste for violence. But he also has his good points. It was his idea to organize Green Rage along military lines and to set up the three envio squads. And he believes in doing whatever is necessary to stop our world from being destroyed."

"Which is more than can be said for most of the others you've let join. Packard, Dean, Slater and the rest are only interested in the money they can make."

"So what?" Creed shrugged. "Think of them as cannon fodder, to do with as we please. They're expendable, we're not." He stretched, then checked his watch. "Using them was another of Hunter's brainstorms, and, I must admit, a good one. He knew who to contact, so I told him to go ahead and try."

"You'd better be careful. Hunter might decide he's the real brains behind Green Rage and dispose of you," Constantine said teasingly, half in earnest.

Creed wasn't amused. He didn't like having his judgment questioned. His genius, and his alone, was the guiding force behind Green Rage. In less than a week he would prove that beyond a shadow of a doubt, both to Constantine and the entire world. "Hunter is a tool. Nothing more, nothing less. If he ever oversteps himself or outlives his usefulness to the cause, I'll deal with him as I've dealt with so many others."

"Be careful, Jason. That man has the instincts of a wild animal. If he ever suspected you would turn on him, he'd turn on you first."

"Have some faith," Creed said coldly. Peeved, he strolled out to the living room. He switched on the television and idly listened to the cable news channel while pouring himself a whiskey. When the anchor mentioned the impending summit, it caught Creed's interest and he sank into a plush easy chair. A panoramic view of Portland filled the screen as a newswoman broadcast live from the City of Roses:

"Authorities are being tight-lipped about reports that a terrorist faction may have targeted the Timber Summit. But rumors continue to circulate of a reputed link between the recent theft of undisclosed military hardware at the Willamette Heights National Guard Armory and the eco-terrorist group known as Green Rage. Undisclosed sources in the Justice Department confirm that a man who died in a shoot-out with federal agents just across the border in the state of Washington was a member of that radical organization."

Creed gulped a mouthful of liquor and scowled at the TV. "What the hell is going on?" he wondered aloud. "Can't I trust those clowns to do anything right?"

"What is it?" Constantine asked, coming up behind him and placing a warm hand on his neck. "Did I hear Portland mentioned?"

"One of Hunter's squad has bought the farm," Creed informed her. "When I left, everything was going as planned. That weasel of a captain had received his money and the logistics had been all worked out." Rising, he polished off the whiskey and set the glass on the bar. "I trusted Hunter. If he blows it, he'll pay. So help me."

"We'll know tomorrow. There's no sense in getting upset. You can't be everywhere at once, and you needed to be here when that call from the islands came through."

"I know, I know," Creed said gruffly. "I shouldn't let it get to me, but I'm only human. Of all the things I've done, this will be my crowning achievement. It will wake the masses up, make them realize that everyone has a stake in the welfare of our planet."

"I doubt that the average person cares."

"Then we'll make them care, whether they want to or not."

In order to be alone so he could think through the newest developments, Creed went back out on the balcony and leaned on the railing. He liked Julie, but she just didn't appreciate the total picture. As dedicated as she was to preserving the planet, she wasn't dedicated enough.

But then, who was? Ever since Berkeley, ever since Creed had been awakened to the plight of the environment on a global scale, ever since, as he liked to say, he'd had his planetary consciousness raised, it seemed to him that he was the only person alive who truly realized the gravity of the situation and was taking steps to fix things.

He never failed to be amazed by the widespread apathy. Millions had to have seen news footage of the rape of the Amazon rain forest, or heard scientists lecture on the dire consequences of the hole in the ozone, yet they went on with their lives as if nothing were happening. Creed figured the corporations and the government were to blame. Acting in collusion, they had duped the American public into thinking the environment was fine. Why, just the other day he had seen where dozens of top scientists went on record as saying they believed the ozone wasn't being depleted, that those who claimed it was were alarmists. Even the man who had invented the device that measured the ozone layer claimed the measurements were being taken way out of context.

What did that guy know? Creed reflected sourly. He suspected that anyone who said the environment was in good shape had been bought off with government or corporate grants. Only an idiot or a traitor would deny the truth.

The wind picked up, rustling trees below, reminding Creed of the first time he had been to the site of a sanctioned timber harvest and seen beautiful pines being toppled right and left. It had brought tears to his eyes, seeing the forest mutilated like that. He'd listened to the timber reps who claimed that for every tree felled, a new one was planted to take its place. But he knew better. Trees were as unique as people. No two were ever alike. Once a precious tree was cut down, there was no replacing it.

So Creed had gotten his start in the ecology wars by sabotaging lumber equipment and spiking trees marked for felling. He'd laughed the first time he'd heard that a lumberjack had lost an arm when the man's chain saw hit one of the steel spikes he had planted. It had served the bastard right, in Creed's estimation.

Eventually Creed came to see that his acts weren't having the desired result. The broken equipment was always repaired or new machines were brought in. And there were always new tree cutters ready to take the place of those who were hospitalized.

More had to be done, and Creed had been just the man to do it. He'd formed his own organization. He'd spent long hours plotting tactics that were intended to make the American public wake up and take notice. In that, he had been partially successful. The kidnapping of the ChemTex executive's daughter had drawn national interest, but for all the wrong reasons.

Not this time. Creed had a one-two-three punch planned that would shock Middle America to its core, that would dramatically point out once and for all that humankind was a grave threat to Mother Earth.

So what if thousands had to die in the process? Creed mused. It was a small price to pay for enlightenment.

CHAPTER FIVE

The sleek McDonnell Douglas Model 500 helicopter swept in low over Forest Park, northwest of Portland. Zooming just above the treetops, it slowed as it neared an open grassy tract where a makeshift stage and podium had been erected and where the delegates to the Timber Summit and privileged members of the press were gathering to hear the President give a speech.

The chopper was on temporary loan to Hal Brognola's department from the Portland National Guard. The Guard pilot, a veteran of twenty-five years, glanced at the muscular man in camouflage fatigues who sat beside him and wondered again which agency the man worked for. He'd like to ask but he knew better. His orders had been precise—do exactly as his passenger wanted, no questions asked.

Mack Bolan lowered his binoculars and pointed at a hill to the west of the meadow. "Let's check that out, Captain Bishop," he suggested.

"Whatever you say, Mr. Belasko," Bishop replied dutifully, banking the aircraft with skill born of long experience.

The drab olive helicopter was similar to those Bolan had seen in service in Vietnam. This one sported a side-mounted General Electric M-134 7.62 mm Minigun linked to an XM-70E1 reflector sight in the observer's seat, courtesy of a last-minute retrofit ordered by Brognola.

Focusing the binoculars, the warrior scanned the hill carefully. They had been patrolling for a half hour without results. In another half hour the President would arrive. If Green Rage intended to strike, they had to show up soon.

Security was as tight as a drum. In addition to Bolan's chopper, another helicopter patrolled to the south, Secret Service agents had been posted around the perimeter of the meadow and police units covered every road leading into the park.

Still, Bolan was uneasy. Forest Park was aptly named. Except for the meadow and a few other open spaces, it was heavily wooded, affording any number of hiding places. Brognola had asked the chief executive to change the site at the last minute, but the President refused. What better place to make a major speech on timber policy than in Forest Park? At least that was the official argument, no doubt put forward by the PR people who were drooling over how it would look on the six-o'clock news.

"Try there next," Bolan said, gesturing at a wooded stretch due north of the stage.

"We checked there twice already," Bishop responded.

"So we'll do it again," Bolan said. "Nice and slow." They flew in low over a small clearing. In the center stood an old log cabin built during the last half of the last century. Most of the roof had collapsed, and one wall had buckled. The rest was overgrown with weeds and brush.

"Hover a minute," Bolan directed, and trained the binoculars on the cabin. It seemed okay, but he wasn't taking anything for granted. After consulting the map in his lap, he pressed a button on his headset and declared, "Command Post, this is Air One. Request Secret Service check homestead at grid coordinates C7. Repeat, C7. Advise when done. Over."

"Roger, Air One," came the reply. "Command Post out."

Bolan tapped Bishop on the arm. "Make a slow sweep of this immediate area."

"Yes, sir."

The terrain was typical. Trees everywhere, laced with briar patches and bisected by a gully. Bolan made a thorough survey of every square foot. As the whirlybird rose from above the gully, his headset sparked to life.

"Air One, this is Command Post. Secret Service reports negative results on that homestead. Do you copy?"

"Copy and acknowledged. Out." The warrior had only to nod and the captain took the aircraft over the cabin once more. A pair of Secret Service agents wearing trench coats and sunglasses glanced up, and one gave a thumbs-up sign. The warrior frowned. "Okay. Let's try to the northwest one more time."

Bolan rubbed the back of his neck to relieve a kink and set the map on the console. He had a feeling that he was missing something, that he had overlooked a crucial detail. But he had no inkling of what it might be. As far as he could tell, the Feds had every angle covered.

Maybe that was his mistake, Bolan pondered. Maybe he should put himself in the shoes of the terrorists, not the Feds. He should look at the tactical aspect as Green Rage would.

One point was apparent. It would be impossible for the terrorists to sneak into the park so close to the start of the summit. If they were smart, they had picked their spot days in advance and were in position long before the security forces converged on Forest Park. That being the case, Bolan speculated that the hit team had probably been in place for at least twenty-four hours, possibly longer.

But in position where? That was the million-dollar question. Bolan recalled the hardware stolen from the armory. M-72s were compact, disposable antitank free-flight missile launchers. The standard rounds were fin-stabilized rockets capped with M-18 warheads fitted with impact-detonating fuses. They could penetrate thick armor plating with ease.

Since the President would be out in the open on the podium, penetration was hardly a factor unless Green Rage intended to attack after the speech, when the President was on his way back into Portland. But Bolan couldn't see them being so reckless. Security would be even tighter along the limo's route, with air coverage every foot of the way. The odds of escaping afterward would be slim to nonexistent, and based on prior performance, Green Rage liked to have a way out of any tight situation.

The warrior leaned back in his seat. If there was an aspect he had overlooked, he couldn't think of it.

In his mind's eye Bolan pictured an M-72. Its range was rated at slightly over a thousand yards, but effective accuracy couldn't be guaranteed past six hundred feet, about the length of two football fields.

Straightening, Bolan said, "I've changed my mind, Captain. Take us back toward the meadow."

They were halfway there when the warrior's headphone blared. "Attention. This is Command Post. ETA of Blue Goose is five minutes. Repeat, five minutes. All personnel be advised. Command Post out."

Blue Goose was someone's quaint idea of a code name for the President. Bolan could see the road that wound to the summit site. The motorcade had appeared about a mile off.

"Now what?" Bishop asked.

The helicopter was at the tree line, holding position like an oversize hummingbird.

Bolan shifted to note the position of the podium, then imagined it at the center of a circle four football fields across. Where within that circle, he asked himself, could the Green Rage members possibly hide? The meadow extended well over six hundred feet to the south, so it couldn't be there. To the west the trees were so tightly clustered that getting a clear shot would be a problem. To the east there was cover, but not quite enough.

The warrior had to lean forward to study the lay of the land to the north. His pulse quickened when he realized the old cabin was almost exactly six hundred feet from the podium, maybe a little less. "The homestead!" he barked.

"Again?" Bishop said, but he promptly complied, dipping lower than ever before.

Nothing had changed. The cabin stood undisturbed except for the brush and weeds being buffeted by the rotorwash. Adjacent to the buckled wall was a clear patch approximately ten feet across. Bolan pointed at it and announced, "I'm going to jump. Take me down as far as you can."

"Jump?" the officer repeated, his eyebrows arched. "What do I do then?"

"Wait up here. If I find anything, I might need you to back me up."

"The Secret Service already checked there once. What exactly do you expect to find?"

"I won't know until I find it," Bolan said. Unstrapping the harness, he twisted to retrieve his M-16. The chopper held steady over the spot he had indicated while the pilot gauged the proximity of the nearest trees and the structure. There was enough room to descend to within about six feet of the ground, but it would take consummate flying skill to manage the feat. One mistake and the spinning rotor blades would shear into the pines or clip the cabin.

The Guard officer was equal to the task. Delicately working the stick and pedals, he slowly sank the helicopter toward the ground. A gust of wind unexpectedly buffeted the craft and he immediately compensated. "This is as low as I can go," he stated.

"It'll do," Bolan said. The door resisted until he put his shoulder into it. Getting a solid grip, he eased outward so he could slip from the cockpit. The wash whipped his hair and plastered the fatigues against his body. Keeping his head tucked to his chest, the warrior lowered a foot to the bar step, slid farther out and transferred the foot to the skid. Once he had both feet down, he bent his body and braced for the next move. He had to let go of the door and duck out of the way before it slammed shut on his arm.

Again the wind picked up, and the chopper drifted toward the cabin. Bolan had to jump while he could, before Bishop was forced to pull up. Allowing his feet to slip off the skid, he released the door handle and plummeted over eight feet.

By bending his knees to cushion the impact, Bolan was able to stay upright. He raised a hand to shield his eyes from flying bits of grass and dust as the rotorwash intensified and the whirlybird arced into the sky. Bishop turned the craft so he could see Bolan clearly.

Unslinging the M-16, the Executioner moved to the buckled wall, which had broken into five sections. He stepped on one and nearly lost his balance when a decayed log crumpled. Going around instead, he stood and studied the ruin. Whoever built the cabin hadn't bothered to include a floor, and the ground was now choked with waist-high weeds.

There was nowhere a person could hide, let alone three men burdened with missile launchers. Bolan was afraid his hunch had been wrong. He advanced toward the middle, surprised at how spongy the ground felt in comparison to the hard-packed soil of the outer clearing. Many of the weeds were dry and crackled underfoot.

Pausing, Bolan was about to signal the Guardsman to head for the meadow when he noticed an odd split in the weeds, a thin break about the width of two fingers that ran from near the doorway to about where he stood. It was almost as if someone had taken a sharp blade and trimmed the growth in a straight line.

Then the warrior looked down and discovered a second line at right angles to the first. Taking a few steps to the left, he saw yet a third line, running toward the front of the cabin. The outline was that of a giant rectangle. Why anyone would do such a thing eluded him.

Bolan studied the variety of weeds and noticed a short, round reed that seemed totally out of place. Reeds grew in marshes and swamps or along rivers, not in the middle of a pine forest. He bent to examine it— and it moved.

The truth hit Bolan like a sledgehammer. He tried to leap back and bring the M-16 to bear, but the ground buckled under him as three men in green *ninja*-style outfits seemed to burst up out of the very earth. Only Bolan knew better.

The Vietcong had used the same ruse time and again. A typical nasty ploy had been for them to dig a pit, embed sharpened bamboo at the bottom and conceal the trap with a thin cover, which in every respect looked exactly like the ground around it.

Someone in Green Rage had come up with a similar idea. They had peeled back the top layer of sod, dug shallow holes large enough for three men to lie in and made a lightweight latticework to support the sod once it was laid back down. To enable them to breathe, they had poked holes in the sod and pushed reeds through the holes. Thin slits had been cut at eye level so they could see.

From the air, even from the doorway, everything appeared perfectly normal. Only a close inspection could have revealed the ruse.

Bolan would have fired on the trio had his legs not become entangled in the buckling latticework. He toppled onto his back and twisted to confront them but was felled by a ringing blow to the jaw. Stunned, he collapsed. Dim voices pierced the fog that clouded his brain.

"What the hell do we do? The President isn't here yet!"

"We're blown! Head for the bikes!"

"Look out for that chopper! Slater, take it out just like I taught you!"

The warrior heard the drum of footsteps, heard a click and a hiss and the high-pitched shriek of a rocket in flight. He knew they had fired at Bishop. He willed his body to rise, but it refused to obey. The explosion, when it came, was too far-off, too faint.

"Damn it, you missed!" a terrorist bellowed. "Do I have to do everything myself?"

Gradually Bolan's vision cleared. He saw the three terrorists just past the collapsed wall. The tallest had raised an M-72 onto his right shoulder and was hastily adjusting the rear peep sight. Suddenly the terrorist lowered the launcher and whirled. "Move your butts! He's coming in for a strafing run!"

On high, the M-134 minigun cranked into operation, whining like a car engine stuck in neutral. Rounds ripped into the ground, stitching a tight pattern toward the terrorists. Two of the three were able to leap clear, but the third was too slow. He screamed as the minigun rounds chewed into his legs. Crashing onto his stomach, he cried out, "I'm hit! Oh, God, I'm hit! Help me!"

Evidently it was every terrorist for himself. The other two never looked back. They sped into the trees, heading to the northwest.

Bolan put his palms flat and shoved himself into a lurching run, hearing shouts in the vicinity of the meadow. Secret Service agents were on the way. So was the second helicopter, speeding in from the south.

The warrior was confident the terrorists would be caught. The woods were dense but not so dense that the pilots would be unable to keep track of them. He skirted a tree, glimpsed the pair roughly twenty yards ahead and made his sluggish legs lengthen their stride.

Without warning the terrorists halted. The taller man trained his telescopic tube launcher skyward; the other pointed his at Bolan.

The warrior took one more step and dived. All hell seemed to break loose. As he hugged the earth, he heard the rocket whiz by a yard above his head. The blast was much too close, showering dirt and bits of wood on top of him. Less than a heartbeat later, a second, louder, explosion occurred, and Bolan craned his neck to see Bishop's shattered bird aflame and falling directly toward him.

The warrior rose and sprinted to the right. He had mere seconds to get in the clear. There was bound to be an explosion when the chopper hit, and unless he was beyond the blast radius he might be incinerated or blown to pieces. A glance showed the copter descending like a blazing meteorite. He veered around the trunk of a spruce, realized he had run out of time and threw himself onto his stomach behind another, wider tree.

The ground itself rumbled and heaved. Metal screamed. Pines were snapped like so much kindling. A hot wind fanned Bolan's nape, and for several seconds he could hardly breathe. The awful sensation passed quickly. He pushed himself to his knees and saw the chopper and the area around it burning.

Captain Bishop was gone, yet another casualty to add to the growing tally racked up by Green Rage.

The pilot of the second chopper, perhaps enraged by the loss of the first, had swooped in dangerously low and cut loose with his minigun. Hardly had he opened fire, though, when a rocket caught his aircraft head-on. Resembling a miniature Fourth of July fireworks display, pieces of the helicopter showered to the ground in a brilliant spectacle of fiery metal.

Bolan had to dodge falling debris. The tail assembly landed to his left, felling a tree as if it were a toothpick. A broken skid thudded into the ground to his right.

By that time the terrorists had gained considerably. Bolan spotted them sixty yards ahead of him. He snapped up the M-16, but the close vegetation prevented him from fixing a sure bead on either target.

Bolan envisioned the layout of Forest Park, trying to guess their destination. North of the cabin the forest extended almost to the Willamette River. Highway 30 separated the park from the waterway. And if he remembered correctly, there were a few dirt roads bordering the park that connected to the highway.

That had to be it, Bolan reflected. There was a car or truck waiting for the terrorists along one of the dirt roads. He ran faster, hoping to overtake them before they reached the getaway vehicle. Yells to his rear signified the Secret Service agents were trying to locate the fleeing pair, but without air support they had no idea where to look. And the warrior didn't have a radio.

The terrorists reached the brink of the gully and took the slope on the fly. By the time Bolan gained the crest, they were a hundred feet to the northwest, racing along the bottom toward a bend.

The warrior figured the terrorists were being cagey. By sticking to the gully, they were well hidden from agents in the woods. He was a dozen yards from the bend when the raucous rumble of a small but high-powered engine resounded through the pines.

At the turn, Bolan slowed just long enough to take in the scene before him. The pair had pulled camouflage netting off three dirt bikes and were about to flee. The tall terrorist gunned his motorcycle and glanced impatiently at his companion, who was frantically trying to start up his bike.

The moment Bolan stepped around the bend, the tall terrorist peeled out, the rear end of his cycle fishtailing wildly. He regained control and zoomed up the slope.

Tucking the autorifle to his shoulder, Bolan centered the sights on the second terrorist's head just as the man looked back and saw him. He went for a pistol at his hip but was slow compared to the lightning muzzle velocity of the M-16. Three 5.56 mm rounds cored his brain and he keeled over, taking the motorcycle with him.

Bolan slung the rifle as he sprinted to the bike. Heaving the corpse aside, he righted the vehicle and slid a leg over the seat. From the smell, he knew the panicky terrorist had flooded the carburetor. Although it seemed hopeless, he tried to start the bike anyway and smiled grimly when it roared to life.

It had been a while since the warrior last rode a motorcycle. He opened the throttle and was nearly pitched off when the bike reared onto its back wheel and streaked up the slope. Leaning forward so the front end smacked down, he stabilized the motorcycle as he shot up and over the top.

A tree loomed in Bolan's path, and he barely wrenched the handgrips in time to avert a collision. Hundreds of feet ahead the terrorist was still racing to the northwest.

Weaving among the trees, avoiding thickets and ruts, the warrior slowly gained some ground.

Then the terrorist broke from the vegetation onto a dirt road. Sliding to a stop, he glanced over a shoulder and spotted Bolan. Immediately he opened the throttle full out and roared away toward Highway 30.

A cloud of dust hung in the air when Bolan reached the road. Hunching over the handlebars, he watched the speedometer climb from forty to fifty to sixty. He would have gone faster but the road twisted back and forth, compelling him to slow for the bends.

Try as he might, Bolan was unable to gain any more on his adversary. The terrorist was good with a bike. Bolan had to settle for keeping the man in sight.

For more than three-quarters of a mile the chase went on without a change, until Highway 30 appeared. The terrorist abruptly tore off his green mask and stuck it in a pocket.

When next the man looked back, Bolan recognized Garth Hunter, the blond powerhouse from the cabin, the former Marine with a penchant for violence. He deduced that Hunter had removed the mask to be less conspicuous once they were on the highway.

Moments later the eco-terrorist did just that, turning a sharp left and merging into the traffic flow.

Bolan thought he saw a chance to make up lost distance. He cut to the left well before the turn, shot across a gravel strip and raced onto the highway. He had seen a truck approaching from the north but judged it too far off to pose a danger. What he hadn't seen, however, was the red sports car that was passing the truck.

It bore down on him like a bright red comet.

CHAPTER SIX

Smith often said that there were two types of soldiers, the quick and the dead. Mack Bolan had survived the vicious killing fields of the world by being not only quick on his feet but quick-witted, as well.

When the warrior saw the sports car hurtling toward him, he had three choices. He could try to scoot back the way he had come, which would put him in the path of the oncoming semi. He could try to reach the far side of the highway, which might backfire if the driver of the sports car veered into him. Or he could do exactly what he did—nothing.

Bolan's razor-keen mind chose the least of the three evils. By staying where he was, he ensured the semi would miss him. And it gave the sports-car driver spare seconds in which to react to his sudden appearance. He glimpsed a young, fear-filled face, saw hands urgently spinning the wheel, and then the red car shot past him on the left, missing him by an arm's length.

Hunter had made the mistake of slowing, apparently in the hope of seeing Bolan splattered all over the asphalt. On realizing his pursuer had escaped unscathed, the terrorist buried the speedometer.

Traffic was heavy. Bolan had to weave in and out of the steady flow in order not to lose sight of his quarry.

Some drivers hardly noticed. Others drove onto the shoulder to avoid a collision. An elderly lady became so rattled that she accidentally strayed off the highway and clipped a tree.

Bolan was doing over ninety when he spotted a state patrol vehicle parked at the edge of the road. The trooper had a radar gun trained on the traffic—not that the man needed one to tell Hunter was exceeding the speed limit. The patrolman spotted the speeding dirt bike, threw the radar gun onto the seat and pulled out onto Highway 30, blocking both lanes.

Hunter wasn't about to stop. He slowed just enough to zip around the tail end of the cruiser, then laughed and raised his left index finger in a mocking salute.

Bolan had to reduce his speed to avoid the patrol car. The trooper was executing a turn to go after the terrorist. Angling in alongside the vehicle, Bolan gave the patrolman quite a start.

"What's going on?" the officer blurted.

The warrior couldn't afford to take the time to explain fully. "Federal agent!" he lied. "That guy just tried to assassinate the President at Forest Park. Call it in if you don't believe me."

Without awaiting a reply, Bolan settled into the proper lane and figuratively put the pedal to the metal. The wind was so strong he had to squint to keep his eyes from watering.

Hunter did the unexpected. It would have made sense for him to follow Highway 30 to the northwest so he could lose himself in a remote rural area. Instead, he braked, took a hard right onto a bridge over the Willamette and crossed into uptown Portland.

Bolan had to give the terrorists credit for their well-thought-out plan. Once downtown, Hunter could easily ditch the cycle and disappear in the heavy stream of humanity that thronged the sidewalks. Within minutes he might be on a bus out of state. Or maybe there was a vehicle waiting at a pickup point. Either way, Bolan had to nail him before he vanished.

The warrior had help. With siren wailing and lights flashing, the state patrol car caught up with him. The officer jabbed a thumb at Hunter, then pulled on ahead. In tandem the three of them flew along Lombard Street.

Since Bolan had seen Hunter discard the missile launcher in the gully, he saw no reason to be concerned for the officer's safety. All Hunter had was a pistol. Or so Bolan assumed, until Hunter groped at the side of his uniform and pulled out an object the size of an apple.

"Look out! Don't get too close!" Bolan shouted, but his words were swept away by the wind. The trooper couldn't hear him.

Hunter shifted, jerked at the object and tossed it behind him. Bouncing and skipping like a baseball, it came to rest in the middle of the street, right on the solid yellow line.

The officer leaned out his window to get a better look. The hand grenade was probably the last thing he ever saw.

With a thunderous roar the bomb detonated. The cruiser was almost on top of it, and the explosion hurled the front end of the patrol car into the air. In a bizarre sort of aerial ballet, the vehicle turned completely around, flipped upside down and sailed ten feet before smashing onto its top, which collapsed as if made of cardboard instead of metal. Screeching like a demented banshee, the car slid to a sideways stop.

There was no need for Bolan to stop and check on the officer. The man's upper torso lay outside the car; the rest of his body was pinned by the crushed roof.

Pedestrians screamed. Cars shot off the street, crashing into parked vehicles. Bolan pierced the heart of the bedlam and set eyes on Hunter, blocks distant. The terrorist took a right onto a side street.

Sirens were howling at several locations when the warrior made the same turn. Hunter hadn't bothered to hide, but was now traveling due south toward the core of the bustling metropolis.

A low hill rose in front of them. Hunter ignored a red light, causing a van to veer off in order to miss him. Brakes squealed, rubber burned and the van slammed into a bus taking on passengers. The blond man threw back his head and laughed. Causing mayhem was as natural to him as breathing, and he reveled in the fear he inspired.

Bolan hit the hill doing sixty-five. He prided himself on his self-control, but he couldn't resist a twinge of anger when Hunter looked back while going over the top, smirked and waved. The warrior shifted, gaining power. If fortune smiled on him, if Hunter stayed on the same street, he would try to drop the killer with the M-16.

Then a second hand grenade arced into sight, the sunlight glinting off its metal body. The bomb struck the street and careened down the incline toward Bolan. He didn't know how long he had before it went off, but since most grenades had only a four- or five-second delay, he acted instantly, jerking the handgrips to the right and shooting like a bullet between a pair of parked cars. The front tire bounced up off the curb, hard, nearly unseating him. He tried to stay on the sidewalk, but the cycle had a mind of its own and landed in a small yard. His momentum carried him up a flight of wooden stairs onto a porch. By throwing his whole weight to the left, he missed a picture window, nearly hit the corner of the house and crashed through the railing. He was airborne when the blast took place.

An invisible hand pushed at Bolan's back as he tried to straighten the motorcycle so he'd land on two wheels. Instead, the concussion tilted the bike. He came down on the front tire and felt the cycle start to somersault. Throwing himself clear, he thudded against the side of the house. The cycle tumbled end over end and smashed into several filled trash cans, making an incredible racket.

The warrior rose, unslinging the M-16 on the run while sprinting up the middle of the street. Dozens of windows on both sides had been shattered by the blast. A few of the residents were cautiously stepping outdoors or poking their heads out windows to see what was going on.

Bolan reached the top of the hill. A taxi driving toward him lurched to a stop, the cabbie gawking in amazement. The warrior took a few more steps, seeking some sign of the terrorist. To his chagrin, the motorcycle was nowhere to be seen. Hunter had turned onto another street.

Hurrying over to the taxi, Bolan said, "I need a ride."

"Hop in, mister," the cabbie replied meekly. "Wherever you want to go, I'll take you. Old Sammy Jones makes it a point never to argue with anyone who can shoot him dead."

JASON CREED WANTED to shoot someone—preferably Garth Hunter. He sat in his damp swimming trunks and stared at the television in baffled fury, listening to the reporter relate how the President of the United States had narrowly escaped being assassinated by a hit squad of fanatics, members of Green Rage.

Julie Constantine stood by the bar and swirled the bourbon in the glass in her right hand. She was also upset, but for a different reason. It had taken her most of the morning to talk Creed into going down for a swim, and they hadn't been in the water two minutes when a woman had rushed out to the pool shouting that there had just been an attempt made to kill the President. Needless to say, their swim had been cut short.

"I had it planned perfectly," Creed snarled. "How could Hunter have blown it?"

"Maybe it wasn't Garth's fault," Julie said, trying to calm him. She knew how Creed could get when events didn't go the way he wanted. He liked to hit things, or people. And she disliked being slapped around, especially when she wasn't the one at fault.

"Since when do you like to defend that muscle-bound clod?" Creed snapped. "Yesterday you told me that you don't much care for him."

"And yesterday you were raving about how fine a job he's done for you. It's not as if he didn't try. You heard the news. Slater was killed. Welch is in custody." She paused. "Which reminds me. How much does Welch know about your big operation? What if he talks?"

Creed came up off the couch as if someone had jabbed him in the rear with a sewing needle. "Damn!" he declared, and put a hand to his forehead. "I've been so mad, I'm not thinking straight."

"Will you have to call it off?"

"Let me think," Creed said, his brow creasing. He rambled on out loud, weighing the consequences of the debacle. "Hunter is the only one I've confided in, and even he doesn't know the whole picture. As for Welch, he was only given information pertaining to the hit on the President."

Constantine took a sip of bourbon. "What about the training sessions you put the three squads through up in the mountains last month? They had two weeks together to compare notes."

"It couldn't be helped," Creed said, defending his decision. "They had to be put through the paces in advance so they'd be able to do their jobs. Slater had never ridden a cycle before. Dean didn't know the first thing about scuba diving. Packard needed to brush up on explosives."

Creed ran a hand through his wet hair while trying to remember exactly how much he had revealed to each envio squad. It had been the basics, nothing more. Certainly not enough to benefit the Feds. "We're safe in that regard," he said, as much to assure himself as her.

"Did you tell any of them about our condo?" Constantine asked. She didn't relish the idea of spending the rest of her life in prison because one of their underlings cut a deal with the government to avoid prosecution.

"What do you take me for?" Creed said. "You know my motto. Trust no one." He glanced at the picture on the TV. A news helicopter was making a pass over Forest Park. "Trust me. I covered our tracks. The only one who knows is Hunter."

"And what if he's caught?"

"He'd never talk. He hates the government for what they did to him."

Constantine remembered the chill she had felt every time she had been in Hunter's presence. The man was like an elemental force of nature, a bubbling caldron of savage violence just waiting for any excuse to explode. But he did have a peculiar childlike devotion to Creed, who was probably the only man Hunter had ever called friend. "Maybe so," she admitted. "But the Feds have ways of making people talk against their will. One little injection will have Hunter babbling like a baby."

Creed had to concede her point, and he wasn't about to be thwarted, not now, not when he was so close to striking a blow for the environment that would be felt from one coast to the other. Future generations would remember his name with awe.

"All right," Creed said. "Pack your bags. We're leaving for Hawaii earlier than I planned. If Hunter eludes the federal dragnet and joins us, fine. If not, Dean, you and I will manage by ourselves."

The woman brightened. She had never been to Hawaii before, and several days of fun in the sun would do wonders for her spirits. Unlike Creed, she needed time to unwind every now and then, to remind herself that there was more to life than Green Rage.

"A few more days, that's all we need," Creed was saying. "If we can keep the lousy Feds guessing for a few more days, it will be too late for them to stop us. Afterward, I don't much care what happens. I'll have made my point. Everyone in America will have seen the truth."

"That they will, lover," Constantine said.

Molding her full figure to his, she remarked, "I just love it when you get on your high horse. What do you say we have one for the road, so to speak? I mean, it's a long flight to Hawaii. You wouldn't want me to be deprived, would you?"

Creed grinned and looped his arms around her slender waist. "Why not? It will be a while before the next time, and I could stand to relax."

Her lips curling seductively, Julie Constantine pulled Creed's face down to hers. "Come to Momma, big man. I'll make you so relaxed you'll melt."

MACK BOLAN HAD WATCHED Hal Brognola wear a rut in the carpet long enough. "You should try to relax," he commented.

The big Fed grunted. "Relax, he says! Six dead, nine injured, untold thousands of dollars in property damage, not including the cost of the two helicopters, the summit disrupted, a whole city in turmoil, and you want me to relax?"

"Beats having a heart attack." Bolan turned, catching a glimpse of himself reflected in the waiting room window. He had changed into a loose-fitting jacket and slacks, and only another professional could have told that he wore the Beretta under his left arm and the Desert Eagle in a special rig in the small of his back.

"I appreciate your concern," Brognola said. "But the attempt today was too close for comfort. If you hadn't stumbled on their hiding place, Green Rage would have done it. The bastards would have killed the President."

"Has he agreed to postpone the rest of the summit?"

"No. Everything has been rescheduled, but they're still going through with—" Brognola broke off abruptly when a white-haired doctor in a white smock entered the waiting room. The man wore the haggard look of someone who had been in surgery for hours. "Well, Dr. Franklyn?"

"We had to amputate both legs. They were shot to ribbons," the surgeon said.

"He'll live, though?"

"That's problematic at this point, Mr. Brognola. He also took a round in the liver. I did my best, but quite frankly, I doubt Mr. Welch will last out the night."

"I'm sure you did all that you could. University Hospital came highly recommended." He didn't add that it had also been the closest. "How soon can we see him?"

"Mr. Welch should revive within the hour, but I can't predict what his mental state will be. He's been wheeled under armed escort to room 303." Dr. Franklyn pursed his lips. "If you're going up, I would suggest that you take the back stairs. The press is all over the lobby, badgering everyone. I swear they have no manners whatsoever."

"Thanks for the tip."

Bolan lengthened his stride to catch up with Brognola. Since the big Fed's own people stood guard outside of the terrorist's room, they were able to walk in without having to show identification.

Ely Welch was as pale as the sheet on which he lay. Intravenous tubes were connected to both arms. Monitors flanked the bed. A striking brunette in a crisp nurse's uniform rose from a chair.

"Any change yet, Agent Weaver?" Brognola asked.

"No, sir."

"I want him to come around, now. Give him whatever will do the job."

"It's risky, sir. We could lose him."

"Better him than the President," Brognola stated. "The summit will only last three days. I need to know if Green Rage will try again."

The warrior admired the smooth, practiced movements of the agent as she turned to a tray and prepared a needle. A slight bulge low on her thigh told him that she could handle herself in more ways than one.

"This will take a few minutes to have an effect, sir," Agent Weaver said. "He might be woozy at first and not be able to understand you." Bending over the terrorist's right arm, she selected a large vein, then injected the drug. "There you go."

Bolan moved to one side and leaned against the wall. Weaver glanced at him inquisitively.

"I don't believe we've been introduced. Theresa Weaver. My friends call me Terri."

"Mike Belasko." Her warm handshake was as firm as any man's would be.

"Where have you been hiding, Mr. Belasko? I've worked for Mr. Brognola for seven years now and never seen you before."

Brognola cleared his throat, beckoning. Weaver stepped closer to the bed in case she was needed. Ely Welch groaned a few times, fidgeted and smacked his lips together.

"It won't be long," Weaver predicted.

Within a minute the terrorist's eyelids fluttered open, and he gulped air like a fish out of water. His pupils were dilated, and he seemed to take forever to turn his head as he surveyed the room. On seeing his visitors, Welch blinked a few times. "Where—" he croaked.

"At a hospital in Portland," Brognola replied. "We're federal agents. We need to ask you a few questions."

Welch gazed dully at the warrior and the bogus nurse. After licking his lips, he said in a ragged whisper, "Why do my legs feel funny?" He tried to raise his head to see the lower half of the bed, but he was much too weak.

Brognola frowned. "You were gravely wounded. The doctors were forced to amputate."

"Ampu—" Welch repeated thickly, choking off the rest of the word when the reality seared him. It shocked him so badly that the dull glaze disappeared, and in its stead raw panic lined his ashen features. "They cut off my legs? How dare they do that without my permission! I'll sue the whole bunch of them. See if I don't!" His tirade ended in a fit of coughing.

"Do you agree to answer us?" Brognola pressed. He was more than willing to have Weaver inject the man with a different substance if Welch refused.

The terrorist acted as if he hadn't heard. "No legs!" he cried, aghast. "I'll be a cripple the rest of my days. I'll have to use a wheelchair to get around. Dear God!"

Weaver took the initiative and gently placed a hand on his wrist. "There, there. I know this has come as a shock, but you must try to calm down or you'll only make yourself worse."

"I can't believe this is happening," Welch moaned. "It wasn't supposed to turn out like this."

"There's something you have to tell us," Brognola persisted. "Does Green Rage plan to make another attempt on the President's life during the Timber Summit?"

"What?" Welch said absently, focusing on the big Fed with difficulty. "Another try? Hell no. Once was enough. We were going to off the high-muck-a-muck just to distract you guys, anyway."

"How's that?"

"Something to keep all you Feds busy, to divert your attention from Creed's main plan."

"Which is?"

"Why should I tell you? Stupid Feds!" Welch closed his eyes and laughed softly. The loss of his legs had unhinged him. He was a man on the verge of losing his sanity. "I will say this, though. If all goes as planned, lots and lots of people are going to die." The laugh rose in volume. "Lots and lots!"

CHAPTER SEVEN

Mack Bolan rolled down the tinted window of the sedan he had rented at the Newark airport and promptly wished he hadn't. The air reeked of a foul odor that smelled like sulfur. He and Terri Weaver were traveling northeast toward New York City, and imposing industrial plants lined both sides of the highway.

The warrior had been to New Jersey several times. On many occasions he had wondered how the people who lived there tolerated the often rank smells that wafted from many of the more than eight hundred chemical plants stretching from near the Hudson River down to Camden.

"We should have brought gas masks," Weaver said jokingly. She looked positively stunning in a lacy dress which would have automatically gotten her arrested on certain street corners in New York City.

"Yeah," was all Bolan said. He had yet to get over his annoyance with Brognola for being saddled with a temporary partner he had neither requested nor desired. It was no secret that he liked to work alone. And on this assignment, given the nature of the opposition, the last thing he wanted was to have another person's safety on his mind.

"Are you always so talkative?" Weaver probed.

"Nothing personal."

"That's comforting. I was beginning to think it was my breath. You hardly spoke ten words to me the entire flight. I don't think it's fair, Mike. You can't blame me for this. If you have to be mad at someone, be mad at Ely Welch."

"I am, but he is dead," Bolan said, and gave her a wry grin that lightened the atmosphere.

In the end, the terrorist had talked. Brognola had merely nodded at Weaver, and she'd produced another hypodermic. Within five minutes Welch answered every question posed, revealing everything he knew. Unfortunately, Bolan mused, the man hadn't known enough.

The basic facts were that Jason Creed had taken up with an unidentified female. The pair went everywhere together, Garth Hunter had confided to his men. Except up into the Phoenix Mountains, where Creed had held a crash course in terrorist techniques for three envio squads.

None of the squads was supposed to know what the others were up to, but around the campfire at night a few facts had slipped out. Clay Packard, the man in charge of Envio Squad Two, had mentioned that Creed was sending him to the state Packard disliked the most, New Jersey.

By a sheer fluke, Welch had learned a little more. On the last day of the training sessions he had slipped away to sneak a smoke, a habit Creed despised. Two other men had strolled past his hiding place, and he had overheard part of their conversation.

Hunter and Packard had been comparing notes. Hunter complained that the trip to Portland might well be his last. Packard had replied that blowing up chemical plants was just as dangerous, and they'd both be lucky if they ever saw each other again. If not for the money, Packard had said, he wouldn't think of sticking his neck out.

Then Packard had made the remark responsible for Bolan being in New Jersey. "As if rigging the explosives without being caught won't be enough of a headache, I have to buy some of the components from the Sandman. I can't stand him."

"Who?" Hunter had asked, and the pair had walked out of earshot, leaving Ely Welch with no idea who the Sandman might be.

The Justice Department computers took up where Welch left off. A rundown of known felons had turned up a two-time loser with the nickname of Sandman, a moniker he received in the joint because he was forever sleeping, even when he was supposed to be at work. There was a reason. The prison doctors diagnosed him as narcoleptic.

His real name was James Potter. An electronics whiz, he had Mob ties and made his money on the shady side of the law, selling things like eavesdropping equipment, security devices, electronic detonators and whatever else his clients needed.

It made sense for Packard to go to Potter. It made sense that Creed planned to destroy the plants by remote control. So, to Hal Brognola, it had made sense to send in Bolan and Weaver, acting the part of Jason Creed and the terrorist leader's unidentified flame. It was a long shot, but it made sense.

Bolan reached into his shirt pocket and pulled out the slip of paper bearing Potter's last-known address. "We're looking for 212 Templeton in north Newark. Check the map again."

Weaver opened the glove compartment and took out the folded map of New Jersey. She spread it open on her lap and traced their route with a finger. "Another ten minutes if the traffic doesn't thin out."

"It won't," Bolan said. Rush hour was in full swing, and the streets and sidewalks of Newark were crammed. He could well believe that New Jersey had the highest population density of any state in the country.

"So you still haven't said," Weaver commented. "If it's not my breath, what's bothering you? Are you a lone wolf at heart? If so, have no fear. I won't step on your toes. Mr. Brognola was quite explicit in that respect. I'm to do as you say at all times, no questions asked."

"I usually work alone and don't want to keep looking over my shoulder to see if you're okay."

"Don't. I can handle myself. It's not like I'm fresh out of the academy. I've been in the field dozens of times. And I earned my marksman rating last year."

Bolan braked at a red light and was nearly hit from behind by a laundry truck whose overweight driver shook a fist at him. "I have no doubt that you're competent, or Hal wouldn't have sent you. But you being a woman—"

"Oh, God," Weaver interrupted. "Don't tell me. You're one of those Cro-Magnons who thinks that all women should be chained to their kitchen stoves. Women shouldn't have careers like men do. Is that it?"

The warrior looked at her. "You didn't let me finish. I started to say that your being a woman has nothing to do with it, in case you were wondering. But in our kind of work, we put our lives on the line each and every day. Man or woman, it makes no difference. A bullet to the brain is just as final. And man or woman, I'd worry about you."

Weaver's mouth had dropped open, but she quickly regained her composure. "My goodness. That's the most you've said to me since we met."

Bolan didn't answer. He'd already said enough.

As if she were psychic, Weaver said, "I understand now. You'd be concerned no matter who Mr. Brognola sent along. Well, you can put your mind at ease. I have no intention of being killed. Not when I'm getting married in four months."

The warrior glanced at her hands. There was no ring. "You're engaged?"

"Yes. But I don't wear my ring when I'm on the job. I don't want anything happening to it."

They shared an awkward moment. Then Weaver laughed, and Bolan smiled, glad the ice had been broken.

"Friends?" she asked.

"Friends," Bolan agreed.

Eventually they entered one of Newark's seamier districts. Dilapidated tenements lined both sides of the road; graffiti covered most walls; many windows were cracked or missing; young toughs hung out on street corners, greedily eyeing the sedan as it drove by.

"I could be wrong, but something tells me that the Sandman isn't one of society's upwardly mobile," Weaver commented.

"Or maybe he likes to keep a low profile," Bolan suggested.

Templeton Street contained an old market, a pharmacy with steel bars in its windows, assorted small stores and a brick building that bore a faded sign that read Potter's Electronics.

"Bingo," Bolan said. He made a circuit of the block, paying particular attention to the alley flanking the Sandman's place. A beat-up two-door was parked at the rear. Satisfied all was as it appeared to be, Bolan pulled to the curb in front of the establishment and switched off the ignition.

"You do realize," Weaver said softly, "that if Potter has ever met Creed in person, we're blown."

"In which case we hold him, give Hal a call and wait for his boys to collect our package."

Bolan slid out and glanced both ways. Few pedestrians were abroad. Three teens wearing gang colors stood on the corner to the west, but they showed no interest in him or the rental car. The warrior smoothed the front of his jacket, ensuring the Beretta was properly concealed.

Weaver joined him. She had a lithe, bouncy step that accented the sleek contours of her shapely figure. "Ready when you are."

As Bolan turned to the iron door, he had his first intimation of trouble. Sneakers padded on the sidewalk; lusty young voices snickered and chuckled. The next moment the three gang members had surrounded them and were openly ogling Weaver. Two were husky blacks, the third a thin white youth whose face had lost a war with acne.

"Will you look at this babe!" Pockmark declared. "Be still, my beatin' heart!"

"Definitely def," said a black with a tiny scar on his cheek.

"Tell us, Momma," the third chimed in. "How'd you like to dog it with three studly types?"

"Why don't you guys run along?" Bolan growled.

Pockmark tittered. "Oh, man! You've got us tremblin' in our shoes!" His expression became flinty. "Why don't *you* run along, dweeb, while we show your lady friend a good time?"

"Yeah, man," Scar added. "You don't want to be rilin' us, or we'll rag on you so bad your face will look like raw meat."

The Executioner's patience ran out. He didn't want to attract a lot of attention, so he was about to take all three down with a minimum of fuss when Weaver gave him a slight nod and sidled closer to Pockmark.

"Chill out, fellas," the woman said soothingly. "There's no need for all this hostility when we can be the best of friends."

"We can?" Pockmark said, expectation erasing the menace from his features.

Weaver touched the tip of a finger to the underside of his chin, smiled sweetly and said, "No way!" Her hand clamped onto his throat and she pivoted, driving her right knee into his groin. Pockmark screamed in pain and clutched at himself. Weaver let him go and spun on one heel to deliver a crisp snap kick to Scar's knee as he produced a switchblade. He went down with a yelp of pain.

As the third gang member lunged at Weaver's back, Bolan stepped between them, caught hold of one of the teen's wrists, twisted and sent the tough sailing into the wall. He whirled to finish off the other two, but his help wasn't needed. Scar was flat on his face, blood trickling from his nose. Pockmark was on his knees, crying pathetically.

"I can't stand his kind of slime," Weaver said, straightening and aligning her dress.

"You handle yourself well," Bolan said, and meant it. She had a natural flair for the martial arts and moved like someone who had practiced to the point where the moves were second nature. "Black belt?"

"Second degree." She offered her arm and nodded at the shop. "Shall we, Mr. Creed?"

Taking her slim elbow, Bolan walked to the door.

"Wait. What about those three? Shouldn't we drag them into the alley before someone notices?"

"In this neighborhood no one will care."

The interior of Potter's was gloomy and stuffy. Long benches were piled high with all sorts of electronic gear, most of it old and in need of repair. A short, obese man was just taking a seat on a stool behind the counter. His pudgy fingers dipped into a doughnut box, and he took a huge bite out of a jelly-filled doughnut, smearing his lips and chin.

James Potter fixed beady dark eyes on them while chewing loudly. He sniffled, then ran an arm across his nose, leaving a streak. "Hello, folks," he greeted with his mouth full. "Jim Potter at your service." His double chin bobbed at the street. "I saw what happened out there. Sorry about that. This neighborhood used to be a great place to live about twenty years ago. It's been going downhill ever since."

"Why do you stay, then?" Weaver asked.

Potter stuffed the last of the doughnut into his mouth. "My pa owned this place before me. Sure, it's a dump, but he paid off the mortgage before he kicked, so I own it free and clear. Keeps the overhead down." He shoved the doughnut box toward them. "Care for a bite? There's plenty. Help yourself."

Bolan planted himself in front of the man. "We didn't come here to eat. We came here for information."

"Oh?" Potter said. "And who might you be, mister?"

Casually slipping a hand under his jacket in anticipation of the worst, Bolan responded, "Jason Creed."

Brognola's plan hung in the balance. If Potter had ever met Creed, it was all over and they would have to track down Envio Squad Two the hard way. Bolan watched the piggish man's eyes for telltale clues.

The Sandman froze in the act of reaching for a doughnut. He glanced at Weaver, his gaze lingering. Swallowing hard, he said, "This is a surprise. I thought you made it plain that we were to conduct all our business by phone."

"There's been a hitch," Bolan said. "Did Packard pick up everything like he was supposed to?"

"You don't know?" Potter asked suspiciously.

"Would I be here if I did?" Bolan snapped. "He never reported in. The last I heard, he was going to pay you a visit."

"He did," Potter confirmed. "Sherman came with him."

"You delivered as promised?"

"Hey, I'm a pro. You wanted four custom-built radio detonators with a range of a thousand feet and a portable transmitter keyed to the same frequency. That's exactly what I turned over to them. I built those units from scratch, and I'll swear on my dad's grave that they'll work or you can have your money back."

Bolan pretended to ponder for a few moments. "Do you have any idea where Packard was headed after he left here? Did he say anything to you?"

"Yeah, as a matter of fact. He mentioned that he needed some C-4 so I sent him to see a pal of mine, Giorgio." Potter leaned forward and lowered his voice even though there was no one else in the store. "Just between you and me, Mr. Creed, I don't think Packard likes me very much. He always treats me as if I'm dirt. And that Sherman called me a fat toad to my face."

"Don't take it personally. Sherman just likes to flap his gums to hear himself talk," Bolan said.

"Is that it?" The Sandman sat back and drummed his fingers on the counter. "Well, it seems to me that your best bet would be to go see Giorgio. Do you have his address?"

"No. Packard dealt with him, not me."

"I have it in the back room. I'll get it for you." Sliding off the stool, Potter plodded to a brown door, crossed the threshold and closed the door behind him.

Weaver pressed her shoulder to the warrior's and spoke out of the corner of her mouth. "Well done. You had me convinced."

"Let's hope our luck holds. Maybe Giorgio knows where Packard is staying." Bolan idled the time away by examining the items piled on the left-hand table. A minute went by. Two minutes. He exchanged glances with Weaver, who shrugged.

"Slugs always move in slow motion."

The warrior let another couple of minutes elapse before he stalked to the brown door and reached for the knob. At the last instant his combat-honed instincts kicked in and he jerked his hand away as if he had been about to grab a red-hot poker.

"What's wrong?" Weaver asked.

"Come on," Bolan said, and hurried to the front. The gang members were gone, a smear of blood marking where one of them had been dragged off. He stepped to the corner, checked to be sure no unpleasant surprises awaited, then hustled to the rear of the building.

The two-door was gone.

"He suckered us," Bolan said in disgust.

"Why? Where did we go wrong?"

"I have no idea." The back door was open a crack, so Bolan peeked inside. Tools and state-of-the-art electronic components covered a workbench. This was where the Sandman earned his real bread and butter making illegal devices for his criminal cronies.

Bolan stepped inside. A file cabinet stood in one corner. As he crossed to it, he glanced at the inner brown door and saw a fine strand of filament wire strung from the knob to a rectangular green metal box on the floor. He bent to examine the trigger mechanism. The wire had been attached to the igniter by a snap hook. If he had opened that door, he would have been blown to bits.

"What is that thing?" Weaver asked at his side.

"An AP-12 antipersonnel mine," Bolan replied. "I haven't seen many of them over here. They're more common in Europe. Manufactured in Sweden, as I recall."

"Potter is a nasty piece of work, isn't he?"

"He has his moments. But he might have out-smarted himself this time."

"How so?"

Bolan indicated the filing cabinet. For a slob, the Sandman kept fairly meticulous records. There were files for his expense accounts, for wholesalers and distributors, for anything and everything that had to do with the running of the shop, even a file containing paid sanitation bills.

Weaver had taken a handful of files and was riffling through them. "What exactly are we looking for?"

"Any mention of Giorgio."

"But if he's a Mob connection, surely Potter wouldn't be stupid enough to keep a file on him."

"You never know. Giorgio might run a legitimate business as a front, just like Potter."

The bottom drawer yielded the prize. Terri Weaver plucked out a file bearing the name Giorgio's Guns and Ammo. "It's on the south side of Newark," she revealed while scanning a receipt for a Smith & Wesson revolver, "at 4242 Stanton Boulevard."

"Bring the file." Bolan ushered her outside, then told her to wait and stepped to the booby-trapped inner door. Working carefully, he removed the loop of wire from the knob, disarmed the mine and left the shop.

Templeton Street was virtually deserted. Bolan peeled out of there, following Weaver's directions as she guided him using the map. They traveled six blocks and turned right. The warrior checked the rearview mirror out of habit, tensing when an old Chevy made the same turn. "You'd better buckle your seat belt," he advised.

"Why?"

"We have a tail."

SPOCKTACTIC

CHAPTER EIGHT

The Sandman wasn't the only nasty piece of work.

A dozen FBI agents found out the hard way that Jason Creed deserved his reputation as a vicious fanatic. About the same time that the Executioner spotted the tail, they were converging on the door to Creed's third-floor condominium.

Fred Winslow, the agent in charge, had conducted the operation by the book. The phone line to Creed's condominium had been tapped in order to monitor any incoming or outgoing calls. The other tenants had then been quietly evacuated. An agent posing as a pizza deliveryman had gone to Creed's door and knocked. No one had answered, but the agent distinctly heard a stereo playing inside.

Winslow figured Creed and his rumored lady friend were enjoying some sack time. He positively tingled at how much of a boost his career would get after he brought down Creed. Already he was looking ahead to a plum assignment in Washington, D.C., to a nice, cushy desk job where his life wouldn't be on the line every minute of every day.

The thickly padded carpet betrayed no sound as the agents crept to the door and spread out with six on either side. At a nod from Winslow, two agents squatted in front of the door and applied a thin strip of C-4 plastique from top to bottom next to both jambs. The agents taped detonation cord in place, backing down the hall as they did, and rigged it to detonate electrically.

Winslow waved his agents off and retreated beyond the danger zone. He was taking no chances with a killer like Creed. Rather than kick in the door the old-fashioned way, Winslow was going in fast and hard using every tool at his disposal. Jason Creed would never know what hit him.

The *crump* of the blast was amplified by the narrow corridor. Fragments of wood whizzed through the air like angry bees. The agents had done their job well, and the only real damage was to the door, which flew inward as if rocket propelled.

"Smoke!" Winslow barked, and saw three of his men toss canisters through the door. Tucking his Uzi to his side, he went in first, legs pumping, an adrenaline high heightening his senses.

The white chemical smoke spewing from the canisters had partially filled the living room. Lively jazz still blared from a pair of speakers.

Winslow had the layout of the condo memorized and dashed toward the master bedroom. Six seasoned agents were right on his heels. The rest had orders to block the doorway and keep Creed from escaping if by some miracle the terrorist slipped past Winslow.

The bedroom door was slightly ajar. The agent went in low, his shoulder flinging the door wide. He dodged to the left to evade lethal fire, but there was none. His back to the bedroom wall, he stared at the neatly made bed. He had been so keyed up at the thought of taking the infamous Creed into custody that it took a few moments for him to realize his trophy wasn't even home.

"Check the other rooms!" Winslow bellowed, rising. "Under beds. In closets. Everywhere."

The agents dispersed.

Winslow stood slowly, wrestling with his disappointment. He happened to glance at the mahogany dresser, at the ornate mirror above it. A large note had been taped to the glass. In black ink two words had been scribbled, two words that sent a stark chill down Winslow's spine: Got You.

For all of five embarrassing seconds Winslow's legs behaved like putty. Taking a breath, he plunged out the doorway. "Get out!" he shouted, too shrilly for his liking. "Everyone get the hell out of here, now!"

Only one agent was in the hallway, and he gave Winslow a puzzled look.

"Do it!" Winslow roared, shoving a man who popped out of another room. He couldn't see the agents barring the door for all the smoke, but he hoped fervently they had heard and were obeying. As he raced toward the outer hall he realized the music had stopped and the condo was deathly still except for the beat of fleeing feet.

The pit of Winslow's stomach compacted into a tight knot, and he knew he wasn't going to make it, knew he would never see his wife and kids again, knew his cherished promotion was a pipe dream that had cost him his life.

Outside the Cheshire Condominiums, two young agents stood by one of the unmarked vans in which the strike team had arrived. They wore body armor and carried M-16s. Both were angry that Winslow had seen fit to leave them behind. True, someone had to watch the vans, but why couldn't it have been someone else?

"This sucks," Billy Mitchell groused.

"You know it," Danzel Edwards agreed. "I had my heart set on making the news. Now I never will."

As if to prove the agent wrong, the entire upper level of the building suddenly mimicked a volcano, erupting in a spectacular explosion visible as far as the distant Phoenix Mountains, a blast so loud that every window within a quarter mile was reduced to slivers. One side of the structure crumpled like a stack of dominoes and came crashing down, showering bricks, beams and stucco onto the unmarked vans and the young agents.

"Look out!" Mitchell cried, just before a chunk of wall the size of a Buick crushed him to the ground.

Edwards frantically backpedaled, his brain denying what was happening while his eyes screamed for him to run.

Something struck Edwards on the right shoulder and sent him flying. He scuffed his hands and knees on the rough pavement, pushed to his feet and spun to behold a disaster.

It would be a long time before the Cheshire Condominiums were fit for human habitation. The upper floor was gone, as was a good portion of the lower levels. The sections still standing sagged terribly and were filled with debris. Smoke curled into the sky. Somewhere in the ruins, a cat meowed.

And it was patently obvious that a lot of damage had been done.

TERRI WEAVER HAD SHIFTED to study the five occupants of the Chevy. "They look like more gang members to me. Bloods, Crips, whatever, I can't tell. But they're definitely wearing colors."

"We don't have time for this. We have to get to Giorgio's before the Sandman warns him about us."

"Do you think he will?"

"Why else would Potter take off like that?" Bolan asked while making a sharp left. Less than thirty seconds later the Chevy appeared in the mirror. Heads bobbed, arms moved. Bolan reckoned that hardware was being readied. "The last thing we want is a firefight in the middle of downtown Newark. Hang on. I'm going to try to lose them."

The sedan leapt ahead when Bolan floored the accelerator. He caught the driver of the Chevy napping and made a turn before the locals got their act together and sped up. The rental car wasn't designed for speed, though, and the best he could do on the narrow streets, with all the cross traffic and pedestrians using the crosswalks, was forty-five to fifty miles per hour.

Whatever the street toughs had under the hood of that old Chevy was another story. The battered gray car squealed around the turn and roared after the sedan as if the driver thought he was qualifying for the Indy 500. He didn't bother slowing for cross traffic and caused two accidents in the first two blocks. Pedestrians were forced to scramble for their lives or be run down.

Bolan saw punks lean out windows on both sides of the Chevy. One appeared to be holding a Heckler & Koch assault rifle, the other an Armalite AR-18.

"They're gaining," Weaver commented matter-of-factly. She reached into her purse and produced a SIG-Sauer P-225. Popping out the magazine, she verified it held the full eight rounds, then slapped the clip back in and fed a round into the chamber. Twisting, she rolled down her window.

The warrior had kept one eye on the gang members, who were less than a block behind now. He saw the kid with the Heckler & Koch snap up the rifle and shouted, "Get down!"

Bullets tore into the rear window, stitched an uneven line of neat holes from one side to the other, narrowly missed the top of the front seat and perforated the windshield. Amazingly both windows remained intact.

Bolan straightened, caught Weaver doing the same out of the corner of his eye and hauled on the steering wheel at the next corner, hanging a left. She eased out the window, her hair whipped by the wind. Adopting a two-handed grip, she took careful aim and waited for the speed demon to show.

So intent was Bolan on seeing her nail the junior-grade hardmen that he nearly missed spotting the two little girls who suddenly materialized from between a pair of parked cars, directly in his path. He jerked the wheel to miss them, swerving to the left, which in turn nearly pitched Weaver out the window.

"Hey! What the blazes are you trying to do?" Weaver saw the girls, and added, "Damn it!"

The gray car had screeched around the corner. Those little girls, riveted in place by the shock of their narrow escape, were watching the sedan, their backs to the Chevy. Neither realized the souped-up vehicle was bearing down on them.

"Terri!" Bolan yelled.

She took one look and brought up the pistol. In steady cadence she banged off four shots as smoothly as Bolan himself could have done. He saw holes blossom in the windshield of the Chevy, saw the car swerve just enough to miss the children.

"Those cold-hearted bastards!" Weaver fumed. "They would have run over those kids without a second thought."

"Hang on," Bolan urged, making yet another turn, this time to the right. Since the opposition enjoyed the advantage of speed and firepower, he had to rely on his wits to stop them. He spied an alley, but the mouth was blocked by an illegally parked truck.

Bolan flashed past several intersections at sixty miles an hour. The ramshackle homes thinned, and the warrior found himself in a warehouse district. Few people were abroad, so at last he could concentrate on the pseudowarriors and not have to worry about bystanders. The crack of Weaver's pistol rang in his ears as he shot through an open gate into a huge parking lot. A loading dock stood off to the right, piled high with pallets and crates.

The Chevy reached the gate just as the sedan neared the end of the loading dock. Bolan shot up the ramp, mentally crossing his fingers that he hadn't boxed them in. The fender brushed one of the high stacks of pallets but didn't knock it over.

The driver of the gray speedster lacked the warrior's skill. He arrowed onto the ramp at the wrong angle, rammed into some crates, overcompensated and smashed into some pallets. In trying to straighten, he nearly sent the car over the edge. Tramping on the brakes at the last moment was all that averted a crash.

It bought Bolan precious seconds. He came to the far ramp. At the bottom he cut to the left and slid to a stop in a swirling cloud of dust. Throwing his door wide, the warrior leapt out, drawing the Desert Eagle as he cleared the seat. He ran to the side of the ramp and had the big .44 fully extended in time to give the gang members a suitable greeting.

The toughs were caught off guard. One of them seemed to be arguing with the driver while the gunner holding the Armalite was awkwardly inserting a new magazine. At a bellow from one of them, all five looked up in a panic.

The Desert Eagle roared twice, the .44 Magnum rounds taking out two gang members. Weaver's SIG-Sauer joined in the lethal litany. Windshield and windows shattered as the would-be killers were reduced to blood-splattered mannequins thrashing about in a macabre dance of death.

The driver had to have stomped on the gas pedal in his final death throes because the Chevy surged forward. It was doing ninety, easy, when it came to the ramp and hurtled into the air, wheels spinning.

About twenty feet from the bottom of the ramp sat a large forklift. The gray battering ram slammed into it, and the vehicles, locked together, slid across the lot. Sparks shot out from the car's undercarriage; the shriek of tortured metal was horrendous.

Bolan sprinted forward as the Chevy ground to a stop. The impact had driven the car's engine into the front seat, reducing the torsos of two of the toughs to pulp. The three in the back seat were mangled almost as badly.

"Good riddance to bad rubbish," Weaver remarked while reloading.

A siren wailed to the southeast.

Bolan didn't intend to spend the rest of the day at a police station answering countless questions. He ran for the sedan and worked the shift lever as soon as Weaver jumped in.

At the gate the warrior bore to the left. Sirens now blared all over north Newark, and in the distance lights flashed. Bolan picked another street. A few blocks farther on he changed course again. By sticking to side streets and slowly but surely bearing to the south, he eluded the net thrown up by Newark's police force and wound up within a few miles of Giorgio's gun shop.

At last they could relax. Bolan stretched and glanced at his partner. "You did well back there."

"For a woman, you mean?" Weaver asked, only half in jest.

"You did well, period."

"Thank you. You didn't do half-bad yourself."

"For a man, you mean?" the Executioner asked dryly.

Weaver's response was cut short by the appearance of a police car cruising toward them in the opposite lane. "Here's where we learn if they have a description of our vehicle."

Bolan spotted an alley and considered ducking into it but discarded the idea since doing so might attract the very attention he wanted to avoid. Feigning a yawn, he put a hand over his mouth and watched the officers on the sly. They were immersed in conversation and didn't give the sedan a second glance.

"Luck is with us for once," Weaver said. "Now if only it will hold when we reach Giorgio's."

It didn't. The gun shop was in a small shopping center, flanked by a printer and a carpet store. A sign in the door announced that the shop was closed, but Bolan walked to the window anyway and peered inside as if admiring the firearms on display. The lights were out, and there was no one inside.

"What do you make of it?" Weaver inquired.

"Either Potter warned him and Giorgio flew the coop, or Giorgio is taking a late lunch. We'll wait."

There was a sandwich shop across the street. Bolan pointed it out and said, "We better grab something to eat while we have the chance."

"Sounds good to me. Lead on," Weaver said agreeably as she slipped her warm hand into his.

"We're supposed to be a couple, aren't we?" the woman said in response to his quizzical look. "We should act the part."

They slid into a booth that afforded an unobstructed view of the shopping center. Bolan ordered a cheese sub while Weaver picked a hamburger with all the trimmings. In short order the food was delivered and the warrior dug in. He raised a querying eyebrow when he caught Weaver studying him. "What?"

"I was just wondering whether you're one of Brognola's special agents, and whether I should give it a shot."

"Special agents?"

"Don't act as if you don't know what I'm talking about. If you've worked for Brognola any length of time, you must have heard the rumors. They say he has a special team of agents stashed away somewhere. The best of the best, as it were. The rumor is that these agents tackle only the toughest assignments."

"You should know better than to listen to gossip," Bolan said, while making a note to talk to Brognola about the connection between loose lips and sunk ships.

It was inevitable, though, he supposed. Stony Man Farm ranked as one of the government's best-kept secrets, but no secret was airtight. The Farm hadn't built itself, and some of the support personnel were bound to have wagged their tongues now and then.

"I'm not asking you to admit whether you are one," Weaver continued hastily. "All I want is for you to consider putting in a good word with Mr. Brognola the next time an opening comes up."

Bolan simply stared.

"Don't look at me like that. I'm serious. My career is everything to me. I'd give my right arm to be part of Brognola's elite team."

"If it exists," Bolan amended.

"Of course. But let's take it for granted for a minute that the gossip is true. How would I go about joining?"

"You might talk to Hal."

"I've brought it up a few times, and in each instance he shrugged off my questions. It's so aggravating. He knows how devoted I am to our government and the principles for which it stands. And he knows I can hold my own anywhere, anytime. Why won't he take the hint and offer me a position?"

The warrior felt a twinge of sympathy. Her frustration was genuine, and understandable given her ability.

"There must be a reason," Weaver went on. She mulled it over a little while nibbling at her food. Abruptly her features became diamond hard. "Wait a minute. Tell me something. To your knowledge, are there any women on this special strike team?''

"You'd have to ask Hal," Bolan reiterated softly.

"That's the bottom line, isn't it? It's a men-only club, I'll bet. Oh, maybe there are a few women on the sidelines cheering the home team on, but Brognola won't put women into combat situations as a matter of course. Yes or no?''

Bolan was actually glad when a black car pulled up in front of the gun shop and two men in sport shirts and slacks got out. He pointed for Weaver's benefit. They watched the shorter of the pair insert a key and open the door. "Ready to go into the trenches again?''

"I'm always ready," Weaver shot back. "But try telling that to Hal Brognola.''

Weaver insisted on going dutch, and Bolan knew not to argue with her in her frame of mind. As they crossed to the shopping center he saw the taller man take the Closed sign from the window.

"How do you want to play this?" the woman asked. "Do we go for the gusto or wing it and try to scam them into telling us what we need to know?''

"I've never been one to do things halfway," Bolan replied. He slipped a hand behind his back to loosen the Desert Eagle as he opened the door. Overhead, a tiny bell tinkled. Neatly displayed racks of guns lined both walls and formed two rows up the middle. A pine scent hung heavy in the air thanks to a pair of green air fresheners hanging from small hooks in the ceiling.

The taller man, who had black hair and a twisted nose and looked to be in his early to mid-twenties, was stacking boxes of ammunition by the cash register. He glanced up and gave them the once-over. "Can I help you folks?"

"Where's Giorgio?" Bolan said, certain the man wasn't.

"Who wants to know?"

"Tell him a mutual friend sent me. The Sandman." Bolan leaned on the counter and observed Weaver place her purse on top of a gun case and remove a small mirror. She fiddled with her hair, her other hand close to the open flap, within quick reach of her pistol. The woman never missed a trick.

"I'll see if Mr. Giorgio is in," the tall man grumbled. Backing through a curtain, he wasn't gone twenty seconds when the curtain was thrown wide and the shorter man strode out. What he lacked in height he made up for in muscle. His salt-and-pepper hair had been cropped short, and his mustache was clipped at the corners.

"I'm Abe Giorgio. Bruno says that you mentioned the Sandman?"

"He gave me reason to think that you were the last one to see an acquaintance of mine, Clay Packard. I'd like to know if Packard picked up the merchandise he needed."

"Is that a fact? And who might you be?"

"My name isn't important. I'm just trying to find Packard."

"Oh, I think you're trying to do more than that, mister," Giorgio responded, and snapped his fingers. Immediately Bruno and James Potter leapt from behind the curtain, each holding a Mossberg pistol-grip shotgun.

The warrior started to make a grab for the Desert Eagle while Weaver's hand darted into her purse, but both of them were stopped cold by the metallic ratchet of two slide handles being pumped.

"I wouldn't do that if I were you," Abe Giorgio said smugly. "Not unless you're partial to being buried in bits and pieces."

CHAPTER NINE

Jason Creed was a new man, figuratively speaking. He had bleached his hair blond, clipped and styled it, and affixed a sandy mustache to his upper lip. Dressed as he was in a new suit and tie, with a shiny black attaché case beside his chair, he looked just like an up-and-coming business executive, which was the image he wanted to convey.

Julie Constantine had gone him one better. Her raven tresses were now shoulder length and a luxurious auburn. The prim dress she wore concealed her ample charms, while the fake glasses on her nose lent her an intellectual air, or so she thought.

Seated in the lounge at Los Angeles International Airport, Creed scanned the front page of the newspaper spread out on his lap. "Listen to this. 'Thirteen FBI agents were slain in Phoenix when they raided a condominium rigged with a massive quantity of high explosives.'" He couldn't keep the corners of his mouth from twitching upward. "Imagine that. How horrible."

"Is there any mention of that awful assassination attempt on the President?" Constantine asked loud enough for those seated near them to hear and appreciate her counterfeit outrage.

"Yes, there is," Creed replied, playing his part to perfection. "The authorities are at their wit's end. All their leads have turned out to be dead ends. And the one prisoner they took, Ely Welch, has died due to complications stemming from the amputation of both his legs."

"What a sorry world it is we live in."

Creed decided to change the subject before Julie got carried away with herself. She always did, given half the chance. Before long she'd be weeping for all those unfortunate federal agents. Julie was a wonderful actress when she wanted to be, much better than he was, although he would never admit it.

"Hawaii is the exception to the rule. Once you've seen those golden beaches and taken a dip in the ocean, you'll forget all your cares and woes."

A middle-aged woman wearing expensive clothes leaned toward them and gave a tiny cough. "Pardon me, I couldn't help but overhear. Is this your first trip to the Islands?"

"Yes," Creed lied.

"Oh, you'll just love it. I can guarantee," the woman said. "I've gone every other year for almost two decades. There's no place else on the planet quite like it."

"Every place is unique," Creed said. "That's why it's a shame to see our natural resources being so grossly squandered."

Some of the woman's friendliness evaporated. "Excuse me for asking, but you're not one of those darned tree lovers, are you?"

Creed had no choice. He knew himself well enough to realize that if the old bat got him started, he'd get more carried away than Julie and start spouting off about the vile rape of the planet and how any act was justified if it was in defense of the world that nurtured them. Instead, he answered, "Certainly not. What do you take me for?"

"I didn't mean to offend you. It's just that all this terrible Green Rage business makes a body want to pull her hair out. How can people be so stupid? What makes those lunatics think that the life of a tree means more than the life of a fellow human being?"

"Maybe they're looking at the whole picture," Creed said lamely.

"I don't see how you can say that. They're crazies, the whole bunch of them. Why else did they try to kill the President after he organized a summit to save the very trees they claim to care so much about?" The woman sniffed. "They must have the brains of a turnip, as my dear departed husband would have said. Either that, or it's the drugs."

"Drugs, madam?"

"Don't tell me you haven't heard? All those radicals spend their free time smoking dope or shooting stuff into their veins and having orgies and such."

Creed couldn't help himself. "Have that on reliable authority, do you, you old biddy?"

"What?"

"You heard me. If you ask me, you're just jealous because no one would invite you to an orgy if you asked them."

An indignant gasp preceded the woman's rising and walking off in a huff to a different seat.

Constantine leaned on the arm of her chair and regarded Creed coldly. "That was brilliant, Sherlock. Why don't you just wear a sign telling everyone who you are?"

"Get off my case," Creed retorted. "You heard her. The snotty bitch had it coming."

"Speaking of coming," Constantine said, nodding, "look who just strolled down the aisle."

A pair of security guards approached. Creed saw the woman spot them and start to rise. He wouldn't put it past her to go over and complain about his rude behavior. The guards would probably laugh it off since he hadn't done anything illegal, but he couldn't take that for granted. They might be self-righteous types who liked to throw their weight around at every opportunity.

The woman sat back down but held herself on the edge of her seat. Creed watched the security team without being obvious. He was confident his disguise would fool anyone, but he didn't care to put it to the test, not when he was unarmed.

Constantine, true to form, was whistling to herself and staring absently off into space as if she didn't have a care in the world.

The security guards stopped. One of them took out a walkie-talkie and spoke softly. Moments later the pair wheeled and hastened back toward the main terminal.

Creed let out the breath he hadn't known he was holding and smiled at his companion, who rolled her eyes to signify he had been worked up over nothing.

None too soon, the departure of their flight was announced. They boarded, and Creed slouched down in his seat, reducing his formidable height by a good five inches. He had claimed the window seat and now made himself comfortable. Once the aircraft was in the air, he could relax totally, a rare luxury.

Constantine put her carryon in the overhead rack before she oozed into her chair. "I could do with a nap. We've been on the go since we left Arizona."

"Might as well. We'll be busy once we land."

"Are you sure this old friend of yours will cooperate? What if we go to all this trouble and he refuses?"

Creed lowered his voice. "You make it sound as if he has a choice. Trust me, babe. If Axel won't go along with the program, the program will go along without Axel. I won't let anyone or anything stand in our way." He tapped the window. "Take a good look at L.A. By the time we're done, there won't be a soul living here. Not for the next thousand years, anyway."

IT WAS RARE for the Executioner to be caught off guard when he knew he might be walking into a trap. The only reason that he was this time was that he had agreed to play along with the program set in motion by Brognola, and there had been an outside chance that the plan would still work despite the Sandman's vanishing act.

Bolan regretted his decision when Abe Giorgio came around the counter and relieved him of the big Desert Eagle and the Beretta. Weaver was disarmed, as well.

"Thought you'd pull a fast one on old Abe, huh? You're none too bright, either of you. I haven't lasted as long as I have, with only one minor drunk-and-disorderly on my rap sheet, by being stupid."

Weaver acted indignant. "What is this all about? We're friends of Clay Packard. We were led to believe that you sold him some C-4. Now he's disappeared, and we were wondering if you knew where he might be."

"Cut the crap, sweetheart," Giorgio said. His thick finger stabbed at the warrior. "Your boyfriend here already blew it for you."

The Sandman chortled. "That's right, foxy. He screwed up when I told him about Sherman calling me a fat toad. Remember? Your friend here said that Sherman just liked to flap his gums."

"Yeah. So?"

"So Sherman's first name is Gloria."

Bolan betrayed no reaction but he was irked by his blunder.

Giorgio leaned his elbows back on the edge of the counter and gave Bolan and Weaver a close scrutiny. "So what are you? Cops?"

Neither answered.

"You might as well fess up," Giorgio prodded. "It won't make a difference. You're dead meat either way."

"You're making a big mistake," Weaver warned.

"No, lady, *you* made the boneheaded move. You see, there's something you don't know. Something even Potter didn't know when he sent you to see me."

"Which is?"

Giorgio smiled cockily. "Another reason I've lasted so long is that I won't do business with just any Tom, Dick or Myrtle who comes down the pike. I don't sell to punk kids, I don't sell to junkies. I don't sell to anyone if it doesn't feel right. Get me?"

"No."

"Then let me spell it out for you. Sure, the Sandman recommended me to Packard. But there was something about that arrogant bastard and his friends that I didn't like. So I put him off twenty-four hours, told him I had to see if my supplier had enough C-4 on hand, and then had Bruno shadow them. He planted a bug in their hotel room when they went out to eat."

Bolan finally spoke up. "You learned they were part of Green Rage."

"You've got it," Giorgio said. "Damned crazies. I hate those freaking environmental wackos. They'll waste anybody over a few stinking flowers or a bunch of stupid owls." He scowled in disgust. "No way would I do business with scuzzies like them. When Packard came back, I told him that I couldn't get my hands on the goods he wanted. He was ticked off until I gave him the names of a few independent operators who might be able to help him out."

The whole time Giorgio talked, Potter had been fidgeting. "Why are you telling them all this, Abe? Shouldn't we waste them while we have the chance? If they're cops or Feds, they might have backups who will bust in here any minute."

"Jimmy, Jimmy, Jimmy," Giorgio said. "First off, Vinnie is outside keeping watch. If these chumps had friends, we'd know it by now. Second, only a grade-A moron wastes someone in his own place. Know what I mean?"

"But what—" the Sandman began to protest.

"Hush your mouth," Giorgio said sternly. "Do I tell you how to run your business? Don't try to tell me how to run mine. I've been doing it for more years than you, and I've never been in the slammer." He walked to the front of the store, giving the warrior a wide berth. After reversing the sign to show the place was closed, he pulled the blinds and locked the door. "All right. Out the back."

Bolan had no choice but to comply. Arms held out where the hardmen could see them, he followed Weaver around the counter and into a large room lined with shelves containing ammo, holsters, cleaning kits and other items of the gun trade. In one corner a rack held lever-action rifles and several pump-action shotguns. On a table sat a stripped-down pistol, in the process of being repaired. All perfectly legitimate.

Bolan had to hand it to Giorgio and Bruno. They were indeed pros. They covered him as they would a stalking tiger. Both stayed at least three paces away at all times and never let the barrels of their weapons dip.

The Sandman opened the rear door and looked both ways. "The coast is clear, Abe."

"Hold up."

Bruno trained the shotgun on Weaver. "Arms in front. Both of you," he directed. "Wrists touching."

Giorgio walked to a cabinet and took out a huge roll of clear tape. Then he walked up behind Bolan and touched the barrel of the Desert Eagle to the back of the warrior's head. "Not one twitch. You hear me? Jimmy, you do the honors. At least ten turns apiece around their wrists."

The Sandman was clearly not thrilled, but he obeyed. Working quickly yet nervously, he did the warrior first.

Bolan contrived to hold his wrists so that there was a slim margin of slack. Not much, but he hoped it would suffice later to enable him to work his hands free—provided they didn't kill him first.

Weaver, oddly enough, grinned sweetly at the Sandman and baited him, saying, "What's the matter, Jimmy? You're sweating like a pig, but it's nice and cool in here. Never been an accessory to murder before?"

Potter blanched and finished taping her. "You have a real smart mouth on you, bitch. I think I'll drink to the memory of it after you've been snuffed."

The Sandman handed the tape to Giorgio. "Is there anything else you need me for? If not, I'd like to split. There's some work I need to catch up on at my shop."

"Go," Giorgio said. "I'll phone you after we get back." He paused while Potter turned. "And Jimbo?"

"What?"

"In the future be more careful who you send my way. I've warned you time and again that you're too damn greedy. You can't go around doing business with every jerk who walks in off the street. Didn't you learn your lesson the last time you were sent to the joint?"

"Sorry, Abe. I guess bad habits are hard to break."

"Beat it. Send Vinnie around before you leave."

Bolan had been watching Bruno for any sign of sloppiness, but the young killer hadn't made any mistakes. The man never dropped his guard. Giorgio, on the other hand, was more relaxed, more casual about the whole thing, yet he was always alert, ready to cut loose if the need arose.

Outdoors, Bolan caught sight of a shiny new blue van. A gun jabbed into his lower spine, and he was goaded to within a step of the sunlight.

Bruno slipped outside and opened a sliding door. The inside of the vehicle was richly carpeted. A pair of plush swivel seats and a small bar showed its owner liked his creature comforts.

In a few moments another young gunner joined them. His black hair was slicked back, and he wore a black leather jacket with bulges under each arm. "What's up, boss?"

"We're going for a ride in the country, Vinnie," Giorgio replied. "Do you remember how to get to that salt marsh where we dumped the traitor and his coke-head girlfriend?"

"No problem, Mr. G."

"Then you handle the wheel. And no speeding this time. We can't afford to be stopped by the cops. Understand?"

The reference to a marsh gave Bolan food for thought. It was a little-known fact that even though New Jersey was densely populated, more than half the state was covered by pine forests, marshes and swamps. One particular region, known as the Pine Barrens, had long been a Mob dumping ground for victims slain in New York City and the gambling resorts.

If Bolan recalled correctly, the nearest salt marshes to Newark were to the south, a good hour and a half away. There was a slim chance he could use the time to his advantage and overpower his captors.

Vinnie pushed Weaver and Bolan into the vehicle. He put a hand on the woman's bottom and pinched hard as he shoved her, then laughed when she glared. "This one has a nice tush, Mr. G. Too bad we can't have some fun with her first."

"Never mix business with pleasure, kid," Giorgio said as he slid into the passenger seat.

Only Bruno sat in one of the plush chairs, his shotgun propped on his lap, the muzzle trained on Bolan and Weaver.

The warrior had eased to the floor with his back against a side panel and his arms between his bent legs. Weaver sat facing front. Seemingly by accident, her dress hiked high on her thighs. The gunner's eyes were drawn to her creamy skin like iron slivers to a magnet.

"You pig," she grated, and shifted so her back was to him. She jerked her dress down, then sagged forward as if distraught and groaned, "What have we gotten ourselves into?"

True to Bolan's hunch, the van traveled to the south. Giorgio turned on the radio and caught part of a newscast detailing the deaths of five gang members in a shoot-out. Shifting to sneer at Bolan, he commented, "Your deaths won't be on the news, I can tell you that. No one will ever know what became of you. Even if you are cops."

Weaver raised her head. "It seems to me that you're not very bright, Abe. I mean, do you always go around killing someone just because you suspect they might be trouble?"

"Always. I have a creed I live by, missy, and so far it's kept me from rotting away behind bars."

"A creed?"

"Never take anything for granted. Never trust anyone. And when in doubt, bury the sucker."

"Let's assume you're right. Let's take it as a given that we're the law. If you kill us, we'll be missed. Others will come looking for us."

"Let them," Giorgio replied. "The chumps will have no idea where to look. And while they're playing footsie with me, my lawyers will have all the time in the world to cook up an airtight defense." He leaned an elbow on the top of the seat. "So come on. Tell me who you work for. It must annoy the hell out of you to know you're going to buy the farm because of a bunch of flakes like Green Rage."

"We're not Feds. We only want to know where to find Clay Packard."

"Liar, liar, panties on fire," Giorgio said, and laughed at his own wit. Lifting her purse into view, he plucked out her badge and ID. He had been holding them all along. "What's this, then, sugar? It says here that you're Special Agent Weaver with the Justice Department." In contempt, he spit on the badge and tossed it to the floor. "I don't like being played for a fool. I may have dropped out of school in the ninth grade, but I know a Fed when I smell one. And, sweetheart, you reeked to high heaven the moment I set eyes on you. You and the big guy, both."

Bolan had no intention of joining in the conversation. He knew a lost cause when he saw one. Instead, he worked at loosening the tape. Without being obvious, he rubbed his wrists back and forth repeatedly, until his skin was chafed and aching. But the pain was a small price to pay when his life and Weaver's hung in the balance.

HAL BROGNOLA STOOD at the window of his office in the Justice Department and saw his patent scowl reflected back at him.

It wasn't bad enough that the Green Rage had made world headlines by nearly assassinating the President. Outdoing himself, Jason Creed had blown apart thirteen FBI agents down in Phoenix. It had been a worse fiasco than that business in Waco, Texas, a while back.

Brognola blamed himself. No, he hadn't been the agent in charge in Phoenix, but he'd given the orders to involve the FBI. The buck stopped at his desk, and he had never been one to shirk responsibility.

Every time the big Fed thought that he had Creed nailed, the bastard up and slipped through his fingers. It was damned aggravating.

His best and brightest hope lay in Striker, and now Bolan and Weaver had gone missing. The Executioner should have contacted him an hour ago, which meant something had gone wrong.

He could still see the twinge of disapproval on Bolan's face when he suggested the warrior and Weaver pair up. Except when working with Able Team or Phoenix Force, Bolan liked to play the field alone. The big Fed knew that, but he had insisted. He thought his clever plan to be foolproof. He should have known better.

Hal Brognola sank into his chair, staring at the phone, willing it to ring. But it didn't. "Come on, Mack," he said aloud. "Don't do this to me." His voice changed to a raspy growl born of frustration and friendship. "Where the hell are you?"

CHAPTER TEN

The van had been winding along a dirt road for the better part of an hour. Mack Bolan kept his back braced against the side panel to keep from being jostled more roughly than he already was thanks to the rutted, pockmarked surface.

Bolan had used the time well. The tape was loose enough that he could almost but not quite slip out a hand. Another few minutes, he figured, should suffice.

Salt marsh surrounded them on both sides. High reeds and cattails bent in the wind. Small, grassy islands broke the flat, shimmering mirror of water that seemed to go on for as far as the eye could see. Lilies floated everywhere. Great, noisy flocks of ducks and geese called the marsh home, and at times the racket they made with their quacking and honking was enough to drown out the muted purr of the van's motor.

Little had been said in quite some time.

Vinnie concentrated on his driving. Based on the way he gnawed his lower lip and cast worried glances at the marsh, Bolan pegged him for a city boy, born and bred, who didn't like being out of his natural element.

Abe Giorgio was reading a newspaper.

Bruno had been fighting off boredom for most of the trip, stifling yawns before his boss noticed. Occasionally he shifted in the chair, which had caused the muzzle of the shotgun to drift to the right.

Their behavior was typical of junior-league players. They thought they knew what they were doing, but they were too sure of themselves. Killing informants and junkies was easy. It had given them a false sense of confidence the warrior was about to dash to pieces on the bitter rocks of reality.

Terri Weaver's behavior, however, wasn't at all typical. Normally a firebrand, she had sat bent over practically the whole trip, as if too upset to lift her head. Several times she had made loud sniffling noises, as if crying. Each time Vinnie had laughed.

Suddenly the road crested a low knoll dotted with rocks. Bolan knew their journey was at an end. A pond choked with water plants glistened below the knoll. All the hardmen had to do was weigh down their bodies with forty or fifty pounds of those rocks and no one would ever find them again.

"End of the line, kiddies," Giorgio said, confirming the warrior's guess. He yanked on the sliding door, then stepped back. Apparently he had taken a liking to Bolan's Desert Eagle because he had it wedged under his belt. Pulling the weapon, he gestured. "Let's go, Bruno. We don't have all damn day."

Vinnie and Bruno flanked their employer, Vinnie with a pair of nickel-plated Colt revolvers in his hands. Evidently he'd seen one too many Westerns.

"Okay, big man," Giorgio snapped. "Out you come. Nice and easy, if you don't mind."

Holding his hands close to his waist, Bolan eased from the van. It made the short hairs at his nape prickle, staring down the barrels of four guns and not knowing when one of them might cut loose. Vinnie was like a racehorse champing at the bit. It wouldn't take much to set him off.

Giorgio motioned Bolan to move to one side, then called out. "Now you, sweetheart. Quit your whimpering and take your medicine like a man."

To Bolan's surprise, Weaver uttered a piercing wail and started to sob.

"No! I won't! I don't want to die! Please, let us go and we'll never say a word! You've got to believe me!"

Giorgio shook his head. "Pitiful. It's always the women who go all to pieces." He leaned inside. "Look, lady. We're not playing games here. Get the hell out, or I'll have you dragged to the marsh on your ass."

Weaver sobbed and sprawled onto the carpet. "No! No! You can't!"

Bolan heard Giorgio tell Vinnie to go in and get her. For a moment he was the only one looking at Weaver, so he was the only one who saw her glance at him and wink. Then she lay flat on her stomach and cried hysterically.

The warrior prepared to spring into action on her cue. He didn't know what she had in mind, but whatever it was, he would back her play. Vinnie stepped into the van and moved slowly toward her, holstering one of his fancy revolvers as he did. Giorgio leaned forward to observe. Only Bruno had a gun pointed at Bolan.

"Come on, bitch," Vinnie snarled, reaching for Weaver's shoulder. "Make it easy on yourself."

The woman glanced up, her face partially hidden by her cascading hair. A feral gleam, not tears, lit her eyes. "That's what I intend to do, stupid." Her right arm streaked up and in. Metal flashed as she buried a knife blade in the young gunner's chest.

Vinnie screamed, a strident, piercing hair-raising sound that froze Giorgio in place and made Bruno spin to see what had happened.

The Executioner couldn't have asked for a better opening. Exerting his strength to its utmost, he tore his hands free of the tape. He grabbed the shotgun with one hand while driving the other into Bruno's stomach.

Too much pasta and pastries had given the hardman a soft belly that collapsed in on itself under the force of the warrior's blow. Bruno collapsed to his knees, dazed but not out. He was able to hold on to the pistol grip, and he tried to turn the shotgun toward the warrior's body.

Bolan kicked him, a precise, tight snap kick to the nose that smashed it flat and split the man's upper lip. He tried to tear the shotgun from the gunner's grasp, but Bruno hung on like a drowning man to a lifeline. By accident, Bruno's finger closed on the trigger.

The blast was like a clap of thunder. Buckshot ripped into the sliding door, missing Giorgio by a hair.

The warrior knew he had to put Bruno out of commission swiftly in order to help Weaver. He arced his right foot at the gunner's face. Unexpectedly Bruno caught hold of his leg and twisted, which sent Bolan toppling to the right. His shoulder was lanced by pain, but he was able to hold on to the shotgun. He had the barrel, Bruno had the grip.

Growling deep in his throat, the hardman threw himself at his attacker. Bolan planted a foot in Bruno's abdomen and heaved in a neat judo toss. The gunner sailed over the warrior's head, slammed down on his back and instantly rose to his knees.

Bolan was a shade faster. He speared his right hand, fingers as rigid as tensile steel, into the base of Bruno's throat, gouged his fingers deep into the yielding flesh and twisted.

Bruno gave out a strangled whine as his jugular was mangled. Forgetting about the shotgun, he clasped both hands to his agonized throat. "No!" he was able to croak.

"Yes," Bolan said, reversing the shotgun with a deft flip and pumping a shell into the chamber in the same move. The tip of the barrel was mere inches from the gunner's brow when he fired.

Whirling, Bolan went to Weaver's aid. He saw that Giorgio hadn't moved since the fight began and didn't understand why until he took a few steps and saw Weaver on her knees in the van, covering Giorgio with one of Vinnie's flashy revolvers.

"Nicely done," Weaver commented, bobbing her head at Bruno. She slid out and pressed the Colt against Giorgio's temple. "What do you want me to do with this guy? If you're open to suggestions, I say we save the taxpayers the cost of a trial. His lawyers would just weasel a reduced sentence, anyway."

Giorgio gulped and tried to sound brave when he said, "Now hold on, you two. I'm worth more to you alive than I am dead. I know where Packard is staying, remember? Maybe we can cut a deal here."

"No deals," Bolan said harshly. Grabbing Giorgio by the scruff of the neck, he flung the man bodily to the ground. The Desert Eagle lay on the carpet just inside the van. Bolan scooped it up, flicked off the safety and set the shotgun down. Moving to the open front door, he searched and found his Beretta and Weaver's SIG-Sauer under the passenger seat. He replaced the 9 mm pistol and handed Weaver her own weapon.

"Thanks. So what are we going to do with Giorgio?" Weaver asked as she jerked the man to his feet.

"Get some answers," Bolan said.

Giorgio puffed out his chest. "Not damn likely, mister! My lips are sealed unless you agree to a deal. Information in exchange for my life. That's the only way you'll get it out of me."

"Wrong," the warrior said, as he leaned in and rapped the butt of his pistol against the man's temple. Giorgio sank to his knees, blood trickling from his wounded head.

"Go to—" Giorgio began, then stopped, his eyes wide as Bolan thumbed back the Desert Eagle's hammer. He licked his lips, winced and said, "All right. I'll give you the names of the referrals. Just don't shoot me!"

"I'm waiting."

Giorgio supplied them with three names and addresses.

"Now the name of the hotel where Packard is staying," Bolan demanded.

Again the hardman narrowed his gaze, his features hardening. "Not so fast, big man," he said, visibly straining to keep his voice level. "That's my ace in the hole. If I tell you, you could kill me. So let's deal, huh? What do you say? Give me your word that you'll let me live and I'll give you the name. What do you say?"

"You're dead if you don't," the Executioner replied.

Giorgio sagged visibly. "The Colonial on Fremont Avenue."

"Thanks." Bolan told the man to stretch out on the ground in a prone position, then removed a pair of plastic handcuffs from a pouch on his belt. In a quick, practiced motion the warrior had Giorgio's hands behind his back and cuffed.

"Someone will be along in a while to pick you up, which is a lot more than you deserve. Be thankful that you didn't suffer the same fate as your friends here. And, Giorgio...if the information doesn't pan out, I'll be back."

WITHIN FIFTEEN MINUTES they were heading along the winding road back to civilization, Bolan behind the wheel. At the first town they came to, Perrineville, Weaver hopped out to place a quick call to Washington. When she climbed back in, she seemed subdued.

"Control patched me through to Brognola. It seems that he was worried about us and gave orders to be notified the minute either of us made contact. You should have heard him. He was very relieved to hear that you were unharmed." Weaver paused. "I get the impression he cares for you a lot."

"We go back a long way." Bolan elected to change the subject before she pried into matters he would rather not discuss. "What about Creed? Anything new on him?"

"He flew the coop and left a present in his condo for the FBI. Enough explosives to damn near level the building. Thirteen agents were killed."

"And Hal has no idea where Creed went?"

"None. He said to tell you that he's plenty worried. Unless we can track down Envio Squad Two in time, he's afraid we'll have a disaster on our hands to rival the catastrophe in India some years back. At Bhopal, I think it was. Thousands could die."

Or more. It wasn't hard for Bolan to imagine a vile toxic cloud enveloping Newark and much of its environs, the poisonous vapors dropping people like flies. If the wind was just right, the cloud would drift over New York City. In which case the death toll might climb into the hundreds of thousands, or even millions should the cloud stall over the Big Apple. It was a chilling scenario.

"Mr. Brognola also wanted me to ask you something," Weaver said rather hesitantly.

"What?" Bolan prompted when she didn't go on.

She averted her face. "He told me to tell you that if you wanted to see this through alone, he'd understand. You only have to say the word and I'm to catch the first flight back to D.C."

Bolan didn't know what to make of the message. It had been Brognola's idea to team him up with Weaver in the first place. The strategy had backfired, but not through any fault of hers. She had acquitted herself well and made an outstanding partner.

It didn't take a mind reader to see that Weaver was upset. Bolan figured that she had taken Brognola's suggestion as a personal rebuke, as yet another example of female agents being shafted because they supposedly couldn't measure up. But he knew the big Fed too well to brand him as sexist.

"What do you want me to do?" Weaver asked softly.

"We've gone this far together. If it's all the same to you, we might as well see it through to the end."

"Thanks for having confidence in me. I won't forget this. Ever."

Once more Bolan changed the subject. "I've been meaning to ask you. Where did that knife you used on Vinnie come from?"

Weaver smiled. "Where no man would ever think to look," was her reply. "I learned a long time ago that a person in our line of work can't be too careful. It pays to have a hideout. I never go out in the field without one or two."

Bolan marveled that she was able to hide anything under the skimpy dress she wore, but he chose not to mention the fact. It did prompt him to say, "Maybe when we reach Newark you should change clothes. There's no longer any need for you to pretend you're my girlfriend, and you might want to wear something more practical."

They made good time until they hit the outskirts of the city. Congested traffic cost them an extra half hour. The rented sedan was right where they had left it. Weaver removed her suitcase from the trunk and they sneaked into Giorgio's shop through the back door so she could change. While she was busy in the bathroom, Bolan scoured the gun shop but found no evidence of illegal hardware or explosives. Giorgio had been too cagey to keep them on the premises.

As Bolan concluded his search, out strolled Weaver. The dress had been replaced by a brown jacket and matching slacks. Her high heels were history. In their place she wore low black leather shoes. And her hair had been tied in a bun.

"I'm ready for action. How do we play this?"

"Fast and loose," Bolan replied as he walked to the telephone. He took a phone book from under the counter and paged through the commercial section until he found the Colonial. Draping a cloth used to clean guns over his hand, he dialed the number. A man with a raspy voice answered.

"Hello," Bolan said. "I'm supposed to meet a friend of mine there in a short while. His name is Clay Packard. Can you tell me which room he's in?"

"Packard?" the man repeated. "He was down here getting candy from the vending machine just a little while ago. Hold on a sec, pal, while I check."

The warrior gave Weaver the thumbs-up sign.

"He's really there?" Weaver whispered. "I half expected Giorgio to lie to us."

In a little while the man came back on the line. "Here it is. I couldn't remember if he was in 216 or 316, but it turns out he's in room 126. I guess my memory isn't what it used to be. Do you want me to ring him for you?"

"No, that won't be necessary," Bolan assured him. "We'll be there shortly. Thanks."

"Our luck has finally changed," Weaver commented as they hastened to the sedan.

Bolan was tempted to exceed the speed limit but opted not to risk being stopped. As before, Weaver navigated. She was a wizard at reading maps and kept them on side streets most of the way. Fremont Avenue lay in a run-down section of Newark. Sleazy motels and bars lined both sides. Women in tight dresses and tighter shorts paraded along the sidewalks or stood on street corners, soliciting customers.

Once, perhaps fifty years ago, before Newark succumbed to urban blight, the Colonial must have been a class establishment. The design was impressive, with flowing arches and recessed windows. But now there were hairline cracks in the stucco walls, and the paint on the arches had peeled in great patches. Only three of the neon lights in the sign worked. And the pool, to judge by its condition, had been closed for years.

Bolan went around the block once, then pulled to the curb on the side of the hotel farthest from the entrance. A few streetwalkers gave him inviting looks, which he ignored. One was brazen enough to sidle up to him and wink.

Someone had considerately propped open an exit door with an empty beer bottle, allowing the warrior and his partner to slip inside unnoticed.

The hallway smelled of sweat and other, less pleasant, odors. Bolan took the right side, Weaver the left. The nearest room proved to be 186. Slowly counting down the numbers, they came to within earshot of the decrepit lobby before they reached their goal.

Placing a hand on the Beretta, Bolan gingerly tried the knob. To his surprise, the door wasn't locked. He put an ear to it but heard no sounds. Nodding at Weaver, he shoved the door with his shoulder and went in low and fast with the 93-R probing the air ahead of him.

The room was empty.

A check of the bathroom, the closet and under the bed turned up no luggage, no evidence at all that anyone was staying there. The bed was unmade, though, and there were two ashtrays full of cigarette butts.

"Shabby maid service?" Weaver said.

"Let's find out."

The grizzled gentleman at the front desk adjusted a pair of crooked spectacles on the tip of his nose and gave them a friendly smile. "William J. Flaherty, at your service. Most folks just call me Billy. What can I do for you? Would you like a room for the night?"

"I'm the guy who called about Clay Packard," Bolan said, and got no further.

"Oh, you are?" Flaherty stated. "I thought you told me that you're a friend of his."

"I am."

"Well, that's mighty strange. Because he walked up right after you called, wanting to know if I knew how to get to a place in East Newark. I told him about you, and do you know what?"

"No."

"I'll be darned if he didn't pay his bill and light out of here as if his backside was on fire, him and the three who came with him. And not a word of explanation, either." Flaherty cocked his head. "He did give me a five-spot to relay a message, though."

Weaver stepped forward. "What was it?"

The old man snickered. "Mighty peculiar message, if you ask me." He paused. "It was just two words. Two words for five bucks. Why, that's two dollars and fifty cents a word!"

"What was it?" Weaver repeated, her patience about to snap.

Flaherty smiled at them. " 'Nice try.' That's all the man said. Nice try." He looked from one to the other. "Does it make any sense to you?"

Bolan sighed and bowed his head. They had been so close. And now Packard knew someone was after him and would be on the lookout for them. "It makes sense," he answered.

"Good. Glad I could be of help, sonny."

CHAPTER ELEVEN

Clay Packard was in a foul mood. He got that way when
things went wrong. A burly man whose huge shoulders
resembled slabs of beef, he liked to boast that in his
younger days he had knocked out eleven straight op-
ponents in the ring with his devastating right hook, the
same right hook that landed him in prison when he
killed a man in a barroom brawl.

Packard had hated prison and vowed never to go
back. Yet for the life of him he couldn't seem to get his
act together. One day, he knew, he'd wind up back behind bars, or worse.

The problem was that decent, steady jobs held no
appeal. He had been making his money under the table, as it were, for so many years that he couldn't shake
the habit.

So when his old friend Pete Slater had phoned him
and told him about this outfit called Green Rage whose
founder was willing to fork out major bucks for dangerous work, Packard had been unable to say no.
Common sense told him to, yet he agreed to fly from
Camden, his home town, to meet with Jason Creed.

Packard had expected the environmental fruitcake to
be a mouse of a man who cried every time a flower was
plucked. He'd been shocked to find that Creed was

bigger and meaner than he was, and even more disturbed to meet Creed's second-in-command, Garth Hunter. Now there was a certified mental case if Packard had ever met one. And, truth to tell, Hunter scared Packard.

When Creed had outlined his plan to blow two chemical plants sky-high, Packard had been all set to decline. He liked to take risks as much as the next guy, but there were limits. Causing the deaths of untold thousands seemed certain suicide because it would bring down more heat on the culprit than a blast furnace.

Then Creed had named the price he was willing to pay to have the job done—two hundred thousand dollars, all in small bills, taken from an armored-car heist and virtually untraceable. It was the score of a lifetime, the bonanza Packard had always dreamed of but never really thought he would reap. With two hundred thousand he could go anywhere in the world. If he used the money wisely, he'd be set for life.

So against his better judgment, Clay Packard had agreed. He'd been put through grueling training sessions. He'd listened to Creed rant and rave about how all the trees, the dolphins and spotted owls were going to be wiped off the face of the planet unless something was done, and soon. He'd let himself be bossed around and worked harder than he ever had before, all for the money that would soon be his.

Provided he lived to collect, or didn't get thrown in jail first. That was the one hitch. Packard was no dummy. He knew the Feds wanted to get their mitts on the members of Green Rage in the worst way. He knew that by throwing in his lot with the fanatics, he had stuck his neck in a noose that might tighten at any moment. And he wasn't going to let that happen.

Packard's key to survival lay in staying one jump ahead of the Feds and anyone else who entered the picture. His life on the mean streets of Camden had given him a raw edge that served him well now. He would take no undue chances.

Which was why, when the desk clerk at the Colonial told him that a man had called and would be right over to see him, a man who claimed to be Packard's friend but hadn't given his name, Packard had rushed to his room and instructed the other members of Envio Squad Two to grab their bags and leave.

That had been twenty minutes ago. Now Packard was seated across the street from the Colonial in a stolen four-door sedan bearing license plates taken from another vehicle. He watched a dark-haired man who appeared every bit as formidable as Garth Hunter and a pretty woman who carried herself as if she was tough stuff emerge from the lobby and walk partway around the block to their car.

"Is that them, you think?" Gloria Sherman asked.

"If it is," Tony Genaro added from the back seat, "I say we leave them be. I don't like the looks of that dude, Clay. He's trouble."

"Tell me something I don't know," Packard growled. Twisting, he glanced at Eddy Miles, the fourth member of his handpicked group. "What do you say? Should we take them out or not?"

"No."

There. It was settled. Packard had picked them because they were reliable, and he wasn't about to buck their input. All three were from Jersey. He'd known Eddy Miles since they were kids growing up on the same block. Tony Genaro was a drinking buddy. And Gloria had been his steady for more than eight months.

They were his friends, the first ones Packard had thought of when Creed asked him if he knew of anyone who would like in on the operation. Each would get fifty thousand for his or her part, more money than any of them had ever seen before.

Sherman drummed her fingers on the dash. She was a plump woman, well past her prime, and had worked in half the taverns in Trenton. That had a lot to do with why she was also as hard as nails. "Maybe we're being hasty. Maybe we should tail them, learn who they work for."

"And if they make us?" Genaro said. "We'll be in Feds up to our armpits before you can blink."

Miles, the smallest of the quartet, leaned forward and commented, "I don't know. That big guy doesn't look like any Fed I ever saw. There's something about him. Hands off, I vote."

"Hands off it is," Packard stated. He motioned for them to duck when the other vehicle's headlights flicked on and the car pulled into traffic. In moments the pair was lost in traffic, bearing south.

"Now what?" Sherman asked.

"Now we find another hotel," Packard said. "We have the detonators, but we can't do a thing until we get our hands on the explosive we need. Tomorrow we'll make the rounds and see what turns up."

SEVERAL BLOCKS DISTANT, Terri Weaver turned to Mack Bolan and asked, "What next? Do we shake down the independents and hope one has a clue or two?"

"It's our best bet," Bolan said. He was keenly aware of the time constraint they were under. They had no idea how soon Envio Squad Two would strike. It might be two days, it might be two hours. Finding the squad quickly was imperative.

The first name supplied by Abe Giorgio was that of a small-time operator rumored to work out of an old warehouse in the most run-down section of the city. Giorgio had known only the man's street name, Big Boom, whose main customers all had gang ties, either in New Jersey or New York City. Giorgio had spoken of Big Boom with contempt, but the man couldn't be taken lightly.

Bolan located the section of the city easily enough. The streets were dark, the industrial sector a shabby specter of what it should have been. The warehouses were in disrepair, fences were overgrown with weeds and piles of trash littered alleys and parking lots.

"It's no-man's-land," Weaver said. "I bet the cops don't come here unless they have no other choice."

"Who can blame them?" Bolan responded. There were similar areas in every major city, war zones ruled by gangs, where the byword was "anything goes." Decent citizens who entered did so at their own peril. Traffic that late at night was sparse, and pedestrians were few and far between.

Weaver surveyed the buildings on her side. "Why do I have the feeling that we're being watched?"

"Because we are." Bolan had yet to spot anyone, but every so often he knew unseen eyes were focused on their vehicle.

Few of the warehouses had numbers on them. Bolan remembered that Big Boom conducted his business at 512 Lavender Place, but he was having a hard time finding the street, let alone the exact building.

For all Bolan knew, Big Boom had already moved on to another location. His type tended to float from spot to spot in order to keep the local law at bay. If that was the case, it would be difficult trying to find the man's new base of operations since the locals weren't about to open up to just anyone. Questioning them would be an exercise in futility.

"I just saw a number on a post," Weaver announced. "It was 411."

"Then we're about a block away." Bolan studied the warehouses on his side. He had to guess which was the right one and wheeled up beside an enormous closed loading door. There was no sign of activity. All the windows were dark.

Weaver opened her purse and palmed the SIG-Sauer. "He must have flown," she said while slipping the pistol under her belt over her right hip.

"I'll go see. You sit tight." Bolan reached for the handle.

"Wait a second. What is this? I thought we're a team. Why should I stay put?"

"Because I'd like the car to be here when I get back. One of us has to make sure no one steals it or strips it, and you're elected."

To forestall a protest, Bolan slid out, pushing down the lock button as he did. He walked to the loading door, which wouldn't budge no matter how hard he tried. In search of another way in, he moved to the west, into murky shadows. Gravel and broken glass crunched underfoot. He passed a barred window and a cluster of trash cans.

A side door stood ajar. The Executioner drew the Beretta and held it close to his right leg so it wouldn't be obvious. A hinge squeaked when he eased the door wider. Slipping inside, he pressed his back to the wall and paused to get his bearings and let his eyes adjust to the deeper gloom.

The warehouse was as still as a tomb. Bolan found it hard to believe anyone was there, yet he had to be sure. To the right a narrow hall led into pitch blackness. In front of him the ceiling seemed as high as the sky. The floor was so much empty space, except for a few busted crates. To the left a flight of stairs led to the second story.

Bolan took a gamble. He had no desire to play cat and mouse with street punks who knew the layout of the warehouse as well as they knew the backs of their own hands. They would simply lie low until he left. So, advancing to the middle of the storage area, he tilted back his head and called out, "I'm not the Man. All I want is to talk to Big Boom."

There was no reply other than a faint rustling that could have been the wind or rodents—human or otherwise.

"I'll make it worth his trouble," Bolan added. "A C-note for five minutes of his time."

Bolan heard more rustling and scurrying. He made no sudden moves. No doubt a half-dozen guns or better were trained on him. Vague shapes flitted at the periphery of his vision, and then someone whispered.

Suddenly a large light switched on overhead, bathing the warrior in a bright circle. Bolan looked up and distinguished the outline of a catwalk. The figures drew closer. Four toughs partly ringed him in front, and he was certain there were just as many to his rear.

A tall, skinny black youth wearing a vest and leather pants strutted into the light, hooked his thumbs in his wide belt and smiled. "You must be out of your gourd, white bread, coming down here like this. Didn't your momma ever tell you that some parts of town ain't fit for white trash after dark?"

Bolan refused to take the bait. "Are you Big Boom?"

"Maybe I am, honky, maybe I'm not," the man said. "Who wants to know, chump?"

Some of the watchers snickered. Bolan knew he couldn't show any weakness or they would be on him like starving wolves on an injured buck. "I need information. If you're willing to answer a few questions, say so. If not, I've got better things to do than stand here while you yank my chain."

The tall man sniffed, his eyes narrowing. "Mouthy mother, ain't you? Maybe you ought to look around. In case you ain't noticed, you and that old Army dude Custer have a lot in common."

Bolan couldn't let the opportunity pass. He noted the positions of the five toughs behind him and the type of hardware they carried. Three had Uzis, one packed a rifle, the third a measly .25-caliber pistol. "Is this how you greet everyone who wants to do business with you?" he asked.

"Do you take me for an idiot, white meat? You claimed that you're not the Man, but I'm not buying. You've got the look, mister. A look I don't like."

"Then I take it that you don't want the C-note?" Bolan said, and shrugged. "Suit yourself. All you had to do was answer a few questions, but if you don't need the bread, that's fine by me." He turned toward the entrance.

"Hold it, sucker!" Big Boom snapped. "You leave when I say you can leave and not before." He took a few strides nearer, his confidence growing. "Why is it white folks are as dumb as bricks? You shouldn't have told us about the money. There's nothing to stop us from taking it and throwing your white ass out of here."

"Sure there is," Bolan said evenly, framing a smile on his own face so they would be caught off guard when he showed them who the real chumps were. Not one had noticed the 9 mm pistol that he held in the shadow of his leg.

"Like what, man?"

"This." In a blur of motion the warrior whipped his arm up and pointed the Beretta at Big Boom's face. Startled, the man recoiled but had the presence of mind not to run. Several of the others cursed and bolts were thrown on the Uzis.

Big Boom riveted his men in place with a strident shout. "Chill! No one does a damn thing unless I say the word! You got that, brothers?"

"We can take this loser," a hefty gunner claimed.

Big Boom looked into the warrior's eyes and swallowed hard. "You'll do no such thing. He might get off a shot as he's going down and I'm right in the line of fire." He raised his voice to emphasize his command. "Lower your pieces, and be quick about it! I ain't taking no chances with you dim bulbs."

Out of the corners of his eyes, Bolan saw the gunners obey. He took another step so that the Beretta's barrel was inches from the main man's nose. "Now then. I take it you'll answer a few questions."

"You've got my undivided attention."

A creak on the catwalk alerted Bolan a fraction of a

second before a shot rang out. He leapt, and the slug bit into the floor at the very spot where he had been standing. Hooking his left arm around Big Boom's throat, Bolan swung around behind the man and bent low, using him as a shield.

"Luther!" Big Boom roared. "I'm going to kick your butt if you don't do as I tell you! Put down your gun, homeboy. You hear me?"

"I hear," came the reluctant answer.

Bolan listened to a metallic rattle from above. Slowly straightening, he pressed the Beretta against Big Boom's ear and backed from the light. One of the Uzi wielders balked at moving aside but did so when Big Boom insulted his lineage. Once they were in the dark, the Executioner let go but didn't lower the pistol.

"So what is it you want, honky?"

"I'm looking for a white man named Clay Packard. He's looking to score some C-4, and I'm told you can grant his wish."

Big Boom laughed. "Who told you that? Some lame sucker with crack for brains?"

Bolan had no time to play footsie with the junior-league gun dealer. A few of the gunners had disappeared, and he wouldn't put it past them to try to flank him in order to stop him from leaving. He jammed the Beretta into the man's neck and said, "Don't play games with me. Not if you want to live."

"Hey, I ain't got no death wish! You dig?" Big Boom was rattled but trying hard not to show it. "You want to hear I deal? All right, I deal. Pistols, rifles, SMGs when I can get my hands on them. But plastic explosive? Do you have any idea how hard it is to find that stuff? Hell, if I had any, I'd keep it for my own use, turkey."

Something in the dealer's manner convinced Bolan. He wondered if the other two names Giorgio had given him would turn out to be equally worthless. Here he was, wasting precious time when at any moment Envio Squad Two might strike. "Let me ask you this. If you wanted to buy some C-4, who would you go to?"

"No way I'll rat on anybody, so you might as well shoot me and get it over with," Big Boom said.

Bolan pondered. He could leave with nothing, or he could turn the situation to his advantage with the right leverage. It all depended on the dealer. "Ever heard of Green Rage?"

"Say what?"

"Green Rage. They were on the news the other day when they tried to hit the President," Bolan clarified.

"Oh, that sick outfit. The tree lovers. What do they have to do with anything?"

"Some of them are right here in Newark. They plan to blow up a couple of chemical plants as their way of showing people how dangerous chemicals are."

"Yeah? So?"

Bolan scanned the warehouse. So far the homeboys were keeping their distance, but that could change at any moment. "So if they succeed, a toxic cloud will spread out over the city. We're talking poison gas.

Thousands will die. Men, women, kids. Maybe even you."

The gun dealer was taken aback. "Are you serious? No lie?"

"That's why I'm after Packard. If I can't stop him, a lot of people are going to suffer. People you know. People you see every day." Bolan paused. "So think about it. Which is more important, ratting or stopping Green Rage?"

"How do I know you're not making this whole thing up?"

"Go with your gut. What do your instincts tell you?"

Big Boom gnawed his lip. "Fair enough. The tree lovers mean nothing to me." Bending nearer, he dropped his voice to a whisper. "If I was looking to buy some C-4, I'd go to one of two people. The first is named Giorgio. He has Family ties, if you know what I mean. The second is a dude named Adams who has a place out along the Passaic somewhere. Some of my suppliers do business with them. They're both big-time. Whatever you want, they can probably get."

"Adams," Bolan said. The name was the third one Giorgio had given him. "Here's your money. I'm leaving now. I hope none of your boys does anything stupid."

"They have the smarts of a brick, but they listen."

Bolan continued toward the entrance. Provided the Feds were on the ball, Brognola should be able to come up with an address for Adams.

The warrior had taken less than four steps when the man on the catwalk shouted, "I see him, Boom! Don't worry! I'll nail the bastard!"

The leader's reply not to shoot was smothered by the thunder of a high-caliber rifle. Bolan darted to the right, spotted a lanky figure on the catwalk and drilled the shooter with a pair of 9 mm slugs. It was the signal for all hell to break loose. Guns opened fire all over the warehouse. He thought he heard Big Boom yelling, but he had his own skin to think of and dived flat. The air was crisscrossed by a lethal swarm of lead seeking his lifeblood.

The warrior took out the light with his next round. Jumping to his feet in a momentary lull, he made for the same door through which he had entered. A shape reared before him and he gunned it down. He spied the outline of the doorway and figured he was in the clear, but he was being premature.

A few yards were all that remained when Bolan glanced to his right and saw a gunner with an Uzi. The man had the weapon on him, had him nailed dead to rights. Even as the warrior weaved to make himself harder to hit, the Uzi erupted.

CHAPTER TWELVE

Jason Creed liked to fly. It gave him a chance to gaze down on the world he loved so dearly, to more fully appreciate all the planet had to offer. It imbued him with, as he liked to think, a godlike perspective.

From the lofty heights Creed could plainly see how small and fragile the world really was. Viewing cars and trucks the size of ants exposed humankind for the insects they truly were. Not ants, though. Creed saw humanity as a plague of vile locusts that would rape the planet to extinction within fifty years unless something was done to draw attention to the world's plight.

And Creed was just the one to do it. Yes, his carefully planned assassination attempt had gone awry, but the best was yet to come. The chemical holocaust in New Jersey would jolt the national consciousness, would make everyone see that all chemical production should be halted while there was still time.

Then would come the coup de grace, an act of terrorism so shocking that the population of the entire planet would sit up and take notice. It was of this act that Creed daydreamed as the aircraft in which he sat banked to land at Honolulu International Airport.

Hawaii. It stirred fond memories in Creed. Hawaii was where he had fled when he went underground after his first acts of eco-terrorism. He'd only intended to stay a few days but had lingered for weeks, entranced by the pristine beauty of the enchanted islands.

Creed had found paradise on earth, the perfect place, the ideal standard by which the rest of the planet should be judged. The Aloha State, with its deep blue seas, brilliant flowers, graceful palms and sparkling waterfalls, all maintained in their pure state, was like an intoxicating beverage. He couldn't get enough of it.

So to be back again, after being away for several years, was like a homecoming. Creed pressed his nose to the window for his first glimpse of Oahu. On seeing it, he grinned like a kid just given the present he had long desired. "How beautiful!" he breathed in ecstasy.

"Can you see the institute from here?"

Creed tore his face from the magnificent scene to frown at his joking companion. "Some people are born with a wonderful sense of humor. Too bad you weren't one of them, dearest."

"My, aren't we touchy. Wake up in a bad mood, did we?" Julie Constantine retorted while strapping herself in as the flashing sign above them directed.

"I'll admit I'm on a short fuse," Creed conceded, "but who wouldn't be in my shoes? We stand on the verge of committing the two greatest acts of enlightenment ever known to mortal man."

"And we stand so modestly, too."

Unwilling to have his fine spirits dashed by her pessimism, Creed gazed fondly out over the glistening wing as Oahu was bathed in the golden glow of the afternoon sun. He was so entranced that Constantine had to nudge his elbow twice, hard, to get his attention.

"What the hell is it?"

She smiled sweetly and bent over as if to whisper tenderly in his ear. But her words were as cold as her heart. "I warned you to keep your voice down but you wouldn't listen. Now there's a guy across the aisle who keeps staring at us."

Laughing as if at a joke, Creed sat back and stretched. In doing so his eyes drifted to the right and he spotted the man in question. The guy was in his thirties, had an athletic build, close-cropped hair and wore a neatly pressed suit.

Puckering to make onlookers think he was about to kiss Constantine, he said in her ear, "If he's not a cop, I'm the queen of England."

"My sentiments exactly, lover. Do you think he's on to us? What should we do?"

Creed slid lower into his seat and leaned back so he could watch the suit through a narrow gap between his companion's head and her seat. She was right. The man kept glancing at them, his brow knit as if he was trying to place them. Their disguises had him fooled, so far.

"What do we do?" Constantine persisted.

"We play it cool, just like we always do. Act as if we don't have a care in the world. And if he tries to arrest us, we take him down and haul butt out of the termi-nal."

Constantine scrunched her nose. "I love it when you make like a criminal mastermind."

Sometimes Creed wondered why he put up with her. She had a knack for making a joke out of everything, which in itself didn't contradict her passion for the environment but often made him question her degree of devotion. How could anyone be so chipper when the world was dying?

The flight attendant launched into the standard routine about buckling up and putting the seat backs in the upright position. She was quite attractive, and it pleased Creed to see that the guy across the aisle tore his eyes off them to openly admire her. It showed the man had other things on his mind and probably wasn't the threat Julie imagined.

Still, it never paid to take anything for granted. Creed reached inside his jacket and took a common lead pencil from his pocket. He had sharpened it himself before boarding. As weapons went it was pitiful, but a quick thrust to the throat would slow down an enemy, if not cripple or kill.

Holding the pencil so the eraser was braced against his palm, Creed impatiently waited for the jet to land. His good humor was gone. Now all he wanted to do was get to safety.

Creed glimpsed palm trees as the aircraft descended to the tarmac. For a brief moment it filled him with an intense longing to stay in Hawaii forever, to forget about his green crusade and live the rest of his days in the nearest thing to the Garden of Eden the planet had to offer. But he couldn't. Not when the fate of the world rested on his shoulders.

As the aircraft angled toward the terminal, the man in the suit pulled out a wallet and consulted a folded sheet of paper.

When the door finally swung open and the pert flight attendant announced they could disembark, Creed touched his companion's hand and shook his head to let her know they should take their time. It wouldn't do for them to rush out. The guy in the suit might become more suspicious than ever.

Creed pretended to fiddle with his jacket, then bent to adjust the cuffs of his pants. On the sly he spied on the suit, who had risen and was slowly filing along the aisle. After the man passed the flight attendant, Creed stood. "Move it," he said.

The terminal was packed. Creed slouched to hide his height as they went through the ritual of claiming their luggage. He made it a point to keep the other man in sight at all times. Just when he was beginning to think they were overreacting, the man looked around, spotted them, then headed straight for the nearest bank of telephones.

"Damn it," Creed rasped, propelling Constantine toward the front of the terminal. Once outside, several natives approached, a smiling woman holding up leis for them to wear. Creed shook his head and practically ran to the cabs.

Not until they were cruising along Kamehameha Highway did the leader of Green Rage allow himself to relax. The driver was listening to a transistor radio, so Creed felt safe in saying quietly, "Whoever it was, we gave him the slip. Tonight I'll give Axel a call and invite him to join us for lunch tomorrow. If Hunter and Dean show up as planned, we'll be all set."

Constantine stared at the lovely scenery and commented, "Who would ever think that out of so much beauty will come so much devastation? I call that ironic."

"I call it poetic justice," Creed said, "and I can hardly wait to get started."

New Jersey

IT WAS NO SECRET that in some cities the police were outgunned by the gangs they were up against. Street punks loved to pack flashy hardware; the flashier, the better. The days of switchblades and pistols were long gone. Nowadays it had to be an Uzi or a MAC-10 to make the grade.

But carrying an SMG and being able to use one were two different things. Many toughs spent their idle hours cleaning and caressing their hardware when the time would have been better spent practicing. Few could hit the broad side of a bank in broad daylight.

Which was the only thing that saved Mack Bolan when the gunner cut loose on him. The tough forgot to compensate for the natural tendency of an Uzi or any SMG barrel to climb when a sustained burst was fired. Added to that was the mistake he made in shooting from the hip instead of from the shoulder. In the movies and on television that was how it was done, but in real life firing from the hip resulted in wasted lead unless the shooter was extremely skilled.

As a result, the gunner hit everything except the Executioner. Rounds tore into the floor, whined off the wall and struck the ceiling. A few chipped concrete almost at Bolan's feet. But not one bullet hit him.

The Beretta chugged twice. As the gunner staggered backward, another pair of shots blasted from the doorway and dropped him in his tracks. Terri Weaver had materialized out of the night.

Bolan reached her in two strides, then paused. Bedlam ruled the warehouse as the gunners let fly every which way. In all the confusion they were firing at one another. Big Boom's roar of pain could hardly be heard.

"I'm hit! I'm hit bad! Somebody help me! Oh, God! I'm dying!"

Giving Weaver a little push, Bolan sprinted to the sedan. He covered her while she slid in and unlocked his door. In moments they were racing down the street while the night air rocked to the battle royal being waged in the warehouse.

"With any luck they'll wipe themselves out," Weaver commented. "What happened in there, anyway? Did you learn anything?"

Bolan gave her a short rundown, concluding, "It looks as if this Adams is our best bet. We know he has a place somewhere near the Passaic River, but that covers a lot of territory. Somehow we have to narrow it down."

"It's a long shot but we can always let our fingers do the walking."

"I'm stopping at the next phone booth. If he's not listed, I'm making a call to Hal."

The Newark phone book listed over a dozen Adamses. None had the first name Chester, which was the one Giorgio had given. Bolan dropped a quarter and put in a collect call to a certain number in the nation's capital.

The big Fed was happy to hear from the warrior but was concerned at their lack of progress. "I don't need to tell you, Striker, that we're pushing the envelope on this one. If it was feasible, I'd have the President declare a state of emergency and call out troops to guard every chemical plant in Jersey."

It brought up a point Bolan hadn't considered. Were the plants targeted by Green Rage actually in Newark, or elsewhere? He'd taken it for granted they were, when for all he knew they might not be.

Brognola sighed. "There's still no word on Creed. We've been able to establish a link, though, between him and the criminal element he has working for him. Slater and Welch both had records. So does Packard. The key is Garth Hunter."

"How so?"

"Hunter was dishonorably discharged from the Marines at the same time and place as another man, George Dean. Dean went on to do time in prison for armed robbery. Apparently they kept in touch. My guess is that Creed decided to hire the talent he needed for his big scheme and had Hunter get the word out through Dean.''

"That would explain why Green Rage hit those armored cars and delved into kidnapping.''

"Yes. Creed was building his war chest. He never misses a trick, which is why he's still at large.'' Brognola was silent a moment. "Give me an hour on Adams. It's late and I'll have to roust a few people from hearth and home to get the job done. Where can I reach you?''

"We'll reach you.''

Weaver had gone into the convenience store and bought two large foam cups of coffee. "Something tells me that it's going to be a long night,'' she said while handing him one.

Bolan sipped and felt the scalding liquid burn a path to his stomach. "We have an hour to kill,'' he mentioned. "We might as well head for the Passaic.''

The river, which formed Newark's northeast boundary, was one of two that emptied into Newark Bay. Bolan cruised along the west bank and gazed to the northeast. Manhattan and Brooklyn were no more than six or seven miles away. A stiff wind would carry a toxic cloud there in minutes.

The Executioner disliked having to twiddle his thumbs while waiting for word from his friend. He had always been a man of action, so when he saw a tavern ahead he turned to Weaver and said, "When was the last time you made the rounds of Newark's watering holes?''

"Watering holes? What are you—" Weaver spied the tavern and grinned. "Oh. Well, I suppose it can't hurt. If Adams is a drinker, someone is bound to know him.''

It took more than a half hour before they hit pay dirt. In that time they visited five taverns. The husky, bald bartender at the last place was wiping glasses with a soiled cloth when they ambled to the bar and Bolan slapped a ten-dollar bill on the counter.

"We're hunting for a friend of ours by the name of Chester Adams.''

The bartender stopped his polishing and arched an eyebrow. "Friend of yours, you say?" He picked up the bill, examined both sides and folded it. "If that's the case, you might want to call him by the same name as everyone else, which is Chet. He hates to be called Chester.'' The man smirked. "Any real pal of his would know that.''

"Where can we find him?" Weaver asked.

"I wouldn't know.''

Bolan held out his hand. "Then give back the ten-spot.''

Placing his forearms on the bar, the man lowered his voice. "Don't be so hasty, friend. I'm not finished yet." He looked both ways. "I don't know where Chet lives. He's not exactly a buddy of mine. My place isn't his usual hangout, but he does come in here every now and then for a change of pace." He stuffed the bill in his shirt pocket. "He's mentioned that he spends a lot of time at a bar called the Meat Grinder. It's about two miles south of here.''

The warrior and Weaver went to leave.

''One more thing,'' the bartender said. ''If you two go waltzing in there, you're asking for trouble. It's the toughest joint in the city. Longshoremen, bikers, ex-cons, you name it, they drink there. And they eat people like you two for breakfast.''

Weaver winked at him. ''Then we'll just have to give them a case of indigestion, won't we?''

THE BAR RESEMBLED its reputation—somber and men-acing. Pickups, hogs and battered cars confirmed the caliber of the regulars. As Bolan watched, the front door was kicked open and a bouncer the size of a Mack truck tossed a drunk customer out on his behind.

''I guess they wouldn't mention this place in the tourist brochures,'' Weaver commented, about to climb out.

''Not so fast. I'm going in alone.'' Bolan twisted to get at his duffel bag in the back seat and removed a pair of jeans and a sweatshirt.

''First at the warehouse, now here,'' Weaver said, sighing. ''I detect a pattern and I can't say as I like it.''

Bolan began to shrug out of his jacket. ''That bartender was right. If we go in there dressed like we are, we'll buy a lot of grief.'' Draping the jacket over the seat, he unbuttoned his shirt. ''Did you happen to bring any old jeans along?''

"No. But I do have some everyday clothes which might pass muster."

"Might," Bolan said. "You stay here." He removed his shirt and placed both hands on his belt.

"I hate this," Weaver groused, averting her gaze as she turned to her window. "If you ask me, you're using this as an excuse to keep me out of danger. And I don't need a baby-sitter."

While Bolan would never admit as much, she was right. He'd been in dives like the Meat Grinder before and they were no place for a lady, even a tough-as-nails lady like Weaver. Besides which, she'd draw trouble like a pot of honey drew bears. He didn't care to spend all his time fighting off roughneck suitors who wanted to impress her with their muscles.

Once he had changed, Bolan transferred the Desert Eagle's holster to the small of his back and slung the Beretta under his left arm. Both were neatly concealed by the oversize windbreaker he pulled from his bag. "I might be a while," he said. "Sometimes it takes a few brews to loosen lips."

"Wonderful. While you're drinking some yokel under the table, I'll break out my yarn and needles and knit you a sweater. How would that be?"

Bolan made her more upset by grinning. He zipped the bottom few inches of the windbreaker, then strolled into the Meat Grinder. The place was crammed with burly types. Country music blared from a jukebox in one corner. On a small dance floor several couples gyrated in time to the music. At one table a pair of men with arms the size of redwoods were arm wrestling to the cheers and hoots of onlookers. A cloud of smoke hugged the ceiling, and over all was the tangy scent of beer.

No one paid any particular attention to Bolan as he walked to the bar. A waitress in an outfit so tight she probably had to hold her breath when she bent over was making the rounds of the tables. As she passed him, she raked him from head to toe with the look a meat inspector might give a haunch of beef. Her smile was as inviting as a greeting card.

"The name's Bertha, handsome. Get yourself a table and I'll treat you right."

"Maybe later," Bolan said, walking on. He bulled his way through the grungy ranks to order a beer.

The bartender was a skinny man who wore a long apron so caked with dirt and grime that it could probably stand upright by itself. He was also as talkative as a clam, as the warrior found out when he tried to engage him in conversation.

Bolan had to find someone else. He saw a couple get up and leave, so he promptly took their table. Mentally he started to count to ten and got as high as seven when a shadow fell over him.

"That was quick," Bertha said. "What will it be? Would you like a bite to eat? The grill stays open until ten."

The warrior didn't have much of an appetite, but he had to keep up appearances so he ordered a cheese steak with the works. Bertha smiled and sashayed off, threatening to dislocate her hips in the bargain.

While he waited, Bolan studied the patrons. They were as motley a bunch as he had ever encountered. Scars and tattoos were as common as clothes. Leather was the favored style. Rowdy laughter and lusty curses mixed with bawdy voices in a chorus as loud as that coming from the jukebox.

In due course Bertha returned with his meal. Bolan had to practically put his mouth to her ear to be heard. "I could use some help. It's important that I find a buddy of mine, Chet Adams. Has he been in tonight, do you know?"

"I don't rightly recall. Let me ask around for you. Maybe one of the boys saw him."

Once Bolan bit into the steak sandwich, his stomach made a liar of him and he finished the whole thing in no time. As he leaned back and took a sip from the cold mug of beer, Bertha returned.

"You're in luck, handsome. Someone remembers seeing Chet earlier this evening. Go on back to the poolroom and ask for Arno. He can help you."

Bolan gave her two dollars more than the cost of the meal. Sliding his wallet into his back pocket, he passed under a low arch into a room half the size of the one in front. Four pool tables were in use, and loungers lined the walls. He stepped up to a man with a butterfly tattoo on his arm and asked, "Where can I find Arno?"

The man grunted and pointed at the doorway on the far side.

Skirting the tables so as not to interrupt the games, Bolan came to a curtain made of stringed beads. It rattled as he parted the strands. A short hallway led to the rear door, which hung partway open in invitation.

"Arno?" Bolan said. When there was no answer, he walked to the door and opened it. A narrow alley separated the Meat Grinder from the next building. He took a few steps to assure himself that no one was out there, and it was then that the trap was sprung.

A lean man holding a lead pipe walked from behind a stack of crates. A second man popped up from behind a trash can, this one holding a tire iron, and a bearded hulk of a man whose fists were the size of hams strode from the bar. He glowered at the warrior, then said, "We hear tell that you want to talk to Chet Adams. Well, friend, first you're going to talk to us. And if we don't like your answers, you're going to wish that you were never born."

CHAPTER THIRTEEN

It had been so obvious that Bolan was inclined to laugh, but he didn't. He simply straightened and held his arms loose at his sides, giving them the luxury of making the first move. His calm demeanor riled the bear.

"Didn't you hear me? We're fixing to bust your skull wide open if you don't do as we say."

Bolan kept his eyes on Lead Pipe and Tire Iron while stating, "You must be Arno."

"That's right." The man squared his wide shoulders, which did little to lessen his pot belly. "Chet Adams is a good friend of mine. We go back quite a ways. Just about everyone he knows, I know. And I've never set eyes on you before. Which makes me think that you're the heat."

"I'm not a cop."

Lead Pipe chuckled. "He expects us to believe him, Arno. The dork must think we're really dumb."

"Shut up, Gavin," the hulk said. He had sized up the warrior and didn't seem to know what to make of what he saw. Scratching his bush of a beard, he declared, "Well, if you're not a cop, then what are you? Why do you want to see Chet?"

Bolan extended his fingers so they could see he wasn't trying to trick them and slipped his right hand into his pants pocket. Their interest perked when he pulled out the small wad of bills Brognola had given him prior to leaving Washington. "Why else? I'm in the market for some special merchandise and I've been told he can help me."

"Is that a fact?" Arno eyed the money like a chocolate addict would eye a jumbo candy bar.

"All I want is a meet. He can name the time and the place," Bolan said, and had an inspiration. "There's fifty in it for you if you'll give him a call and ask him to see me. That's all you have to do. Just ask him. If he says no, I'll live with it. No hard feelings."

Tire Iron had to voice his opinion. "I don't trust this guy, Arno. Let's crack his head and go back in. I left Marcy alone and you know I hate to do that. The others will be all over her."

Arno didn't like getting advice. "I'm the one doing the thinking here, peabrain. And I say fifty bucks will buy a lot of beer." His pudgy thumb stabbed at Bolan. "You stay put, mister. I'll go make that call and be back in a jiffy. But first, the fifty."

Bolan peeled off five tens and held them out. The big man took hold of them as if they were fine china, then hurried back in.

"Gavin, Renny, you keep an eye on moneybags. Don't let him go anywhere until I get back."

"Will do," Renny promised, smacking the tire iron against the palm of his hand.

Little did they realize that Bolan had no intention of leaving, not until he obtained the information he wanted. He could do it the easy way or the hard way, but since he would rather not initiate a fight, he opted to play the part of a buyer until they called his hand.

Renny, though, wasn't content to leave well enough alone. Wagging his rusty tire iron, he came closer. "I don't care what the big guy says. I don't like your looks. Maybe I should rearrange them to suit me."

"Back off," Gavin declared. "Arno won't like it if you don't do as you're told."

"Screw him. He's not my mother." Renny suddenly lashed out, poking Bolan in the shoulder with the tip of the iron. When the warrior stood there and took it, Renny sneered and poked him again. "Look at this, Gavin. I don't see what the big deal is. The wimp is scared to death. He's not going to do a thing."

"Wrong," Bolan said. Pivoting smoothly on the ball of his left foot, he drove his right foot into the man's groin. Renny screamed and doubled over, his face as red as a beet, his mouth wide enough to inhale a melon. Bolan blocked a feeble blow aimed at his thigh, then countered with a right uppercut that laid the man out as flat as a board.

"No!" Gavin belatedly sprang into the fray. Holding the lead pipe with both hands, he tried for a home run, swinging at Bolan's head.

The warrior ducked and the pipe swished over him. Before Gavin could swing again, he snapped his elbow into the brawler's ribs. Gavin staggered but recovered much faster than Bolan had anticipated, and attacked.

His features contorted like those of a feral dog, Gavin swung the pipe wildly. His fury made him careless. Had he taken the time to set himself and swing precisely, he would have fared better.

Bolan backed into the trash can. As the pipe cleaved the air in a downward arc, he leapt to the right. A resounding crash echoed through the alley and the trash can went down. The warrior ducked around a hasty thrust, coiled and jumped to the rear. Inadvertently he slammed into the high fence.

Gavin, sensing victory, advanced slowly. He feinted to the right, feinted to the left and went left.

It would have been easy for Bolan to draw and fire before the pipe touched him, but shooting the man would have accomplished nothing. This wasn't a hardened criminal, just a moron of a bar lizard who thought he was protecting a buddy. Killing him would anger Arno, and Bolan needed Arno's cooperation.

So rather than shoot, Bolan resorted to the combat skills he had honed in more fights than he cared to remember. His left wrist blocked the pipe. His right knee knifed into Gavin's thigh, high up, even as the rigid fingertips of his right hand sliced into the edge of Gavin's neck. The double whammy brought Gavin to his knees. Gamely he tried to raise the pipe, and he was still trying when a chop to the base of his skull rendered him numb from head to toe. Then his face kissed the ground and the world faded to black.

Bolan wasn't even breathing hard. He brushed himself off and leaned on the rear wall of the bar. It was a good thing, he decided, that the trio had lured him to the alley. They undoubtedly had many friends inside who would have rushed to their aid if the fight had taken place indoors.

A minute or so elapsed. Arno bustled out the doorway and nearly tripped over Renny. He gawked at the prone forms, too flabbergasted to speak.

"Don't blame me," Bolan said. "Your friend Renny tried to brain me. Gavin joined in on general principles."

Arno checked both men to verify they were alive. As he rose, he regarded Bolan suspiciously. "You could have cut out, been free and clear. Why didn't you?"

"We've already been through that. I want to do business with Chet."

"Speaking of which, he says that he doesn't know you from Adam. Usually he likes to set up a meet with a customer in advance to take their measure, if you get my drift. But he'll make an exception in your case only if you agree to two conditions."

"Which are?"

"One, my pals and me take you to the spot. Two, we keep you blindfolded the whole time." Arno prodded Renny with a boot to revive him. "Those are Chet's terms. Take them or leave them."

Bolan had half a mind to leave them. Being blindfolded would put him at the trio's mercy, and Renny had already made it plain that he wanted to smash his skull in. Even worse, they might demand to frisk him first, which he dared not allow.

"What's the matter? Getting cold feet?"

Pointing at Renny, Bolan said, "You want to cover my eyes and put me in the same vehicle with him? How do I know I'll reach Adams alive?"

Arno tugged at his beard. "Hmm. Good point. So I'll tell you what. These two bozos will ride up front and you'll ride in the back with me. I gave Chet my word that I'd bring you to him, and I'll give you mine that no one will lay a finger on you while you're blindfolded. Is it a deal?"

Biker honor. A man's word was supposed to be his bond. Bolan gave the hulking brute a close scrutiny and concluded he would put his life on the line. The stakes justified the risk. "We have a deal."

"Hold on, then, while I bring the Boobsey Twins around." Arno stalked into the bar and returned moments later with a pair of opened beers. Chuckling to himself, he upended the bottles over Renny and Gavin, pouring the contents into their partly opened mouths. The two toughs spluttered, gasped and snapped bolt upright.

"What the hell are you doing?" Gavin spit. "You got me soaking wet, you big ape!"

Renny let his lead pipe do his talking. He came up off the ground in a rush, zeroing in on Bolan, who braced himself. But Arno was faster than Renny. His ham of a hand clamped on to his friend's left shoulder and closed like an iron vise. Renny cried out and nearly buckled.

"Let me go, damn it!"

Releasing his hold, Arno tapped a huge thumb on both of their chests. "Listen up, dimbulbs. Chet wants to see this guy, and I gave my word he'd get there in one piece. So you lay off him, Renny, or by God you'll answer to me."

Gavin snickered at Renny's expense. The latter glowered but lowered the lead pipe.

"Did you hear me?" Arno pressed.

"Yeah, I heard," Renny rumbled, "but that doesn't mean I have to like it."

"Just so you live with it. I won't be crossed on this, man. If you push, I'll break both your arms off and shove them where the sun don't shine." Arno motioned. "Okay, mister. Let's go. Out front to the parking lot."

"After the three of you," Bolan said. He wasn't about to turn his back on Renny if he could help it. Arno or no Arno, Renny would strike the second the huge man's back was turned. Staying a few paces to the rear, he followed them. A few of the patrons seemed surprised to see him walking under his own power. And Bertha swayed up to him as he passed the bar.

"For joy! They didn't hurt you like I feared they would." She gave him an inviting wink. "No hard feelings I hope, lover?"

"None."

"Good. The next time you come in, the drinks, and whatever else you might like, will be on me."

"I'll be counting the minutes," Bolan said dryly.

An antique pickup was parked close to the front door. The paint had long since oxidized; the whole truck was the color of rust. Four bald tires, a cracked windshield and a crumpled tailgate completed the picture.

"My pride and joy," Arno declared, smacking the derelict on the hood. "I've had this for pretty near half my life." He passed his keys to Gavin, saying, "You drive. And if you put one dent in her, I'll dent your face."

With the cab filled, there was only one place left for Bolan and Arno to sit. The warrior climbed onto the bed and took a seat with his back to a tool storage box. In the opposite corner was a pile of crumpled beer cans mixed in with various odds and ends—an old shoe, a hubcap, a broken rake and assorted rags.

Arno stepped to the pile and rummaged through it. "I know it's here somewhere," he said to himself.

"What is?" Bolan asked.

"Your blindfold. Close your eyes."

The warrior did so and couldn't help but tense when a rough cloth was applied to the upper half of his face. Arno had to stretch it to tie it, and even then it was loose. Bolan inhaled and wished he hadn't. "What the hell did you use?" he demanded. "It smells like an old sock."

"Good nose."

Unable to see, Bolan relied on his other senses. He heard Arno thump his fist on the top of the cab as a signal to the other two, then the pickup slowly cranked to life. Seconds later a car elsewhere in the lot turned over.

The shocks squeaked as Arno's massive bulk settled to the bed. "You'd better hang on, mister. My baby shimmies and shakes a lot and has this knack for tilting some when she takes a turn too sharp."

Fortunately Bolan heeded the advice. Gavin didn't know the first thing about driving a stick and made the gears grind every time he had to shift. On turns, the pickup keeled like a rowboat in a hurricane.

The wind shifted the blindfold, allowing Bolan to peer out. He saw Arno glaring at Gavin. As they wound northward, he made note of prominent landmarks. Blocks distant, a pair of headlights paced them. Predictably none of the bar boys noticed.

Bolan half expected Chet Adams to live in a shabby tenement or to operate out of an old warehouse as Big Boom had. But fifteen minutes after leaving the Meat Grinder, the pickup pulled to the curb in front of a modest frame house on a quiet residential street. No sooner had Gavin killed the engine than Arno vaulted over the side and hauled him from the cab.

"Where did you learn to drive, you idiot? If you stripped my gears, you'll pay for a new tranny. See if I ever let you handle my wheels again."

It was so preposterous, it was almost comical. But Bolan didn't let down his guard. All three were as dangerous as coiled rattlers and would kill him in a New York minute if Chet Adams gave them the word. Bolan figured they received a cut for directing new business to the gun dealer, and for protecting Adams when muscle was called for.

Arno yanked off the dirty sock and tossed it back in the corner. "Okay, dude. Hop on down and you can meet the main man."

Bolan paused to stretch after sliding out and spied the sedan about four blocks off. Weaver had just parked. He counted on her not to show herself until after he learned whether Envio Squad Two had paid Adams a visit. Adjusting the windbreaker so it fully covered the Desert Eagle, he trailed the three men up a walk to a porch lit by a solitary bulb swarming with insects.

Arno knocked and moments later a thin hand parted the curtain. The bolt was thrown, and a mouse of a man in jogging clothes threw open the door. "Come in, gentlemen. Straight back to the kitchen, if you don't mind."

Bolan nodded at Adams as he entered. The man had cold, flat eyes and a pale, sickly complexion. "Thanks for seeing me on such short notice. I'm told that you'll be able to help me."

"Oh? Who told you?" Adams queried.

Since hedging would arouse suspicion, Bolan answered, "Another under-the-counter gun dealer by the name of Big Boom. Ever heard of him?"

"The black guy," Adams said in disgust. "You went to him before you came to me?"

"What can I say? I'm new to the area and had to go by the word out on the street," Bolan said to appease him. "You keep a lot lower profile than he does, so you were harder to find."

The flattery brought a fleeting smile. "I keep a low profile because I don't have bricks for brains like he does. Mark my words. Before long the cops will punch his ticket and I'll have one less competitor."

The kitchen was small, with barely enough room for the five of them. Chet Adams sat at one end of an imitation oak table and indicated Bolan should sit across from him. Arno went right to the refrigerator to help himself to a beer. Gavin took one, too, but Renny shook his head, his eyes shooting fireballs at the warrior.

"Now then," Adams began, "tell me your needs. Whatever you want, I can get for you so long as price is no object."

"C-4."

Adams didn't miss a beat. "I have a source. It takes up to a week to obtain, and you'll pay through the nose because a third of what I make goes to him, but it can be arranged."

"How much can I buy?"

"As much as you want, provided you have the money up front."

Bolan felt an intense dislike for the runt of a dealer. Money was all the man cared about. Adams didn't give a damn about all those who lost their lives further on down the contraband chain of death and destruction. "What about det cord? In large quantity?"

"No problem," Adams said smugly. "I compute the price by the foot, so the more you buy, the more I make."

Bolan casually lowered his right hand to his lap. He was about ready to make his move. Of the three goons, only Renny was watching him, and none had a weapon. Adams had his arms resting on the table.

"Before we go on," the arms dealer said, "I'd like to see the color of your currency. Don't take it personally. But I've had clowns buy merchandise before and then not have the bread to pay for it at delivery. I like to be sure."

"I understand." Bolan pulled out his wallet and set it on the table. For a moment all eyes were on it, not him. He straightened in his chair while lowering his arm again, only this time he reached clear around to the small of his back and palmed the Desert Eagle.

"Look out!" Renny bellowed, springing forward.

How the man knew, Bolan would never learn. He had the pistol only halfway around when Renny reached him. Callused hands swooped at his windpipe. The Executioner whipped his right foot into Renny's stomach and the tough bent at the waist, exposing Gavin behind him. Gavin had produced a knife from somewhere and was leaping in for the kill.

Bolan pushed his chair back into the wall to give himself a little more room to maneuver while simultaneously rising and triggering a shot. The hollowpoint slug caught Gavin high on the chest and flipped him into Arno, who had recovered his wits and was about to attack. They both crashed to the floor but so did the table, which Chet Adams hurled at Bolan.

The warrior pushed against the tabletop with his free hand to stop it from smashing into him. Adams fled past, toward the hallway. Bolan shifted to put a round into the man's leg but Renny was suddenly on him, his clawed fingers on the Executioner's right wrist to keep him from firing while Renny flailed at his face with his other fist.

It wasn't Renny who Bolan was concerned about. He wanted to avoid going hand to hand against Arno, who was trying to disentangle himself from Gavin. The Executioner tried to drop Renny quickly with an open palm blow to the sternum, which rocked the man on his heels but didn't force him to let go.

"Hold the bastard for me!" Arno raged, halfway to his feet.

Bolan dipped at the knees and drove his shoulder into Renny as if going for a block against an oncoming linebacker. He lifted his adversary off his feet and knocked him into a chair, but still he clung tenaciously, preventing him from using the Desert Eagle. Renny's plan was transparent. He intended to keep Bolan occupied until Arno joined in.

The warrior wasn't about to let him. He pretended to punch at Renny's face, and when the man jerked back, he reached across his chest and took the pistol in his left hand. Renny grabbed for his left wrist, but Bolan wasn't to be denied. Holding the Desert Eagle low, he stroked the trigger twice.

At each blast Renny tottered backward. He tripped over the overturned chair and fell, his body convulsing in its death throes.

Meanwhile Bolan had shifted to bring the big .44 to bear on Arno. But the man was on him before he could. The hulk slammed into him like a living bulldozer and he hit the wall so hard the breath gushed from his lungs and his ears rang. The pistol was torn from his fingers. Then, before the warrior could catch his breath, he was swept up into a bear hug.

"Got you!" Arno cried.

Bolan was lifted bodily off the floor. He attempted to break free, but the hulking biker's arms resembled the trunks of stout trees. Swinging his legs, he kicked Arno in the shins and tried to knee him in the groin, but did no real damage.

Arno just laughed. "I'm going to crush you so bad the law will think a python got a hold of you!"

It felt that way to Bolan. The strain on his ribs and spine was incredible, the agony excruciating. Sucking in what air he could, he made one last effort to fling his arms wide. Arno's arms never budged. In a minute it would be all over. Bolan's ribs would splinter and shatter and he would die slowly, perhaps stomped into oblivion or gutted with Gavin's knife.

Bolan couldn't permit that to happen. He stared into Arno's laughing eyes, bunched his neck muscles and smashed his forehead into the bigger man's nose. Arno yelped, his grip slackening slightly. Encouraged, Bolan tried another head butt. Blood splattered onto his face and neck.

"Damn your bones!" the bear roared. "You'll pay for that!"

The next instant Bolan was pile-driven into the wall. Stars exploded inside his head and the kitchen did a crazy jig. Grating laughter registered dimly. Arno's face floated in front of him, a great pale blur. He twisted and kicked but had no effect.

Arno shook the warrior as a grizzly might shake its prey. "You tried a fast one, partner, but it didn't work. Now you pay the piper."

The words were hollow, faint. A veil of darkness nipped at Bolan. He was poised on the brink of a vast chasm, and he knew if he made the plunge he would never awaken. He shook his head, which only made him dizzy. His chest seemed half its usual size, and his lungs screamed for air that he couldn't draw in, no matter how he tried.

The truth was undeniable. Inexorably the Executioner was having the life crushed out of him.

CHAPTER FOURTEEN

Axel Fagan was director of the prestigious National Oceanic Institute in Honolulu, Hawaii. He had held the position for seven illustrious years of dedicated service. To his colleagues and the world at large he was every bit a success, a scientist with a heart, as those who knew him best liked to say.

But like many knights in shining white armor, Fagan's image stood in peril of being tarnished if the truth about him was known. He had a dark secret that he shared with no one, not those who worked with him, not his wife, not even with his reflection in the mirror. And if that secret was to become common knowledge, he would lose his position and spend the next five to ten years behind bars.

Fagan's secret had a name. It was Jason Creed. No one knew they had attended Berkeley together or that they had been friends ever since. During the early days of Green Rage, Fagan had been Creed's bread and butter. No one knew that it was Fagan who often passed on sensitive information he gleaned in his capacity as director.

If he heard through the rumor mill of a corporation allegedly harming the environment, he passed it on so Creed could target the company for prime payback. Or if Fagan learned of individuals who merited attention, he did the same. The truth was that he had been one of Creed's main sources of intelligence for years, and not a living soul suspected.

On this warm evening the two eco-warriors sat across from each other under a spinning overhead fan. Julie Constantine was in the middle. They had a table with an ocean view at the renowned Liliha Restaurant and drinks had just been served.

"I can't believe you're really here," Fagan said. "You didn't call or anything."

"It was a spur-of-the-moment decision," Creed lied, one ear tuned to the small stage nearby, where a Hawaiian on a ukulele and another on a steel guitar were playing distinctly native melodies.

Fagan fidgeted in his chair, nervously surveying the restaurant. "I also can't believe you have the nerve to parade out in public like this. What if someone recognizes you?"

"Relax," Constantine interjected, resting her hand on Fagan's. "Trust us. We know what we're doing. Our own mothers wouldn't recognize us." She patted him. "We're very grateful that you agreed to see us on such short notice. So let's unwind. Enjoy ourselves."

Taking a long, hard swallow of his gin and tonic, the scientist smiled sheepishly and said, "I guess I am acting like a dolt. The authorities have no idea the two of you are on the Islands, or I'm sure I would have heard." To fortify himself, anyway, he polished off the drink.

Creed was glad that Julie was on hand to calm Fagan down because he had little patience with the man, and never had had much to begin with. Oh, they had been friendly enough during their college days. But when the time came for them to act on their beliefs, only Creed had been brave enough to step into the eco-war trenches. Fagan had stayed on the sidelines, whimpering about how he wanted to do more but how he just couldn't, not if it meant ruining his precious career.

Axel Fagan liked to hide behind a veneer of respectability. It was, Creed believed, the ruse of a coward, of someone who gave lip service to a cause but lacked the heart to devote himself one hundred percent. If Fagan could read Creed's mind, he'd discover that his old friend rated him as beneath contempt.

Julie's laughter shattered Creed's reverie. "So tell us," she said, "what have you been up to at the institute?"

Warmed by the liquor and the topic, Fagan told them about current projects. One involved a study of seal habitat in the South Pacific, another had to do with the migration patterns of gray whales, yet a third with mapping deep-sea trenches for future exploration.

Creed let his old chum blather on for over a half hour before he brought up the topic he was most interested in, saying off-handedly, "What about that new bathyscaphe I read about in a magazine? The bio-something-or-other?"

Fagan grinned like the proud father of a new baby. "It's called the *Bio-Ark*. I came up with the name myself. It's a contraction of *biosphere* and *Noah's Ark*. Appropriate, don't you think?''

Creed thought it was the dumbest name for a submersible he had ever heard, but he grinned and replied, "Very apropos. Tell us about it."

"She's a beauty," Fagan said grandly. "We had to finagle a grant to cover eighty percent of the cost, then begged, borrowed and bent a few arms to get the rest. It put our budget way over limit but—"

"We don't care about how you raised the money," Creed interrupted. "Tell us about the *Bio-Ark* itself. Can it really dive deeper than any bathyscaphe ever made and cruise faster than most surface ships?"

"Can it ever!" Fagan exclaimed. "Actually *Bio-Ark* looks more like a submarine than a typical bathyscaphe. She most resembles those X-craft midget subs the British used during World War II." He gazed dreamily out to sea. "She can dive to the bottom of the Mariana Trench if need be, and her cruising speed is rated at thirty-eight knots."

"Imagine that," Constantine said, grinning slyly at Creed.

Fagan never noticed. "That's not all," he went on. "The best part is that she's solar powered. Thanks to a revolutionary new storage system, a prototype unlike any in existence, *Bio-Ark* is fueled naturally. She's environment friendly, you might say."

"Amazing," Creed commented. "But doesn't it have to surface often to charge its cells, or whatever?"

The director glanced sharply at him. "Don't refer to her as an 'it.' Traditionally ships are entitled to be called by feminine pronouns."

Creed caught himself in time to keep from rolling his eyes to the ceiling. "Whatever," he said. "Am I right about the problems you've had recharging?"

"Where did you hear that? On the news? Yes, there were a few kinks that had to be worked out, but they've all been resolved. Now four hours of charging time permit *Bio-Ark* to travel submerged for twenty more. I can't wait to go out on her again. Her maiden voyage a month ago was a marvelous success. She's been at the institute ever since, having tests run to see how well she held up. So far she's passed with flying colors."

"I envy you," Constantine said. "What I wouldn't give to get a look at your pride and joy."

Creed reacted as if she had just come up with the idea, when the fact was that he had told her what to say weeks ago. "There's an idea. Why don't we, Axel? Is there any chance you could let us have a peek at *Bio-Ark*?"

Fagan's fine mood evaporated like dew under a blazing sun. "I don't know," he hedged. "As a general rule we don't allow the public on board. It's not like she's a tourist attraction."

Laughing good-naturedly, Creed said, "Since when are we the general public? It's us, Axel. Two of the best friends you have. Are you telling us that you won't bend the rules just a little for our sakes? Hell, you know we're not going to damage any of your expensive equipment."

Instantly Constantine leaned toward the director and added, "Please. I'd be so grateful. It would be a treat. I've never been on a bathyscaphe before, and I've always wanted to see one."

Creed could tell that Axel was weakening. Extending his leg under the table, he nudged Julie's leg. She got the message and sidled closer to the director, who was flushing a deep pink.

"Just one quick look. What harm can that do? Pick a time after the institute is closed for the day and no one will ever be the wiser." Her fingers lightly caressed the back of Fagan's hand. "Please. For me."

The director licked his lips, nodded and stated, "Sure. Why not? It can't hurt. How about tomorrow evening?"

Jason Creed felt all warm and tingly inside. The long months he had spent in careful plotting had just paid off. His dream was going to be realized. In a few short days he would commit the greatest act of eco-terrorism ever known, and all thanks to the simpleton sitting across from him. Lifting his glass, he beamed and said, "I'll drink to that."

New Jersey

MACK BOLAN WAS the consummate warrior, a distinction he had earned the hard way on the killing fields of every continent. He was the best at what he did simply because he would do whatever it took to bring down the opposition.

When Bolan found himself in a situation where he was outnumbered or outgunned or, rarely ever, outclassed, he dug deep down inside himself and called on his limitless reservoir of experience. So it was in this instance, with Arno about to crush his chest in a mighty bear hug.

Bolan's hands had been neutralized. His feet were next to useless. Head butts had no effect. None of the usual hand-to-hand tactics sufficed.

When Arno threw back his head to laugh, Bolan resorted to the only weapon he had left, his teeth. He clamped down hard on the man's neck. Whisker hairs filled his mouth and the warm, tangy taste of blood touched the tip of his tongue as his teeth bit through skin and flesh.

Arno roared and squeezed harder, so in turn Bolan bit harder. The bear of a bruiser screamed and swung the warrior every which way. Crashing their way around the room, they slammed into the table, then into a chair, Arno growing more hysterical with each passing second.

Bolan's head was clearing rapidly. In desperation the bigger man rammed him into a wall, but Arno's coiled arms took the brunt of the impact. Bolan jerked his head to the right and felt more flesh give.

Howling like a wounded wolf, Arno suddenly flung the warrior from him and clasped both hands to his torn throat. "You're crazy!" he thundered. "You ought to be put away!"

Bolan had fallen to one knee. He glanced up at the towering hulk, gauged the angle and hooked his right foot into Arno's left knee. The crack was as loud as the breaking of a tree branch.

Arno staggered to the left to get out of range and Bolan went after him, arms raised in a classic boxing posture.

"You're dead meat!" Arno raged. Bunching his fists, he clubbed them at the warrior's head. There was no finesse involved, no exhibition of boxing skill. Arno was accustomed to overpowering his foes through sheer brute strength.

The Executioner was the exact opposite; his skill was second to none. Ducking under his adversary's onslaught, he landed a flurry of lightning jabs that jolted Arno enough to make him back up.

Circling slowly, Bolan feinted, pivoted and ripped a solid right to the hulk's ribs. It was like striking a brick wall, but Arno felt it and grunted in pain. The warrior moved out of range of a series of wild blows.

For a few moments they stood apart, Arno wheezing like a beached whale, Bolan's body like tensile steel about to explode into action.

The warrior followed Arno's glance at the kitchen counter and spotted cooking utensils, among them a butcher knife and a meat cleaver.

Moving with astounding speed for one so enormous, Arno darted to the counter and scooped up the cleaver.

He hefted the heavy blade and smirked. "I'm going to cut you into little pieces, little man."

The first rule of unarmed combat was to keep one's mouth shut. Talking distracted a fighter, slowing his reflexes when he needed them the most. This time was no exception. For no sooner did Arno get the words out of his mouth than the warrior slid in close, dropped low and kicked his adversary in the ankle.

Arno bellowed in anger and pain. Raising the meat cleaver high, he came at the warrior like an insane butcher.

Bolan evaded the blade with a pencil's width to spare. He lunged to the right to dodge a second attempt. The third nearly clipped his arm and thudded into the tabletop, so deeply that Arno had to grip the handle with both hands to pull it loose.

Gliding in so close that he could see tiny beads of sweat dotting the man's face, Bolan delivered a solid cross to the jaw, which rocked Arno on his heels. The big man retaliated with a backhand that struck Bolan across the shoulder and hurled him into the counter.

Jerking the cleaver free, Arno spun and spit blood onto the floor. "You're like a mosquito, little man, a mosquito I'm about to swat." Lumbering forward, he wagged the cleaver a few times mockingly.

Bolan was set to take the bruiser down. The fight had lasted far too long. By now, he figured, Chet Adams was probably halfway to Trenton. He sagged against the counter to make the biker believe he was winded, and when Arno seized the moment by windmilling the cleaver at his forehead, the Executioner glided to one side. Again the cleaver missed, embedding itself in the counter instead.

Almost in the same motion Bolan speared the long butcher knife into the bruiser's barrel chest. It sliced in, clear to the handle.

Arno grunted and stiffened. He tried to pull the cleaver from the wood, but his limbs were weakening fast. A puzzled look on his craggy face, he blinked at Bolan and said, "I never thought it would be like this, runt. Always expected to go in my sle—"

Pulling the knife out, Bolan stepped aside and crouched, in case it was a ruse. But Arno wasn't faking. The bearish tough melted to the floor and lay quivering and groaning. Not until Arno's mouth went slack did Bolan unwind.

Immediately, from the doorway, came the scrape of a shoe sole. Bolan whirled, his fingers flying to the Beretta. As he cleared the shoulder holster he set eyes on Chet Adams, standing there with his arms up in the air. A familiar face appeared behind the arms dealer.

"You'll never guess who I bumped into, out on his late-night jog," Terri Weaver said, her pistol fixed on Adams's backbone. "And he's so kind. I mentioned that I could use a cup of coffee, and he invited me in."

"Smart-mouthed bitch," Adams snarled.

Weaver hit him between the shoulder blades with the butt of the SIG-Sauer. "Now, now. None of that vile language when a lady is present."

Bolan retrieved the Desert Eagle and jammed it in its holster. "I wondered what was keeping you," he commented. "I would have gone after him myself, but I was busy."

"So I see," Weaver said while contemplating the bodies. "Has anyone ever pointed out that this seems to be a habit with you? Some people drop bread crumbs to mark their trail. You leave corpses all over the place."

Adams was looking from the warrior to Weaver. "Who are you people? What the hell do you want?"

"Answers," Bolan said.

"Go to hell. I know my rights. If you're the law, I get to make a phone call. I demand to talk to my attorney."

The automatic resort of the legally impaired, Bolan mused wryly. He pushed Adams into a chair and held the Beretta low, at his waist. "Whether you get to call your lawyer depends on whether you live. And whether you live depends on whether you're willing to help us out."

Adams bit his lower lip, his exasperation mounting. "You can't do this!" he cried. "The courts would throw out my confession in a second!"

"Who said anything about confessing?" Bolan said quietly to calm the man. "We're interested in one of your customers, not in you."

The revelation restored some of Adams's courage. "You're wasting your time. Ask anyone. I never squeal on my clients. I'm a man of integrity."

"You're in trouble," Bolan replied, rapping the Beretta on the man's knee. Adams yelled out, then doubled over. "And we don't have time to waste. One way or the other, you will tell us."

Weaver stepped over to the chair. "Does the name Clay Packard mean anything to you?"

Adams glanced up. "No," he said gruffly. "Why? Should it?" He saw Bolan start to raise the Beretta and added, "I'm telling the truth! I never heard the name before. If he's a customer of mine, then he goes under an alias." He paused. "Lots of them do, you know. It's not like they're ordering hamburgers from a fast-food joint. They don't want anyone to know who they are."

"The guy we're after wants to get his hands on C-4, lots of it," Bolan elaborated. "You're the only one in Newark who can supply it."

Adams shook his head. "Flattering, but hardly true. I'm sure that I'm not the only game in town. Go make life miserable for my competitors instead of hassling me."

"You have no competitors."

"What do you mean?" Adams asked. As the truth sank home, he blanched and said, "Listen, I'll be straight with you. No one has wanted plastic explosive in a dog's age. The average schmo has no use for it. And the gangs can't be bothered, either. They like to blow each other away, not blow each other up."

Bolan smacked the barrel of the Beretta against his own palm.

"I swear to God!" Adams said. "No one has bought C-4 in ages. It's such a slow mover, I don't even keep any on hand. Search my house if you want, from top to bottom. You'll find plenty of hardware and ammo, and that's it."

The man was convincing. Bolan believed him about the demand, since only professionals—or fanatics—used explosives regularly, and there was a shortage of both in Newark. Yet it left him with a dilemma. Adams had been his last potential link to Envio Squad Two. How was he to track them down now that he had lost that link?

As if the man were psychic, he said, "Maybe the person you're after will show up soon. How about if we cut a deal? I help you in exchange for immunity from prosecution. I call that fair."

Weaver snorted. "You would, slime bucket. But we're not authorized to cut deals with you or anyone else." She tapped his temple with her pistol and looked at Bolan. "What do you want me to do with the trash? Take it out and toss it in a garbage can? A night spent with real rats might do this rodent some good."

The warrior moved to the sink and leaned against it, pondering. "Do most of your customers get in touch with you the same way I did?" he asked.

"Eighty-five percent do," Adams said. "I pay six different guys at six different night spots to keep their ears peeled for anyone looking to score a few guns or ordnance. They get a small commission." His gaze strayed to the puddle forming around Arno. "The big guy there was one of the best. He brought me ten, maybe fifteen thousand worth of business every year. I doubt that I'll be able to replace him."

"Do you always work out of your house?"

"Sometimes," Adams said, frowning. "More often than not I set up a meet in a public place. But tonight I was tired and didn't feel like going out again. And Arno promised to off you if you turned out to be a phony."

Bolan had been listening closely to the dealer's voice, to the tone, inflection and accent. It wouldn't be an easy voice to mimic, but he could do a decent enough job to fool someone over the phone. Nodding at Weaver, he said, "Tie up our friend and stuff him in a closet."

Adams nearly jumped up. "Wait a minute! Confined spaces make me sick to my stomach. Couldn't you put me down in the basement?"

"Show us," Bolan directed, hauling the man out of the chair. A short hall brought them to the cellar steps. Besides a furnace and washer and dryer, it was crammed with enough guns and ammunition to stock three sporting-goods stores.

Weaver whistled as she moved along a narrow aisle between high stacks of ammo. "Didn't it ever occur to you that if your furnace were to act up, there could well be a crater where your house is standing?"

"It's one of the risks of the trade," Adams said. "I wasn't about to waste good money on a storage facility."

There it was again, Bolan reflected, the real reason thugs like Adams got into the illegal arms business;

namely, the almighty dollar. He walked to a wall where some of the masonry had crumbled and several pipes were exposed.

"I had a bad leak there once," the dealer said. "Fixed it myself."

Bolan gripped one of the pipes and gave it a shake. "You did a good job," he said, then yanked the man over to stand next to the spot. "Put your hands on the top one."

Weaver knew what was expected of her. She had handcuffs out and on Adams before he could protest, the chain looped around the pipe. "That should hold our sterling citizen."

"Gag him, too."

"Will do." Weaver moved to a pile of dirty towels and washcloths over by the washer. "What then?"

"We keep our fingers crossed. If Packard has another source for the explosive, we're royally screwed."

CHAPTER FIFTEEN

San Francisco was Garth Hunter's favorite city. He'd gone there on a whim after his discharge from the Marines and grown to love the quirky atmosphere. Home became his small apartment on Minna Street, the nest he flew back to whenever he needed some R and R.

On this night, though, Hunter wasn't sprawled out on his sofa in front of the tube. He was waiting on a street corner near his place for the man he had handpicked to be a member of Envio Squad Three. A check of his watch showed Dean was already fifteen minutes late.

Hunter was perturbed. It might not seem like much, but fifteen minutes could throw off the whole schedule. And if they failed to reach the rendezvous point off Honolulu as expected, Jason Creed would want both their heads on green platters.

A horn honked, then a car swerved to the curb and George Dean leaned out his window. He was short, wiry and as hard as railroad spikes. "Sorry, man," he said. "I ran into some construction on Highway 24, and then there was a damn traffic jam on the bridge. A truck rear-ended a bus and tied everything up."

"Just hope our pigeon hasn't left," Hunter said as he walked around to the passenger side and climbed in. A police car was coming up the block toward them and he automatically slid a hand under his coat, reaching for his pistol. But the two cops hardly gave him a glance.

"A little high-strung, I see," Dean commented while merging with the traffic. "Guess I can't blame you. It isn't every man who's wanted for trying to blow away the President." He pointed at Hunter's head. "Nice touch, the black hair. It gives you a whole new look."

"Creed told me to dye it," Hunter said. "If it was up to me, I'd just wear a hat. But he doesn't want us taking any chances, not when he's so close to making the history books."

Dean was heading for 101. "He'll do that, all right. And if they ever nab him, he'll spend the next three thousand years behind bars."

Hunter didn't like to be reminded of the prison terms they would draw if apprehended. He'd hated being locked up and would rather die than go through that hell again. "Step on it," he said. "See if you can make up some of the lost time."

Traffic was sparse once they put South San Francisco and the international airport behind them. A quarter moon hung in the sky and was reflected off the still bay.

Never one to waste a minute, Hunter double-checked his Irwindale Arms AutoMag. It had seven .45 Winchester Magnum rounds in the magazine and another in the chamber.

"Plan on dropping a rhino?" Dean asked, joking, as he often did over Hunter's preference for serious stopping power. "Or should I say a blue whale?"

"Poke fun all you want. Just remember it takes two shots from your wienie 9 mm to match one of mine." Hunter tucked the AutoMag into its specially crafted quick-draw shoulder rig.

They drew abreast of Coyote Point, then Dean got off at the next exit and pointed the car toward San Mateo. "You always did go in for overkill, even when we were in the Marines," he commented, then chuckled. "It's funny how life turns out sometimes. Who would have thought that two former grunts like us would wind up helping a fruitcake wage eco-war on the good ol' U.S. of A.?"

"Speak for yourself. I happen to believe in a lot of what Creed says. Hell, all you've got to do is look around you. Pollution is everywhere."

"So is pollen, but you don't see people sabotaging flower beds because they don't want their hay fever to get worse."

"You're missing the point," Hunter chided.

A marina appeared ahead and they fell silent. Dean parked, then reached under the seat, producing a Browning. Wedging the pistol under his belt, he covered it with his jacket before climbing out.

Hunter tucked his chin to his chest whenever they passed under lights. He had memorized the layout of the docks and knew right where to find the *Speed Demon*. To his relief, the speedboat's owner was pacing back and forth. "Sorry we're late, Carter."

"Another two minutes and I was going to leave," the bearded salt replied crustily. "I know we had an agreement, but I can't be too careful."

At the apartment Hunter had counted out three hundred dollars in twenties, which he now handed over. "Here it is. Every cent. Let's get going or we'll miss him."

Carter cast off the line, let the *Speed Demon* drift out a ways and fired up the powerful engine. Both Hunter and Dean had to grab for support when the front end lifted out of the water and the speedboat rocketed northward.

Hunter caught his friend shaking his head and could guess the reason. Dean didn't understand why he had arranged to hire Carter when they could have hired a speedboat operator out of San Francisco and made the trip that much shorter. But then, Dean had always been too lazy for his own good and took as few precautions as necessary, which was why Dean had been in prison twice already.

Creed had come up with the idea. On a short hop from San Francisco, he had pointed out, it would be easy for the Feds to tail them without being spotted. Traveling up the bay past Treasure Island and then westward under the Golden Gate Bridge to the open sea would take four times as long, yet it gave Hunter ample time to assure himself they weren't being shadowed. No craft could dog them that long without giving itself away.

So Hunter stood facing aft, alert for moving shadows or reflections where there shouldn't be any. Carter concentrated on steering and didn't pester them with prying questions. Little did the man know that Creed had given orders to take care of all loose ends.

Treasure Island eventually came into sight, followed by Alcatraz. By then Hunter was convinced they weren't being pursued. Creed would be happy to hear that the Feds had no inkling of his master plan and it could proceed according to schedule.

Shortly the Golden Gate reared above them. Hunter watched the lights of vehicles sweep back and forth and wondered how the citizens of San Francisco would react when they heard that Los Angeles had been rendered unfit for human habitation for the next few thousand years.

Minutes later the *Speed Demon* hit the choppier waters of the Pacific. Carter opened the throttle all the way, and the boat roared into the vast ocean.

Dean had taken a seat and lit a cigarette. His right hand was never far from the Browning. He knew what had to be done and had no compunctions about doing it.

The wind blasted Hunter's face. He inhaled, the scent of saltwater strong in the air. A choppy stretch caused the sleek craft to dip and shimmer, and he held on to the rail until it had passed.

Carter was navigating by his instruments and the stars. "Another twenty minutes," he called out.

Hunter nodded. He had become used to the rolling rhythm of the speedboat and found himself liking the sensation. To the south the lights of a large vessel were so clear it gave the illusion he could reach out and touch them. To the north a fishing boat was puttering homeward after a long day.

Having been a Marine, Hunter had been trained in how to pinpoint grid coordinates on a map using a compass and landmarks. But it amazed him that Carter was able to reach the exact pickup point on the open sea. There was so much emptiness it seemed endless.

In due course the *Speed Demon* slowed to a crawl and Carter switched on a spotlight that he pointed at the sky to the west and blinked on and off three times. He repeated the signal every fifteen to twenty seconds.

Hunter glued his eyes to the heavens. Not that he expected to see much of anything other than a moving shadow. Old Red Simmons would be flying without lights, which was illegal but par for the course for a man who was known from Vancouver to Baja as the best smuggler in the business. Minutes went by. He began to think they had arrived too late, that Simmons had been there and left. Then the rumble of four high-powered engines throbbed overhead.

Dean stood. "Should we tell Tom here?" he said loudly to be heard above the growl of the idling speedboat.

The speedboat owner looked at them. "Tell me what?"

A nod from Hunter was all it took.

George Dean smiled, stepped up close to Carter, and when the other man leaned forward to hear better, Dean drew the Browning in a blur, pressed it against Carter's stomach and squeezed off three shots. The blasts were partially muffled by Carter's body, which would have slid to the floor of the cockpit had Dean not grabbed it from behind, lugged it to the gunwale and made ready to heave it overboard.

"Hold it," Hunter said. Stepping to the body, he patted Carter's pockets until he found their three hundred, plus another wad of bills.

"Fifty-fifty?" Dean asked.

"As always."

The body of Tom Carter hardly made a ripple as it slipped beneath the surface.

New Jersey

IT WAS TWO O'CLOCK in the afternoon when the anticipated call came. Mack Bolan was at the kitchen table, sipping his fifth black coffee of the day and listening to Terri Weaver tell about her childhood spent on a farm in Illinois.

Bolan liked her a lot, and although an attraction existed, he made no move to capitalize on it. He had learned the hard way that personal entanglements were luxuries he couldn't afford. And even if he wanted to, the woman was already spoken for.

When the telephone rang, Bolan pressed the receiver to his ear and tried to imitate Chet Adams's voice. "Yeah? Who is it?"

"Chet, this is Billy over at the Bull's Head. I've got a live one for you. He's from out of town, and he's put out the word that he's lookin' for someone who can supply him with explosives. Do you want to set up a meet?"

Bingo, Bolan thought. It sounded like Clay Packard. "Sure do. You've done good, Billy." He gave Adams's address. "I'll be expecting you within the hour."

"No problem." Billy paused. "Say, Chet, what's with the stuffed-up voice? You got a cold or something?"

"I'm getting over the flu."

"Geez. I hate all that pukin', myself. See you in thirty."

As Bolan hung up, he said to Weaver, "Pay dirt."

"Let's do it. Just like we worked it out."

They went to the living room. Bolan opened the front door and left it ajar. The screen door he left unlatched.

Weaver made herself comfortable in the closet, leaving the door open a crack so she could see whoever entered. "You be careful, Mike," she called out. "The second they see that you're not Adams, they're liable to go for their guns."

"Just watch yourself," Bolan advised. He gave the street a cursory inspection before returning to the kitchen. The bodies were down in the basement keeping the gun dealer company, and the blood had been mopped up, so all would appear normal for the new arrivals.

Moving a chair against the wall close to the jamb, Bolan straddled it and drew the Desert Eagle. The big clock above the stove ticked loudly, and somewhere outside, kids whooped and laughed, at play. For some reason that made him think of Weaver and he shut her from his mind.

Sometimes the waiting was the hardest part of any job. Bolan had honed his patience on the razor-edged killing fields and paddies of Vietnam, but he still had times when the minutes dragged on. This was one of those times. He listened for the squeal of brakes, the slamming of doors. More than twenty minutes elapsed before he heard them.

Rising, the Executioner put his back to the wall and held the Desert Eagle next to his chest. The sound of footsteps on the front porch was followed by a hard rap on the screen door.

"Chet? It's Billy."

"Come on back. I'm in the kitchen," Bolan answered, and cocked the big .44 while crouching. Focusing on their approaching footsteps, he firmed his stance. A shadow appeared on the floor, growing longer and longer.

A scrawny young tough in a black leather jacket entered first. He had short sandy hair and acne, and a scar where his right earlobe should have been. Grinning stupidly, he stopped a couple of paces past the warrior and stared at the empty table. "Chet? Where did you get to?"

Bolan was hoping the second man would enter before he had to commit himself, but the customer stopped short of the doorway. He saw the punk start to swing toward him and knew he could hold off no longer. Leaping, the warrior seized hold of the tough's arm and pressed the Desert Eagle to the side of his skull. His plan was to get them both to freeze so they could be disarmed. But, as with many a best-laid plan, it went awry.

The fault wasn't Bolan's. The well-dressed, towering black man who filled the hallway was in motion the moment Bolan appeared, shoving his hand under his jacket and hauling out a Ruger Redhawk revolver.

The warrior dived for the floor as the Redhawk boomed. The slug from the .44 Magnum weapon, meant for him, caught the young tough in the side and flung him a half-dozen feet to land in a disjointed tangle on the tiles.

Two more shots echoed in Bolan's ears as he rolled to the right. Snapping his arm out, he fired and nailed the customer in the shoulder.

The man twisted but stayed upright. Sneering, he snapped his arm up to take aim at the warrior.

"Drop it!" Weaver shouted. She was at the other end of the hall in a combat crouch.

Trapped between the two of them, with no way out, the man hesitated, glancing from one to the other.

"No!" he roared, then swung toward the lady Fed and banged off a hasty shot.

Bolan and Weaver opened up simultaneously, the Desert Eagle and the SIG-Sauer combining in deafening drumfire. At each shot the customer rocked. The Executioner aimed high so none of his shots would pass through the target and hit Weaver.

In the abrupt silence that ensued, the man's death wheeze was like the rattling of a sidewinder. He did a slow pirouette to the carpet and wound up on his face, his chest and head riddled with bullets.

"Damn our luck," Weaver said, advancing as she slapped home a new clip. "Every time we think we have this one nailed down, it blows up in our faces."

"Check the other guy's pockets," Bolan directed as he knelt beside the man called Billy, who hung tenaciously to life but wouldn't last long. Blood trickled from his mouth and nose.

"What can you tell me about him?" Bolan asked.

Billy struggled to work his lips. "You're not Chet," he gasped, then died.

"Look at what I found," Weaver said, brandishing a wallet she had removed from the customer's jacket. "He has a New York license. Mustafa Kaleem, age twenty-nine, Harlem address. Since you don't see many gang members, bank robbers or crackheads with such a flair for fashion, ten will get you twenty he's a member of one of those fringe black-pride groups that believe in changing the status quo through violence."

"Could be," Bolan allowed. "Not that it matters. We know it isn't Packard, since Hal said he's white." He rose. "We also know we can't stay here any longer. Last night we were lucky. Either no one heard the gunfire, or if they did, they didn't bother to phone the police." Bolan hurried along the hall. "I doubt we'll be so lucky this time."

True to the warrior's prediction, on hastening onto the porch they spotted people up and down the street who had stopped whatever they were doing to stare at the Adams place. A husky man pointed at them and called out, "Hey! What's going on over there? Hold it, you two!"

Bolan wasn't about to listen. Nor did he care to tangle with a bunch of irate do-gooder neighbors. "Back inside," he ordered.

They rushed indoors, the warrior assuming the lead. He vaulted over Kaleem, ran the length of the kitchen and barreled out the rear door. A fenced yard bordered an alley. Bolan went out the gate, turned to the right and broke into a dogtrot. He figured that they had given the neighbors the slip since it would take a while for the good citizens to get up their nerve and enter the gun dealer's house.

The warrior stayed low so none of the people out front would catch sight of him. Too late, he spied an elderly woman in a rocking chair on the back porch of a nearby residence. She had been fanning herself, but on seeing them she craned her neck like a stork that had spotted a tender morsel.

"Hey!" she cried loudly. "Why are you two skulking around?"

A man out front bellowed, "Did you hear that? It was Aunt Bessy! Those two must be in the alley!"

Bolan nodded at the town crier as he sprinted past. So much for keeping a low profile, he mused. "Is the car still four blocks away?" he shot over a shoulder.

"Yes," Weaver answered. "I didn't want your friends to see me."

Weaver drew even with the warrior and side by side they raced to the side street and across it into the next alley. Hardly had they gained the alley mouth than four or five figures pounded around the corner of the block and a man in pink shorts and a purple tank top showed that his lungs were the equal of sweet old Aunt Bessy's any day.

"Here they are! This way! Come on!"

Bolan tried not to dwell on how ridiculous it would look if they were to be run down and half-beaten to death by an unruly mob of self-styled vigilantes. He increased his stride and Weaver followed his lead. When they reached the end of the alley, they both looked back.

Nine men were in earnest pursuit. Seconds later more appeared, all eager to be in on the capture.

The street was deserted so Bolan darted across without breaking stride. He stuck to the alleys for the time being, since they could make better time.

By now the whole neighborhood was in an uproar. In the distance sirens added to the din. It wouldn't be long before the local law arrived.

Bolan and Weaver had traveled three blocks when he suddenly grabbed her wrist and veered into a back-yard. A pit bull tied to an iron stake growled at the intrusion and tried to nip at their legs, but the rope jerked him up short.

Passing between two houses, Bolan reached the sidewalk. The car was parked half a block to the left. A small crowd had gathered in front of Adams's house.

Weaver went around the warrior on the fly, her hand in her purse, seeking the keys. Bolan heard a garbage can crash over and glanced around to see five of the fleetest men stampede into the yard.

"Stop, you!" one shouted.

Sprinting the final yards, Bolan waited for Weaver to unlock the passenger door from inside, then yanked it wide and prepared to slide in—just as Newark's finest screeched into the next intersection and bore down on them.

CHAPTER SIXTEEN

Bolan thought fast and acted instantly. Facing the crowd, he jabbed a finger and yelled, "There, officers!" One of the cops waved in acknowledgment as the cruiser sped past.

The warrior lost no time in piling into the sedan. "Get us out of here."

The five Good Samaritans had arrived on the scene just as the patrol car zipped by. They were jumping up and down and flapping their arms in a vain bid to get the officers to turn around.

Terri Weaver knew how to drive. She whipped the car in a U-turn and spun the wheel at the first junction. Coming to a major thoroughfare, she blended into the flow. "What now?"

"When we're sure no one is after us, pull over and I'll call Hal to tell him we've blown it, that Envio Squad Two is still on the loose."

Unfortunately Brognola wasn't in, and his secretary had no idea when he would be back. Bolan gave his code name and stressed it was urgent. Saying she would attempt to contact Brognola, she took his phone number.

Three minutes later the call came. Bolan grabbed it on the second ring, prepared to deliver the bad news. But Brognola spoke first.

"I was just about to try and reach you at that house Weaver called from last time. We've had a break, and you need to act on it right away." Papers rustled in the background. "I've had my people calling every hotel and motel in Newark and within a ten-mile radius. A few minutes ago we lucked out. Four people answering the description of Packard and his playmates have checked into a one-star bump and grind called the Excelsior. The address is 411 West Side Avenue in Jersey City."

"Then all this time we've been spinning our gears. They weren't even in Newark."

"Afraid so. And there's more. Packard is using the alias of Ned Wilson. The desk clerk told us that this morning he placed a lot of calls to Queens. Shortly after that he bought a map of New York City and left for several hours. Do you know what that means?"

Bolan did. Packard had found someone in the Big Apple who could supply the C-4.

"The good news is that Packard and his people showed up over half an hour ago and are still in their rooms. If you hurry, we can end this thing once and for all."

"We're on it."

CLAY PACKARD WHISTLED to himself as he packed his shaving kit. Now that he had finally obtained the explosives Envio Squad Two needed, they could wrap up their assignment and be on their way to Denver before midnight. That was where the three envio squads were to rendezvous after completing their missions. More to the point, that was where he would receive the balance of the money due him. And Creed had better fork it over, or else.

Sherman, Miles and Genaro waited in the bedroom, all set to go.

"At last we're getting this over with," Eddy Miles commented, voicing the sentiment they shared.

Gloria Sherman nodded. "Jamaica, here I come. I'm going to lay out on a beach and guzzle margaritas until I drown."

Packard raked them with the same kind of look prison guards used to give him when he was in stir. "Don't get ahead of yourselves. We have a job to do. Stay frosty. One mistake and we could go up with the chemical plants."

"Relax," Genaro said. "We've been through the routine so many times, we can do it in our sleep. It's a done deal, as those Hollyrot types like to say."

At a gesture from Packard they filed out. A wide corridor brought them to the lobby, where the pert desk clerk gave them a friendly smile.

"Are you folks checking out already?"

Packard liked her. She was young and pretty, and reminded him of his cousin Zelda, who had taught him about the birds and the bees above her daddy's pawn shop in north Camden back when he was fourteen. He would have liked to ask her out, but Gloria would cut off his privates if he dared show any interest in another woman. "We have work to do," he said as he placed the key before her.

"What business are you in?" the woman asked innocently.

"That's none of your concern, honey," Sherman told her.

"Now, now," Packard said. "There's no need to be nasty. The fact is, we're troubleshooters for a local company, SynCorp Chemicals. Maybe you've heard of them?"

"They have a big plant up near Hoboken. I pass it every time I head into Manhattan."

Touching her hand, Packard said, "The next time you do, think of us." Smiling, he made for the double doors, studiously ignoring Gloria. Once they were outside, he took the offensive, snapping, "That was brilliant, Sherman. Treat her like dirt for no reason. Give her cause to remember us later."

"Me? You were the one fawning all over the nymphet."

"I was just being polite."

"Your ass."

Miles boldly stepped between them. "Enough, already. I didn't hire on to listen to you two bitch and moan. You can tear each other apart later for all I care. Right now, think of all the crisp green bills waiting for us if we get through this in one piece."

"I'm with Ed," Genaro said. "So let's go snuff out a few hundred thousand nobodies."

SYNCORP CHEMICALS owned one of the largest industrial complexes along the Hudson River. Tall separation towers, large conduits and a bewildering network of pipes formed a virtual maze, covering acre after acre.

Directly across Merrit Street from SynCorp was an equally imposing concern run by DuBane Cyanamid, one of the top-twenty U.S. chemical companies. Beyond DuBane flowed the sluggish Hudson, and beyond the river reared the skyscrapers of greater Manhattan.

Parked on a shoulder of the road one hundred yards from SynCorp's main gate, the Executioner scanned both complexes. Thanks to the desk clerk at the Excelsior, they had a solid clue as to one of the plants slated to be hit. It seemed logical to him that Jason Creed would want the second plant to be close by so the toxic clouds would mix, thereby becoming many times more deadly.

"Dear Lord," Weaver said. "Finding Envio Squad Two in there will be harder than searching for a needle in a haystack."

"Maybe not," Bolan replied. They had contacted Brognola from the hotel, and he had promised to get on the horn to the CEO of SynCorp. "Give me twenty minutes," the big Fed had said, "and you should be able to walk in the main gate with no problem."

Those twenty minutes were up. Bolan drove to the gate and pulled in. A middle-aged man in a drab gray uniform was seated on a chair in the guard shack, reading a newspaper. The guard reluctantly set the paper down, rose and hitched at his cartridge belt. A nameplate above his left shirt pocket read Petersen.

"The main office is closed for the day," the man said with an imperious tone, implying they had no business being there and would be better off returning during office hours. "What can I do for you folks?"

"Mike Belasko and Terri Weaver," Bolan said.

The guard glanced at each of them in turn, then shrugged. "Is that supposed to mean something to me, mister?"

Just then the phone rang. Sighing in annoyance at having his paper reading interrupted twice in thirty seconds, the guard stepped inside, twisted so he could watch Bolan and Weaver and answered. He immediately went rigid. "Who did you say this is?" he blurted.

The call was late. Bolan gazed out over the complex, hoping the CEO would make it short and sweet since every second counted.

"Yes, sir," Petersen said, sounding subdued. "I will, sir. No, sir. Petersen, sir. Art Petersen. Twelve years, sir. No problem, sir. My full cooperation. So long."

It was a shaken man who set down the receiver and turned to the sedan. "Sweet Jesus! Do you know who that was?"

"Yes," Bolan answered wryly. "How many other guards are on duty?"

"Just Mark Fisher. He's making the hourly rounds. We take turns."

"Hop in," Bolan said, indicating the rear door.

"I can't. Someone has to be on duty here at all times. It's company policy."

Bolan had no time to quibble. "You're supposed to give us your full cooperation, correct?" When the man nodded, he said sternly, "Then get in, now. We have reason to suspect that eco-terrorists have targeted this facility for destruction."

Petersen looked as if he would keel over. "Oh, God. This can't be happening."

The moment the door closed, Bolan sped fifty yards to the office building, a small modular affair caked with grime. West of it a narrow parking lot flanked an array of separation towers. Hopping out, he drew the Beretta and checked the clip. Weaver mirrored him with the SIG-Sauer.

"I don't know what you have in mind, Mr. Belasko," Petersen said timidly, "but I'd be awful careful with the hardware. One shot in the wrong spot and we won't have to worry about any terrorists. It'll do the job for them."

The guard had a point. Bolan lowered the Beretta, thinking of the tremendous pressure many of the pipes were under. A single rupture might set off a chain reaction that would be every bit as disastrous as deliberate sabotage. Frowning at Weaver, he said, "We'll have to take them down without firing a shot."

"Easier said than done. I doubt these Green Rage fanatics will let us take them without a fight."

Petersen's mouth fell. "Green Rage? The ones who just tried to kill the President? Those environment loons?" When Weaver nodded, he swallowed hard and nervously rubbed his palms together. "They'll kill us without a second thought. We should go back to the shack so I can phone the police and have them saturate the area."

"No time," Bolan said, stepping to the guard's side. "Listen to me," he went on, trying to calm the man. "A lot of lives are at stake. We have to do this right because we won't get a second chance. Take a few deep breaths and steady yourself."

"I'm okay," Petersen claimed. "Really, I am."

"You had better be, because I don't know a lot about chemical plants. I need your help." Bolan waited a few seconds so his words would sink in. "Try to put yourself in their shoes. If you were a terrorist, and you wanted to make a toxic cloud big enough to wipe out half of a city, where would you plant your bombs?"

Petersen wrung his hands. "Where? Well, I could be wrong, but my guess would be the two main lines that feed into the separation towers. I know that's where the inorganic acids and organic chemicals are in their most unstable state. One of the chemical engineers once told me so. He used those very words."

"Take us there," Bolan said, and fell in behind the guard, moving at a brisk jog along a walkway. A sulfurous smell hung heavy in the humid air. Dim bulbs spaced at irregular intervals cast feeble light that accented the shadows. Often conduits bordered the walk, making it impossible to see more than a few feet to either side.

Bolan had no idea if Envio Squad Two had already penetrated the chain-link fence that surrounded the facility. If not, he would arrange a suitable reception. If the charges had already been set, he would do his best to disarm them before they went off.

The security guard was an anxious wreck. He slowed every twenty feet to listen, bobbing his head like a sand crane, his hand on the butt of his revolver. At a junction he went north; at the next he turned to the west.

Pipes of all sizes were all around them and overhead. Bolan saw catwalks connecting many of the separation towers. If he had a good rifle and a night scope, picking off the eco-terrorists would be like dropping ducks at a shooting gallery.

Suddenly Petersen slowed. Another junction lay ahead, directly under two huge pipes. Whispering, he said, "Those are the conduits I was telling you about. Around the corner and to the right are where they feed into the towers."

Bolan motioned for him to lead on. The warrior moved silently, as did Weaver, but Petersen scraped the soles of his shoes a few times.

Then they reached the junction. The guard started around without stopping to look first. Bolan tried to stop the man by reaching out and grabbing his arm, but his fingers were just closing on the sleeve when there was a muted metallic click from past the corner. In the next heartbeat something struck the guard with a loud thump.

Mouth agape, Petersen swung toward Bolan. Jutting from the center of his chest was the feathered end of a crossbow bolt. He tried to speak and failed. He was dead on his feet.

Bolan gave Weaver a push and threw himself to the right as a second crossbow fired. The bolt whistled past and bounced off a pipe. Lying flat under a conduit, the Executioner sought a target. The terrorists were too well hidden.

The use of crossbows was unexpected, but Bolan told himself it shouldn't have been. Jason Creed was a careful planner, and Creed had been bound to realize that using firearms in the middle of a chemical facility was like playing Russian roulette. Crossbows might puncture pipes, but they were less likely to cause an explosion.

A glance showed Weaver was gone. The warrior backed up, slid out from under the pipes and crept to the nearer separation tower. A slender metal ladder took him to a catwalk barely wide enough for a cat. He headed for the spot the guard had pointed out.

Up high, the wind was brisk, the smell stronger than ever. Bolan hugged the catwalk to reduce his silhouette. Halfway between towers, he paused, certain he had glimpsed movement but unsure whether it had been Weaver or one of the terrorists.

Advancing slowly, the warrior attained a vantage point affording a view of the feeder lines. A pair of dark figures were huddled at the base of the towers to which the lines connected, working feverishly to set charges.

The angle was just right. Any shot that missed or passed through a terrorist would hit the ground, not a pipe. Bolan took precise aim with the Beretta. The suppressor chugged twice and one of the figures rose, clutched at his back and toppled. The other one immediately darted under cover.

Bolan held himself still. The terrorist would be scouring every nook and cranny and he didn't want to draw attention to himself. After a short interval, he slid to the left, to the next tower. He rose into a crouch and was about to descend when a shadow sprang to life and a short sword stroked at his neck.

Most men would have been beheaded on the spot. Bolan managed to skip backward while sweeping up the Beretta. By chance the sword hit the pistol and nearly knocked it from his hands. As it was, his fingers went numb.

The figure attacked, swinging recklessly, trying to end the fight quickly. Bolan backpedaled as fast as he was able on the narrow walk. The swordsman, he saw, was dressed in *ninja*-style garb, a green uniform complete with a hood.

Bending, the terrorist slashed low, attempting to take Bolan's legs off at the knees. The warrior had only one way to evade the blade. He leapt straight up, and when the sword passed underneath him, he dropped down again. But in dropping he lost his balance on the slippery metal and his left foot slipped out from under him.

Bolan grabbed hold of the cable to steady himself. The terrorist, seizing the advantage, arced the sword at the warrior's forehead. He had to let go of the cable, then jerked aside. The sword missed, but Bolan had nothing to hold on to and fell onto his back. He nearly missed the walk. Teetering on the brink, he saw his adversary rear above him with the short sword poised for a final thrust.

Feeling had returned to Bolan's right hand. It was a simple matter for him to point the Beretta and stroke the trigger three times before the sword descended. Since open sky was all that surrounded the terrorist, the warrior wasn't concerned with causing an explosion.

The terrorist spilled over the side, falling silently to the ground. Somehow he retained his grip on the sword and landed on top of it, impaling himself through the abdomen.

Bolan caught only a glimpse of the fall as he pushed to his feet and hastened to the end of the catwalk. As he started down the ladder a crossbow bolt slashed out of the night and ricocheted off the tower. He couldn't tell where it came from.

Taking it for granted that the terrorist had his position pegged, Bolan shoved the Beretta under his belt, gripped the side rails, pressed the outsoles of his shoes against the rails and let himself fall. Gravity took over and Bolan plummeted, the friction searing his palms. If not for the braking pressure of his shoes, both palms would have been badly blistered.

As it was, the warrior was hard-pressed to slacken his speed as he neared the ground. Falling too fast, he hit hard but absorbed most of the impact by tucking his knees and rolling. Another bolt swished above him.

Bolan eventually came to rest under a conduit. He looked, but there was no sign of the third terrorist. Lying low in an attempt to lure the man into showing himself, he wondered where Weaver had gotten to and hoped she was all right.

Seconds weighted by millstones went by. Bolan knew he had to do something, and soon. He couldn't give the terrorists time to rig the C-4 for remote detonation.

Crawling under the pipes, the Executioner angled toward the feeder lines. Soon he saw Petersen, sprawled near the junction. The first terrorist who was shot lay where the slugs had dropped him. He appeared to be a short man.

Of more interest to Bolan was the flight bag at the base of the separation towers. He guessed that it contained the detonators Envio Squad Two had bought from the Sandman, as well as the plastic explosive. He had to get his hands on that bag. Without it, Envio Squad Two was hamstrung.

Rather than approach across the walk, the warrior opted to crawl along under the pipes and loop around to the base of the towers without having to step into the open. He had made it less than halfway when another shape materialized.

Bolan stopped, unable to determine if it was Weaver or a terrorist lying in wait for him. Whoever it was, he or she was as motionless as a brick. With an effort he was able to distinguish a few more details and knew he could go on.

The other guard, Fisher, had been jumped from behind while making his rounds. His throat had been slit, and for good measure the terrorists had put a bolt into his ribs. The body had been stashed under the conduit.

Snaking by, Bolan drew close enough to the flight bag to see that it hung wide open. He inched to the edge of the pipes, then stopped. It occurred to him that he might be playing right into the hands of the surviving terrorists. They could be lying out there, waiting for someone to show. Yet he had no choice.

Sliding out from under the pipes, Bolan crouched and looked both ways. No movement betrayed lurking killers. Exploding into motion, he sprinted to the bag and grabbed hold of one of the handles. As he did, a tall terrorist sprang out from behind the towers, a sword held above his head.

Bolan couldn't shoot, not with the towers directly behind his adversary. Nor could he leap out of the way, so close was the terrorist. Improvising, he did the last thing his attacker would expect—he flung the flight bag at the man's face.

The killer had already begun his swing and couldn't stop. His sword sheared into the bag, becoming briefly entangled. A powerful wrench was enough to tear the sword free, but by then Bolan was on him.

The Beretta caught the terrorist flush on the temple and he sagged. Bolan clubbed him again, then executed a spin kick that sent the man flying into the nearer tower. The hardman lost his sword and fumbled in his uniform for something else.

Bolan ducked as a *shuriken,* poorly thrown, whizzed past his head. He saw the sword, grasped the hilt and straightened as the terrorist threw a second throwing star. It hit the blade instead of him, which deflected it to the ground. Taking a long stride, the warrior swung.

The sharp edge struck the man's wrist as he was about to reach into his hidden pocket for another *shuriken*. He screamed when his severed hand hit the walk, a scream that ended abruptly when the sword bit into his heart.

Bolan whirled, but the fourth envio squad member had yet to appear. Toting the bag, he moved warily toward the junction. Weaver's prolonged absence was proof positive something had happened to her, and he wanted to find her quickly.

Less than a minute later, he did.

Terri Weaver was flat on her back, the last terrorist on top of her. And neither showed any signs of life.

CHAPTER SEVENTEEN

The bathyscaphe was everything Axel Fagan had claimed. Jason Creed stood on the private dock at the National Oceanic Institute and had to repress an urge to bend over and kiss the glistening metal hull. Spotlights illuminated the craft from stem to stern.

The sun had gone down more than three hours ago, setting the Pacific ablaze with a riot of colors. Two hours ago the institute had closed and the staff had gone home for the day, leaving the way clear for the director to show off his pride and joy.

"What do you think?" Fagan asked.

"It's beautiful," Creed answered. And it was. Sleek, powerful, state-of-the-art, it was the ultimate in underwater craft. More than that, *Bio-Ark* was going to serve as a gleaming angel of death, bringing long-overdue retribution to those who polluted the planet.

Constantine had worn a revealing top and shorts, which clung to her body as if painted on. She knew exactly what to do, and molded herself to Fagan's arm. "Can we take a peek inside, Axel? Please?"

The director grinned like an idiot, flattered by her attention. "I guess it can't hurt. But we can't dally. Some of the staff like to come back after supper to wrap up paperwork, and I don't want them to catch me breaking the rules.''

"Neither do we.'' Creed caught Constantine's eye on the sly and she raised her chin to show she understood. They had to move swiftly. Anyone else who showed up would have to be disposed of, which would make Fagan that much harder to manage.

The scientist climbed down the ladder to the short deck. "As you can see,'' he rambled on to impress Constantine, "the control station resembles a miniature conning tower. A computer study showed that, hydrodynamically speaking, it was the best design.''

"Maybe that's why they've used it on subs all these years,'' Creed cracked, but Fagan had eyes, and ears, only for Constantine.

"This is the top hatch.'' The director stated the obvious while slipping a leg into the opening. "Watch your step.''

Creed went down last. He had to scrunch his shoulders to make it through, and once below discovered the quarters had been designed with midgets in mind. The passageway was cramped for someone his size, and if he rose to his full height he bumped his head.

Fagan moved toward the bow, rattling off information about various instruments. "This is our sonar. Its range rivals that of the newest nuclear subs, and the definition is incredible. If you were to stand on a boat ten miles away and toss a spoon overboard, I would know what it was before it hit bottom.''

Constantine put a hand on the cockpit chair and asked in a little-girl voice, "Would you take us out for a short ride, Axel?"

The director looked at her as if she were insane. "I'm sorry, but that's just not possible. If anyone should find out, I'd risk a reprimand, or worse. Being the director doesn't mean I have carte blanche to do as I please."

Smiling seductively, Constantine traced the outline of his jaw with a tapered finger. "How would a few minutes hurt? We'll be back before anyone notices."

Fagan almost gave in. He opened his mouth as if to say yes, then clamped it shut again and vigorously shook his head. "I must put my foot down, my dear. I've already done much more than I should have."

"Allow me to show our gratitude," Creed said, and drew a Heckler & Koch P-7 M-13 from under his jacket. "This farce has gone on long enough." He stalked forward and shoved Fagan into the chair. "Start this puppy up and take us out onto the open sea."

The director sputtered in anger and began to rise. "How dare you—"

Creed reached the limits of his patience. He backhanded Fagan across the face, gouged the pistol into a cheek and growled, "Not another word, you stupid bastard. Do as you're told, or so help me I'll make you suffer as you've never suffered before."

Craven fear filled the man's eyes. The only sound he made was a pathetic mewing.

Constantine had drawn a Raven .25-caliber pistol from between her sleek thighs. "I'll get the hatch," she offered, and hastened off.

"I'm waiting," Creed growled.

Fagan was pale. His lower lip quivering, he swiveled the chair to face the console and flicked a series of switches. Instruments hummed to life, panel displays lit up. The bow viewing port, which resembled a picture window, afforded a clear view of the ocean.

Amidships, the hatch clanged shut, and a tiny red light on the control panel changed to green.

Fagan reached for the stick but paused. He had to steady his lips before he could speak. "What about the aft line? We haven't cast it off."

"Is it rope or a cable?"

"Rope."

"Then get going. We'll rip the sucker right out of its mooring."

Some people never learned. Fagan turned as if to object, but a ringing slap to the jaw changed his mind in a hurry. Resigned to the inevitable, he sank deeper into the cushioned seat and pushed a few buttons. Aft, motors kicked in with a vibrant hum. When he applied the stick, the whole bathyscaphe surged forward a few feet, then shuddered as it strained against the line and the line lost.

Creed smiled smugly when the vessel cleared the end of the dock. Squeezing into the copilot's chair, he gave the top of the console an affectionate slap. "After all these years, you finally did something right, old buddy.

Acquiring this submersible is the only smart thing you've ever done."

Fagan's hands trembled. "It seems to me that you're going to extreme lengths just to enjoy a short ride. Once we're back, I don't mind telling you that our association is at an end. No more money. No more inside information. You're on your own from here on out."

"Jackass," Creed said. "I've been on my own since day one. I don't need your money, and you can keep your lame gossip." He stopped when Constantine's hand fell on his shoulder. "One more thing. I hate to be the one to break bad news, but we're not going back."

The director was shocked. "What? Where are we headed, then?"

"Los Angeles."

New Jersey

TERRI WEAVER STRUGGLED up out of a clinging black fog into the glaring light of a hospital room. She started, remembering the last sight she had seen, that of a charging green *ninja* about to cleave her skull. Bewildered, she glanced around and saw Mike Belasko in a nearby chair, dozing. The stubble on his chin made him more ruggedly handsome than ever, and her heart jumped.

As if he sensed her eyes on him, Bolan snapped awake and rose. "How do you feel?"

"Like I was run over by a tank." Weaver saw a tube sticking from her arm and felt a bandage on her head. "How did I get here?"

"I brought you. The doctor says you were lucky. A few inches deeper and your fiancé would be attending your funeral, not a wedding."

The reminder jarred her, and Weaver couldn't look him in the eyes. "What about the bruiser in the pajamas?"

Bolan had a charming smile when he chose to do so. "That bruiser was a woman, Gloria Sherman." He placed a hand on the bed rail and studied her features. "Don't you recall shooting her?"

Weaver tried to remember, but the sequence of events was fuzzy. She seemed to recollect extending her arm to shoot just as the terrorist reached her. Perhaps, she mused, the pistol had gone off at the same moment Sherman struck. "I think I do."

"Give yourself time. The doctor told me it will be three weeks before you're up and about."

"Oh, no," she said, but not because of the extended hospital stay. She realized that she might be seeing Belasko for the last time, and it twisted her insides.

In confirmation, he said, "I talked to Hal while you were out. He's sending someone to pick me up." He glanced at the wall clock. "They should be here any minute."

"Where are you off to, if I may ask?" Weaver said, her throat oddly constricted.

"Hawaii."

"I envy you. The beaches there are gorgeous. Are you taking some time off?"

Bolan's face clouded. "We have a lead on Creed and Constantine."

"Oh." Weaver clutched the white sheet at her side until her knuckles turned white. "Well, I appreciate your hanging around to see how I did. It was considerate of you."

The big man offered his hand. "I liked working with you." He paused, as if trying to find the right words to say, and simply added, "I can't say that about too many people."

"Thank you. I'm flattered." With a sinking sensation in her chest, Weaver watched him walk to the door. "Mike," she called out weakly. When he turned, she said, "Maybe we'll work together again someday. I'd like that."

"I wish you a happy marriage," he responded, and was gone, the door swinging silently closed behind him.

JACK GRIMALDI WAS the pilot. One of the best in the business, Hal Brognola relied on him when the situation was urgent. It was Grimaldi's job to wing the Executioner and other members of Stony Man wherever they had to be in as short a time as possible.

Mack Bolan had known Grimaldi since the early days of his war on the Mob. The ace pilot was as good a friend as Bolan had, and one of the few people Bolan would open up to, within limits.

But on this day the warrior didn't feel much like talking. He sat in the rear cockpit of a stripped-down McDonnell Douglas F-4E Phantom II, one of the fastest fighters in the U.S. arsenal, capable of hitting Mach 2.17. From over thirty thousand feet up, the countryside below resembled a child's tiny play set.

Bolan was annoyed with himself. He was having a hard time shaking thoughts of Terri Weaver. It had been ages since he let a woman get under his skin, and he couldn't understand why she had succeeded. Maybe it was the fact they were so much alike in their dedication.

Whatever the cause, the warrior resolved to clear his head and devoted his full attention to the mission. Brognola had sounded excited on the phone, with valid reason. The Feds finally had a break in the case, which had come about by accident.

A young FBI agent named Swan had had vacation time coming. Having heard so much about sunny Hawaii, Swan booked a flight from Los Angeles to Honolulu. En route, his interest had been piqued by a couple of fellow passengers. One had been a blond guy, the other a stunning woman with auburn hair.

Swan's interest stemmed from Wanted circulars that had been faxed to all FBI field offices on the heels of the Phoenix debacle. Jason Creed and Julie Constantine were now at the top of the Bureau's Ten Most Wanted list, and every agent had been apprised to be on the lookout for them.

So when Agent Swan saw a couple who somewhat resembled the infamous duo, he had studied them carefully. The Bureau had no photos of Constantine and only one old one of Creed to go by. Sketched likenesses of the pair, based on witness descriptions, left little to be desired. All of which explained why Swan couldn't make up his mind whether the pair across the aisle from him were the suspects.

Swan had concluded the man wasn't quite tall enough. And since, so far as was known, Creed's accomplice didn't wear glasses, that eliminated the woman.

A more experienced agent would have waited until the plane landed and tactfully questioned the pair. But Swan had gone straight to the telephones and tried to get more information. It cost him dearly, because the suspects were long gone by the time he went looking for them.

To the young agent's credit, he had then phoned in a report. Before long, older agents arrived at the airport and after careful questioning established a high probability that the couple had in fact been Creed and his paramour. A dragnet had been thrown out, without result.

Brognola felt the Intel to be credible. He wanted Bolan on the scene in case there were late-breaking developments.

No one had any clear idea why Creed had gone to the Islands. But it was known that the attempt on the President and the New Jersey episode were but two prongs of a three-pronged terrorist onslaught planned by Green Rage. So the powers that be thought it perfectly feasible that the third attack would take place in Hawaii.

Except for a short nap at the hospital, Bolan hadn't slept much in several days. He availed himself of the chance now, saying to Grimaldi, "I'm going to catch forty winks. Wake me when we refuel on the West Coast, Jack."

"Roger that, Sarge. Don't forget to put your food tray in the aisle for the flight attendant to trip over when she comes by. And if I step out to relieve myself, you'll have to fly this bird for a while."

The warrior drifted off with a faint grin tugging at his mouth.

Hawaii

JASON CREED STOOD on the upper deck of the *Bio-Ark* and scanned the blue vault of Pacific sky. Other than a few pillowy cumulus clouds, the blue background was unbroken. He halted in front of Axel Fagan, who sat hugging his skinny knees to his skinny chest, and cocked the pistol. "So help me, you moron, if you've brought us to the wrong coordinates, I'll feed you to the sharks."

Fagan's fear was as palpable as ever. He gazed out over the tranquil aquamarine sea, to where a solitary fin was visible a few hundred feet away. "I swear on my mother's grave," he said plaintively. "These are the exact coordinates you gave me." He gestured at the ocean. "Although why you would want to stop in the middle of nowhere is beyond me. I thought you told me that we were going to Los Angeles?"

"We are," Creed confirmed.

Constantine had been sunning herself, her back to the conning-tower control station. Clearing her throat, she commented, "Maybe something happened, Jase. That old smuggler might have changed his mind. Or maybe Garth and Dean were taken into custody."

"Not likely on both counts," Creed said. "I paid that old fart thirty thousand up front, and he gave me his word he'd be here." Creed spied a distant speck to the east that turned out to be a gull. "As for the other two, if the police had them in custody, we'd have heard it on the news."

"Is that them?" Constantine asked, shading her eyes and pointing westward.

Creed was inclined to be skeptical until the combined rumble of four engines assured him it was. From out of the sun soared a fully restored Martin China Clipper, which had been modified by adding large pontoons for amphibious operations. The sunlight glinted off the oversize but streamlined fuselage as the huge airplane banked. "At last," he said.

Fagan had jumped to his feet to gape at the juggernaut. "My word! That thing dwarfs the *Bio-Ark*."

"Can you guess why?" Creed taunted. Simmons had told him the aircraft would be able to handle the load, but he held lingering doubts. Even with a wingspan of 130 feet and a length of over ninety, Creed didn't see how the jumbo antique would be able to transport so much weight.

Red Simmons was a consummate pilot. He soared in low once and circled to check them out. Then he rose and swooped in from the southeast, against the wind so he could bring the *Condor,* as he liked to call the bird, to a stop that much sooner. The cockpit window opened. A square, rugged face framed by thinning red hair poked out. "Here we are, as promised."

"You're late," Creed mentioned. "And I was expecting you to come in from the east."

Simmons had already ducked into the cockpit. He applied enough thrust to the engines to coast the Clipper alongside the submersible. Moments later a small door in the side of the aircraft swung outward, revealing Garth Hunter and George Dean.

Hunter secured the door, then shoved out an inflatable. The raft ballooned swiftly to its full size, and Hunter jumped in to steady it with a short paddle. Moments later Red Simmons joined him.

The pilot was one of the last of his breed, an aviator who flew by the seat of his pants but always made it to his destination intact. It was rumored he had every cove and inlet along the West Coast memorized, and that he had smuggled in enough goods, people and weapons to fill a chain of warehouses.

Creed had learned of Simmons from Dean, who in turn had heard of the man through a contact made in prison. Getting word to him had taken money and time, but at last Creed had done it. They had met once, briefly, in Seattle, and Creed hadn't been all that impressed.

Up close, Simmons had the florid features of a borderline alcoholic. He was overweight from lack of exercise and liked to walk around with an unlit cigar chomped between his lips. Only five foot six, he hardly presented an imposing picture.

The man's reputation was another matter. Everyone Creed had talked to about Simmons swore that the old coot was the most dependable smuggler in the Pacific, a throwback to an earlier era when a man was as good as his word no matter what line of work he might be in.

Now, shaking Simmons's callused hand, Creed said, "I was about ready to give up on you."

The smuggler didn't like being criticized. "We hit some foul weather halfway here and had to swing wide to the south to avoid turbulence and conserve fuel. I warned you that sort of thing could happen."

Simmons walked a dozen feet along the deck of the bathyscaphe, then sighed. "When you told me I'd be transportin' a small submersible, I was thinkin' along the lines of a minisub. This thing is bigger, by half, and must weigh as much as a tank. We'll be pushin' it, Mr. Tyler, I don't mind tellin' you."

Axel Fagan had been listening intently. On hearing the name Simmons used, he snorted and declared, "Is that the name he gave you, mister? Well, it's not Tyler. It's—"

Creed was on Fagan in a flash. He slammed the pistol against the man's head and he slumped, unconscious, a nasty gash in his temple.

Simmons placed his hands on his hips and chewed the end of his cigar a moment. "Tyler, I don't care if you gave me an alias. Most people in this business use them."

"I'm not most people," Creed said as he kicked Fagan once for good measure. He had given a phony name because he knew all too well that even a hardened criminal like Simmons might balk at working for someone like him. He'd found that out when Dean and Slater had tried to recruit talent from the ranks of ex-cons they knew. More than two-thirds of the felons wanted nothing to do with a pack of "Green Freaks," as the cons branded Green Rage. It had made his blood boil.

Simmons shrugged and went on to other matters. "Another reason I'm late is because I slipped into Oahu last night to top off my tanks. Something told me I'd need every gallon of gas, and by gum, I was right. We'll wing into L.A. on vapor fumes, if I'm any judge."

Creed regarded the aircraft critically. "But we will make it, right?"

"Not to worry," Simmons said. "She was built to carry tons of cargo. And those engines are the finest money can buy. All we have to do is line up this guppy, hook it to the winch and reel it up the ramp into the cargo bay."

And that was exactly what they did. It took them the better part of four hours because the first hoist broke and they had to jury-rig a second out of steel cable, but in due course the job was done, the cargo bay was closed and Simmons took his place in the pilot's seat.

Becoming airborne was an undertaking in itself. The *Condor* covered twice as much distance as usual before the wings gained enough lift to take the aircraft aloft. Simmons sweated bullets until they were at a thousand feet, then whooped and hollered for joy.

Creed would have been just as happy except for a minor incident. Just as they took wing, he happened to glance out one of the small, square windows and saw a fishing boat less than a quarter mile away. He was sure the occupants were staring at the plane. All he could do was keep his fingers crossed that they wouldn't report the strange goings-on to the authorities. He had come too far to let anything stand in his way now.

In forty-eight hours it would all be over. The U.S. Navy would have suffered a crippling blow, and the City of Angels would be inhabited by ghosts.

CHAPTER EIGHTEEN

The Executioner never made it to Hawaii.

Jack Grimaldi touched down at Edwards Air Force Base in California to refuel for the next leg of their flight, and while the pilot stayed with the Phantom II, Bolan checked in with Brognola.

The big Fed was excited about new developments. The first concerned Director Axel Fagan of the National Oceanic Institute. The director and an expensive new submersible, the *Bio-Ark*, had disappeared. In itself, that was hardly significant, until it became known that Fagan obtained his degree at Berkeley, and a computer check revealed that he and Creed had been classmates.

Then came the next break. The crew of a fishing boat heard about the *Bio-Ark* on the news and contacted Hawaiian police to report that they had seen a vessel answering its description being loaded onto an amphibious aircraft, which had then flown off in the direction of the mainland.

Brognola had been quick to put two and two together. He had galvanized federal agencies up and down the West Coast into digging for more information. The name Red Simmons came up, a twice-arrested but never convicted smuggler who specialized in fixed-wing amphibians.

Bolan agreed with Brognola's deductions. Creed was headed for the West Coast with the intent of using the submersible in a terrorist act. But they had no idea where he would strike or the nature of the attack.

Thanks to the DEA, Brognola learned of an acquaintance of Red Simmons's, a former partner who had quit the trade after losing a hand to a propeller. The man's last known address was in San Diego, just down the coast from L.A.

So instead of rocketing over the broad Pacific, the warrior found himself in a rental car barreling south on Interstate 15. South of Miramar Naval Air Station he turned west on the Soledad Freeway, which brought him to the San Diego Freeway. Again he pointed the vehicle southward.

Bolan had always liked San Diego. It was a clean, sterling city spread out over almost three hundred square miles. There was none of the mass crowding seen in Los Angeles or in New Jersey, and little of the urban blight that turned any city into a policeman's worst nightmare.

After passing Mission Bay, Bolan took an exit and headed east into Old Town. He had to consult a map to find the exact address, which turned out to be within two blocks of Balboa Park.

The apartment house had three stories and a front yard the size of a flower bed. Bolan found the name he wanted and was about to ring when a woman emerged.

Slipping inside before the door closed, he paused to adjust his eyes to the dim interior. Then he padded to the stairwell.

The merry laughter of children floated down from above. Bolan climbed to the third floor, loosened the Beretta in its shoulder rig and walked to room 311. He rapped lightly and waited, but there was no answer. As he knocked a second time, the next door opened and a woman whose face was layered thick with cold cream smiled at him.

"Excuse me. Are you looking for Mr. Donovan?"

"Yes. I'm a friend of his."

"How sweet. He doesn't have very many." The woman exposed more of herself, showing she wore a bright pink robe and yellow bunny slippers. "Well, Charley is never home at this time of day. He likes to go to the park and feed the pigeons and squirrels."

"Thank you," Bolan said, and turned to go.

"You shouldn't have any trouble spotting him."

"Ma'am?"

"I mean, with that hook of his, he does tend to stand out in a crowd."

Smiling, Bolan hurried off before she thought to invite him in for tea. Since he had been cooped up for so long, first in the jet and then in the car, he chose to walk to Balboa Park.

The warrior guessed the park to be roughly two miles long and more than a mile wide. Scores of people were out soaking up the sunshine. Others walked pets or enjoyed picnics with their families. Teens were tossing

Frisbees or playing ball. At one spot several young men were throwing a boomerang.

The warrior concentrated on those feeding animals. San Diego was a retirement community, so there was no shortage of older women and men who brought bags of peanuts or bread crumbs every day. He counted twenty of them before he spotted the man he was after.

Charley Donovan was a small, wiry man with a pencil mustache and a Vandyke. He leaned against a tree not far from where the world's largest outdoor organ was pumping music into the warm air, feeding a pack of four lively squirrels from a brown bag impaled on the end of his steel hook.

Bolan had to exercise restraint. Donovan wasn't accused of any crime. Answers were all the warrior wanted, information that would help him nail Jason Creed. He approached the tree in a roundabout fashion so as not to draw Donovan's attention. With his hands clasped behind his back, he strolled up close, stopping when the man glanced at him. "Hello."

"Hello," Donovan said while flinging more peanuts.

"I need to talk to you," Bolan stated, not making any sudden moves, "if you have a minute."

Donovan stopped flinging and stepped away from the trunk. "Do tell. Who are you? And what do you want to discuss?"

"Red Simmons—" was all Bolan said, when suddenly Donovan hurled the bag at him, wheeled and took off toward the Zoological Gardens.

Bolan ducked instinctively as the spray of peanuts struck his face and chest, giving Donovan a few seconds' lead. He gave chase, knowing it would be futile to yell for the man to stop.

Regular exercise and constant activity had given Bolan formidable stamina and the speed of a sprinter, but he was hard-pressed to keep the former smuggler in sight. Donovan weaved among the park-goers and the trees, his size making him hard to keep track of. Bolan knew he had to overtake Donovan before the man reached the gardens. There, the crowds were so heavy, he might well lose sight of his quarry.

The Executioner also had to keep his eyes peeled for police. If the two of them were taken into custody for questioning, Donovan would scream for a lawyer, who would have him back out on the streets in no time, allowing the man to go underground until the heat was off.

A kid on a bike blundered into Donovan's path and the two collided. The bicycle crashed to the ground and the kid cursed a blue streak, but wiry Donovan stayed on his feet and raced on.

More than one hundred acres of semitropical trees and flowers made up the Zoological Gardens, and the area was almost junglelike. Donovan glanced back to grin in triumph as he dashed in among the flower lovers lining a path.

Bolan wasn't far behind, but it might as well have been a mile. He came to the same shrubs and strained to see over the heads of tourists crowded in front of him. Forty feet off, Donovan vanished around a turn.

Frustrated, the warrior hugged the foliage and squeezed by. He sped to the turn, but Donovan was long gone. The wily man had given him the slip.

Or had he?

Rather than conduct a long and fruitless search, Bolan hastened out of Balboa Park and went to his car. Sliding in, he dipped low behind the wheel so that no one could see him unless the person was right on top of the vehicle.

It wasn't long, not more than ten minutes, before Charley Donovan appeared. He had the air of a cagey wolf, walking slowly and stopping every few feet to look in all directions. Once, he halted and studied the cars parked along the street, starting with those nearest him, which forewarned Bolan.

Ducking lower, the warrior mentally counted to ten, then eased high enough to see the apartment building. Donovan had paused at the entrance and was scouring the area one last time. Producing a key, the man darted inside and made certain the door locked behind him.

Bolan made no move to follow. Confronting Donovan there would endanger innocents. Besides which, he doubted Donovan would remain very long; his kind would rather flee than fight.

Not eight minutes after entering, Donovan reappeared, a small travel bag in his left hand. He checked the street carefully before venturing into the open, then hurried along the sidewalk, approaching Bolan's car.

The warrior lowered himself to the floor, twisting so he could keep his eyes on the windows. A shadow flitted across and he caught sight of the back of Donovan's head. When it was gone, he rose and watched the former smuggler go three blocks and take a left.

Starting the car, Bolan pulled out and followed. He wondered if maybe he was wrong in thinking of Donovan as a former smuggler, when for all he knew the Intel the Feds had was outdated and the man might still be in league with Simmons. It would pay to shadow him, to see where he ran to.

As luck would have it, a van in front of Bolan made the same turn he had to make, and he followed closely behind. By craning his neck, he spotted Donovan a block and a half to the west, hiking at a brisk clip. Bolan slowed to give him a larger lead.

Apparently Donovan believed he had given the warrior the slip because he looked over his shoulder only twice in four blocks. Eventually he arrived at a busy avenue and a bus stop.

Bolan pulled to the curb behind a station wagon. The angle was such that there was very little likelihood Donovan would spot him. In a few minutes a bus appeared, and he let it get a considerable lead before he followed.

They were now heading north. The bus rumbled past Old Town, past the University of San Diego, until, on a nearly deserted street flanked by a large self-storage facility identified as the Mini Storage Warehouse, Charley Donovan got off.

Bolan was ten car lengths back and had nowhere to pull over. Raising a hand to his mouth as if he were stifling a yawn, he was all set to speed up if the man recognized him. But Donovan made a beeline for the facility, removing a key from his shirt pocket as he did, then hurried around a corner.

Left with no other option since there were No Parking signs the length of the street, Bolan drove into the parking lot. The manager's office was closed, and a thin cardboard clock posted in the window indicated he or she wouldn't be back for almost an hour.

Bolan moved quietly to the corner. He heard a metal door rattle and rasp as it was raised, and peered out. Donovan had just opened a storage unit and was going inside. The warrior catfooted to the opening and placed his hand on the Beretta.

The unit was crammed with boxes, most filled with old books and magazines. Donovan was bent over one of the boxes, throwing magazines right and left in fevered abandon. He grunted, bent lower and lifted out a small gun case. Setting it on a different box, he worked the tiny latch.

The case contained a Ruger revolver. As Donovan started to reach for the gun, Bolan stepped inside and leveled the Beretta. "I wouldn't if I were you," he advised.

At the first word, Donovan cried out and whirled. He raised his good hand to his face as if to ward off a bullet, and said, "Who the hell are you? What do you want from me?"

"I told you the first time," Bolan replied, gesturing with the 93-R so Donovan would move aside. To remove temptation, he plucked the Ruger from the case and stuck it under his belt. "I want to talk."

Donovan scowled, his dark eyes shifting desperately in search of a way out. "Who do you work for? Who sent you? How much are they paying you to bump me off?"

Backing up a few strides, Bolan shook his head. "Do you need a hearing aid, Charley? All I'm interested in is your old friend, Red Simmons. Or do you still work with him?"

"What's Red got to do with anything?"

"Answer the question."

Regaining some confidence now that he realized he wasn't going to be killed right then and there, Donovan lowered his arm. "I used to work with that old coot. Everyone knows that. But we had a falling out. He went his way, I went mine."

"The two of you were paired up for over a decade. What could have caused you to break up?"

Donovan's chin jutted out. "I'm not telling."

"Yes, you are," Bolan said, taking slow aim.

"All right! All right!" Donovan looked past the warrior, clearly hoping someone would happen by. When no one did, he continued, "Yeah, Red and I worked together for a long time. We were the best damn smugglers ever. Guns, booze, contraband records and clothes, you name it, we brought it into the country.

Then one day we were approached by a man who wanted us to smuggle in dope.''

"There's a lot of money in that."

Donovan snorted. "Tell me about it. I was all for taking the job, but Red, he didn't want anything to do with drugs. Drugs were poison, he'd say, and even though I tried to persuade him until I was blue in the face, he flat out refused."

Bolan had never heard of an ethical smuggler before. "So that's why you broke up?"

"In a nutshell. I figured I could do just fine alone, so I got my own plane and was all set to make my first flight to Colombia for the goods when one of my engines acted up. I climbed onto the wing to see what was wrong and got a bit too close." Donovan held the hook out. "I was laid up for months. Needless to say, I lost the contract."

"Have you seen Red since?"

"A few times. Why? It's him you're after, isn't it? What for?"

"I'm holding the gun, remember?" Bolan said. "When was the last time you saw him?"

"About a year ago. We had a few drinks for old times' sake. The last I heard, he was bringing in loads of fake designer clothes and stuff up near Seattle."

Bolan mulled the information, debating his next move. It would appear that Donovan knew little of value. But it paid to remember that smugglers were just like everyone else—they were creatures of habit. And if Simmons was going to drop off the *Bio-Ark* somewhere along the West Coast, it stood to reason he would pick a place he was familiar with, somewhere the bathyscaphe could be unloaded in secret without risk of being detected by the authorities.

Making up his mind, Bolan motioned at the entrance. "Let's go."

Donovan made no move to obey. "Now hold on, mister. I've told you all I know. What more do you want?"

"For you to show me all the spots where Simmons brings his contraband in."

"Are you nuts? He doesn't use the same drop-off points we did back in the old days." Donovan flinched when the Beretta swung toward him. "Well, maybe a few of the same ones. But they're scattered all along the coast, from north of San Diego clear to Vancouver."

Bolan nodded at the boxes. "Better bring some magazines to read, then. We have a long ride ahead of us."

LEUCADIA LIES between San Diego and Los Angeles. North of this coastal community, in the vicinity of South Carlsbad State Beach, is a small, secluded cove rarely visited by beachcombers or swimmers during the day and never visited by anyone after dark.

But from a rise east of the cove, which hid it from traffic and prying eyes, Mack Bolan saw several small lanterns and spied figures scurrying about. The furtive activity suggested one thing. And since this was a spot used by Red Simmons, he felt that he might have hit pay dirt.

The sun had set hours earlier. Bolan should have been there sooner, but Charley Donovan had taken forever to find the cove, pleading a faulty memory. Donovan claimed it had been years since he was last there, and it was hard for him to remember the exact location.

None of which Bolan bought. Just as professional gamblers never forgot big winning hands, old smugglers never forgot prime smuggling sites.

Turning to the duffel he had lugged from the trunk, Bolan unfastened the zipper and took out an M-16.

"God in heaven!" Donovan exclaimed from where he was crouched a few feet away. So far he had behaved himself, other than to grumble a lot, and stall. "What the hell are you fixing to do with that? Go to war?"

"You took the words right out of my mouth," Bolan said, stuffing three spare magazines into his pockets. Shifting so Donovan couldn't see, he added a smoke grenade.

"And what am I supposed to do while you're gone?"

"Get some beauty sleep," Bolan answered, training the rifle on the smuggler. "On your feet, and turn around." At gunpoint Bolan marched Donovan to the car, which he had pulled into a stand of trees. The empty trunk was wide open. "Climb in."

Muttering nonstop, the man complied, lying on his left side and curling into a ball. "I won't forget this, mister. I can carry a grudge forever."

"Save it." He closed the trunk and leaned on it to make doubly certain it locked and held. Jogging to the rise, he went over it on his belly, then rose and advanced through waist-high grasses and weeds to the edge of the beach.

Bolan studied the six men and the craft they had arrived in. He should have known it was expecting too much to think it would be Simmons and Creed. The craft was a speedboat, not an airplane, and the men, all of whom spoke Spanish, were unloading drugs, not a submersible.

Taking them down wasn't part of Bolan's mission, but he couldn't let the opportunity pass. He caught the Spanish word for cocaine, which told him they were smuggling drugs. From the size of the shipment, they had enough to keep every cokehead in Los Angeles, San Diego and San Francisco happy for quite some time.

Bolan had to stop that blow from hitting the streets. Tucking the stock to his shoulder, he slipped his left hand into his jacket and palmed the smoker. As with conventional grenades, it utilized a pin, lever and striker-type ignition system. He jerked out the pin with his teeth but held the lever down, waiting for the right moment.

The smugglers were half-finished transferring the cocaine to a parked Jeep. Four were busy working while the fifth stood at the controls of the boat, and the sixth stood guard near the vehicle, an SMG tucked to his side.

It surprised Bolan how casual they were about the whole business. None betrayed nervousness except the speedboat operator, who fidgeted, eager to depart. The guard was smoking a cigarette, and the men unloading the coke chatted back and forth as if they were out on a Sunday stroll instead of engaged in a highly illegal activity.

In order to sow a few moments of panic on which he could capitalize, Bolan cocked an arm, waited until the quartet was halfway between the boat and the Jeep and hurled the smoker with unerring skill.

The grenade was in midair when the pyrotechnic starter ignited the smoke, which spewed out in a roiling yellow cloud. It hit the ground and spun, generating more and more smoke.

Stunned, the burly guard simply stared. The other four were frozen in place, as well. Only the speedboat operator had the presence of mind to face the controls and turn the engine over, which woke up his companions. The guard unlimbered his subgun and started toward the smoke cloud instead of seeking cover as he should have done. The quartet came to life, but they couldn't make up their minds whether to head for the boat or the Jeep. One by one they drew pistols.

Bolan took out the guard first, coring the man's brain with two tightly spaced shots. He swiveled to drop another smuggler but had to flatten when the four cut loose with handguns, banging wildly into the night. Inspired by fear, they shot at shadows or waving stems of grass.

From the prone position, Bolan sighted on the speedboat driver. Already the craft was easing away from the shore and would shortly be in water deep enough for the driver to punch the engine into high gear.

One of the lanterns was in the boat, and it cast enough light for Bolan to fix his sights on the middle of the driver's back. He slowly applied pressure to the trigger. The man dropped just as he opened the throttle.

Out of control, the speedboat skewed to the right in a tight circle, slowed to a crawl and sputtered toward the beach. The smooth bow slid up onto the damp sand, digging a deep furrow and wedging the craft fast.

All this Bolan caught out of one eye. He had something else to occupy him, namely the four gunners. Apparently they were aware that the best defense was always a determined offense, because with one accord they raised their pistols and charged. Fanning out, they fired on the run, spitting lead in a wide arc.

The warrior was taking aim when he discovered that he had overlooked a second guard, a man armed with an Uzi who was bearing down on him from the right. The instant Bolan spotted him, the guard opened fire.

CHAPTER NINETEEN

With the guard rushing toward him from one direction and the four gunners from another, the Executioner held his ground. Lying there with lead zinging above him and chewing into the earth at his side, he sent a short burst into the guard, who buckled at the waist. Then he swiveled and blistered the quartet with a sustained burst.

The 5.56 mm hailstorm mowed down the drug runners from right to left. As the last man fell to his knees, he fired wildly into the air, screaming in agony. In pure reflex he emptied the clip, then expired.

The Executioner swapped the spent magazine for a new one and rose. After verifying that each smuggler was dead, he walked to the speedboat. The driver lay on his back, his blank eyes fixed on eternity.

Stepping onto the boat, the warrior searched the various compartments and came across several spare gas cans. He upended one over the controls and the bow. Another he splashed onto the stern section, dousing the cocaine thoroughly.

The contents of the third gas can he poured on the Jeep and the kilos of coke inside.

Bolan stepped to the man who'd been smoking, searched his pants pockets and found a pack of matches.

Since the fires were bound to attract attention, the warrior knew he had to move quickly. Striking a match, he cast it into the Jeep, spun and raced off as flames flared to life. He had a lit match in his hand as he drew abreast of the speedboat and flicked it over the round-bottom hull.

The weeds suddenly seemed a long way off. Bolan raced across the sand, his shoes slapping hard. The flames shooting from the Jeep were as high as he was tall, those in the boat roaring skyward. It wouldn't be long before one or the other blew.

The Jeep took the honors. The warrior was a few yards shy of the vegetation when the explosion occurred, followed a half second later by the speedboat. A warm, invisible hand slapped Bolan in the back and flung him into the weeds and grass. He lost no time in scrambling to his feet and speeding up the incline to the crest, where he paused to grab the duffel bag.

Bolan had the keys out before he reached the car. Donovan would have to wait, he decided, until he had put some distance behind them. Throwing the duffel onto the floor in the back so it wouldn't be obvious if he was stopped by police, he replaced the M-16, zipped the bag closed and jumped in the front.

Dust curled out from under the rear tires as Bolan sped from the stand, across a field and onto the shoulder of the highway. Looking in the rearview mirror, he saw orange fingers of flame visible above the rim.

Five vehicles had stopped along the highway and three or four people had climbed out.

Bolan never slowed. Someone shouted at him, but he floored the pedal and soon reached the speed limit. At the next intersection he cut the wheel to the right. On reaching Interstate 15, he turned north, toward Los Angeles. He passed the Pala Indian Reservation and Rancho California. When the exit for Lake Eisinore and the Cleveland National Forest came up, he took it.

It wasn't long before Bolan discovered a dirt road that suited his purpose. On a secluded stretch he finally braked and turned the key. Drawing the Beretta, he stepped around to the trunk and thumped twice. "Are you still alive in there?"

A string of curses greeted the question.

"Hang on," Bolan said. He had to reverse the key to insert it in the lock. There was a loud click and he leaned down to raise the lid.

Without warning the lid shot up of its own accord, slammed into the warrior's chest with brutal force and knocked him backward. The Beretta spun away. Bolan stayed on his feet and settled himself as Donovan sprang from the trunk and slashed at him with his steel hook.

"Die, you bastard!" Donovan raged, striking in short, fast strokes, his slicing hook hard to see in the dark.

Bolan retreated, staying one step ahead, and tried to grab the Desert Eagle. Donovan saw the motion and closed in swiftly, aiming a vicious blow at his chest. The warrior blocked it with a forearm but before he could seize Donovan's wrist and execute a shoulder toss, the smaller man skipped out of reach.

A six-inch hook was a deadly weapon, and Charley Donovan used his with skill born of long experience. The hook weaved and flashed, never still for a moment, never giving the warrior a respite. Donovan never overextended himself, nor left himself open to a countermove.

The Desert Eagle was Bolan's best bet, but he dared not take his attention off the dully glittering hook or he would pay a dear price. Nor could he look behind him to see what was there. So he was taken unawares when his right heel slipped on the crumbling edge of a deep pothole, and he fell.

Like a jaguar leaping in for the kill, Donovan pounced, the hook cleaving the air in a smooth stroke.

Bolan got both hands up and caught hold of the man's wrist even as he jammed a foot into Donovan's gut and heaved. The man flew head over heels and slammed onto his back. The warrior pushed to his feet and cleared the big .44 in a lightning draw. Cocking the pistol, he pointed it at Donovan's head as the man rose.

"Hold it right there."

Anyone else would have been shot dead in his tracks. But Bolan gave the former smuggler one last chance because he had taken Donovan against his will and forced him to cooperate at gunpoint. Legally he had no right to do so, although morally he had all the right in the world.

Bolan would never know why the other man didn't listen. Maybe Donovan feared he would be slain in time, anyway, or perhaps he thought Bolan worked for an old enemy. Or maybe it was that Donovan had killed before and thought he could do so again and no one would be the wiser. Maybe he thought he could beat a bullet.

Donovan was wrong.

When the man kept coming, Bolan was forced to shoot. He stood over the limp form and shook his head. Not over the outcome, but over the fact that he had needed the man to show him exactly where the rest of Red Simmons's favorite smuggling haunts were.

The cause wasn't hopeless. During the ride up from San Diego, Bolan had given Donovan a pen and a map and made him mark all the drop-off points he could recall. There were four in California, three in Oregon and two in Washington. Any one of them might be where Simmons turned up with the submersible. And since Bolan couldn't cover them all by himself, he needed some backup.

After rolling the body into the trees, the warrior drove to the interstate. A half hour later he was taking the Corona exit and pulling up beside a public phone at a service station. He dropped a coin and dialed a special number known only to Able Team, Phoenix Force and a few other privileged souls. The agent who answered patched him directly through to Hal Brognola.

"Striker! Any news?"

Bolan gave a recap of his activities from the time he parted company with Grimaldi until he picked up the phone. He explained about the loss of Donovan, and the map.

"It could be the big break we've been waiting for. God knows, we can use it," Brognola said. "All the planes and ships we have out hunting for the amphibian have turned up diddly so far. It's as if the aircraft vanished off the face of the earth." He sighed. "Which shouldn't surprise me. Red Simmons is the best at what he does. He knows every trick in the book. My guess is he's flying so low, the waves are lapping at the bottom of his plane."

"So how do you want to handle this?" Bolan asked.

"Bring the map to the Justice Department branch office in L.A. I'll have someone on hand to meet you and fax copies to me. Tell me which site you want to stake out. Field operatives will cover the rest."

"Give me the address. I can be there within the hour."

"Let's just hope that this time our luck holds. If Simmons isn't using his old haunts, we're screwed."

"Royally," Bolan agreed.

THE OBJECT OF ONE of the most intense manhunts in U.S. history was at that moment steadily winging his way toward the West Coast.

Jason Creed hummed softly to himself and stared out over the starlit seascape. From so low a height, the ocean resembled an immense inkwell. He couldn't see waves, but he knew they were there because every so often whitecaps broke the black monotony.

Shifting, Creed looked at Red Simmons, who sat relaxed but vigilant in his chair. "I've got to hand it to you. This bird of yours is everything you claimed it would be."

The smuggler gave the control panel an affectionate pat. "The *Condor* and me go back a long way, mister. She's like the sweetheart I never had." Simmons checked the fuel gauge, then the altimeter. "I made all the modifications myself to be sure it was done right."

Again Creed shifted. Huddled on cushions on the floor were Julie, Fagan, Hunter and Dean. Julie appeared bored. Fagan hung his head in exaggerated misery. The two former Marines were playing stud poker, using toothpicks for chips. "I see that creature comforts weren't high on your list."

Simmons chuckled. "They don't have many creature comforts in prison, either, and that's where I'd be if I weighed the Blue Goose down with a lot of fancy frills. Keeping her light is the key to my survival."

"Ever smuggled a submersible before?"

"Can't say as I have," Simmons said. "This is one to brag to my friends about." He caught himself, then added quickly, "Not that I would, you understand. It was a figure of speech, nothin' more. Once I drop you off, I'll forget I ever saw you."

"I'm sure you'll never tell anyone," Creed said casually, almost too casually.

Simmons glanced sharply at him but made no comment. Slipping on headphones, he reached for a dial and remarked, "A little music will help to keep me awake. But this far out, it's hard to find a station I like."

Creed waited until the smuggler was whistling softly and tapping a foot before he leaned to one side to speak to Garth Hunter. "As soon as we have the *Bio-Ark* under lock and key, I want you to head into Los Angeles and buy the mines."

"No problem," Hunter said without looking up from his cards. "It's all been arranged, just like you wanted. Cash on the barrelhead, and you get the detonators and the six underwater mines. Enough to sink the *Queen Mary*, if you wanted."

Axel Fagan raised his head. His eyes were bloodshot from anguish and lack of rest. "Is that what you plan to do with my submersible? Sink a ship?"

Creed frowned at Hunter. "You talk too damn much." Then, to the director, he said, "What if I do?"

Fagan jutted out his chin in feeble defiance. "You need me to pilot the *Bio-Ark*, you know. What if I refuse? What if I'd rather die first than be a party to spilling blood?"

"I doubt you have the balls to stand up to me," Creed said. "But just in case you get a hair to try, I'll let Mr. Hunter here explain the consequences."

"What do you mean?" Fagan asked timidly.

It was Hunter who answered, his tone so matter-of-fact, there was no denying he meant every word. "I'll start with parts of your body that you don't need to pilot the sub. Say a toe here, a finger there. Maybe an ear and part of your nose. I'll use pruning shears to take them off, and I'll do it nice and slow. By the time I'm done you'll be blubbering like a baby in a pool of your own blood, but you'll live. And you'll do as Jason wants you to do, anyway, so why give yourself the grief?''

Fagan tried to shrivel into a ball. "I understand. Believe me. Your wish is my command."

Creed smiled smugly. "That's what I like to hear."

THE FOUNDER OF GREEN RAGE would have felt a lot less smug if he had donned a pair of headphones and heard the same news report Red Simmons was listening to. The old smuggler did nothing to give his reaction away, but inwardly he seethed.

Green Rage, the kidnapped director, the stolen bathyscaphe—all the pieces fit, and Red Simmons wanted to beat his head against the control yoke for getting involved.

Ordinarily Simmons asked no questions about his clients. Prying wasn't part of the game. He took customers as they came, unless he suspected they dealt in drugs, in which case he wouldn't touch their business with a ten-foot pole.

His old partner, Charley Donovan, had never been able to understand his attitude. "We can get rich in no time!" Charley often argued before they went their separate ways. But Red had always refused, and would go on refusing to deal in dope for as long as he lived.

Donovan had accused him of being too old-fashioned, and Simmons supposed to a limited degree that was true. There were lines he wouldn't cross. He wouldn't smuggle heroin or cocaine, he wouldn't kill. And, given a choice, he wouldn't become involved with a bunch of rabid fruitcakes like those who made up Green Rage.

Simmons told himself that he was growing too old for the trade, that he should have been more suspicious when the man who called himself Jim Tyler arranged a meet and offered him a small fortune to pick him up off Oahu and transport a minisub to the States. Creed had been clever, though. He'd led Simmons to believe that he was some sort of high-tech hardware bandit who went around stealing corporate prototypes for rivals.

Now Simmons knew the truth. But knowing it and doing something about it were two different things, especially when he had already spent some of the advance money. As much as he would like to dump the whole lot of them in the ocean, he figured that he had to see it through.

But then what? Simmons wondered. The Feds would pull out all the stops to take him into custody. Maybe, he reasoned, he should go to them and strike a deal. They might be willing to drop all charges in exchange for bagging Green Rage.

It was worth some thought.

The music came back on, a Tommy Dorsey big band tune, and Simmons whistled along with the song. He caught Jason Creed eyeing him like a chicken ripe for plucking and resolved to keep his eyes on Mr. Creed for the duration of the trip. He wouldn't put it past a nasty piece of work like Creed to put a slug in his back once the bathyscaphe was safely unloaded.

It had been bound to happen eventually, Simmons mused. Many of his clients were wanted somewhere, or on the run, or plain mean like Creed. It was a wonder one had never tried to snuff him before.

Suddenly a blip appeared on the Ferranti ARI 5979 Seaspray radar unit Simmons had paid an arm and a leg for. He had fitted the scanner into the nose of the Clipper and mounted the bright screen to the right of the control yoke. He reached out to adjust the gain while studying the blip.

Creed had noticed. "What is that?" he asked.

"My guess would be an Air Force or Navy jet on a grid sweep of this sector," Simmons said, "lookin' for us."

That got everyone's attention. The woman, whose name Simmons had yet to learn, stepped up behind the copilot's chair. "How close is it?"

"Over the horizon, which in our case is only about three miles because of our low altitude," Simmons explained. "Don't worry. The jet is way up there, about five thousand feet. I doubt we have anything to worry about."

As if to prove him wrong, a few seconds later the blip dipped lower.

Simmons knew what that meant. The jet was dropping slowly toward them, probably because the pilot had seen a ghost reflection of the *Condor* on radar. He activated the RadAlt aerials for the Honeywell AN/ APN 171 altimeter, one of the most sensitive ever built. He'd be able to tell how high he was, down to a fraction of an inch. "Hang on, folks, this might get rough," he announced.

"What are you doing?" Creed demanded when the Clipper descended a few more feet.

"That fly-boy up there isn't one hundred percent sure we're down here," Simmons said. "I aim to make sure he doesn't find us."

"By putting us in the drink?"

Simmons ignored the man. He kept his eyes on the screen, ready to take whatever evasive action was warranted. A green light blipped to life on his left and flashed as regularly as a heartbeat.

As usual, Creed was quick to see it. "What does that mean?"

"The pilot has turned on his radar and is trying to find us," Simmons revealed. "So far, he doesn't have a lock. And he won't, not if I have anything to say about it." Turning to a display panel, he flicked a series of switches and listened to a growing hum as the unit powered up. It was his last resort for dealing with unfriendlies, a device he'd had to purchase overseas, since the government kept tabs on sales made in the States.

The ECM central integrated system had been cobbled together but functioned as well as a working military model. Simmons waited for the multisensor to tell him the jet pilot had a lock, and the very moment it beeped, he switched a toggle, putting the EW jamming equipment on-line.

"I hate this," Creed growled. "We're like sitting ducks down here."

"It could be worse," Simmons said just to rattle him.

"I don't see how."

"We could be dead ducks."

The Seaspray showed the fly-boy had switched to an S-pattern and was flying wide to the north and south. Simmons nodded. He had eluded the pilot, but he knew they were somewhere in the area. Jamming his radar had proved that. Now came the crucial part. If the jet happened to be outfitted with a counterjamming device, the *Condor* was literally cooked.

Simmons watched the radar warning receiver but the multisensor didn't register another lock. He breathed a little easier and glanced out his window at the surface, which the Clipper was practically skimming. They were almost out of danger.

Then a second blip appeared on the Seaspray screen. It was another jet flying in from the northwest. Simmons saw it join the first. The pair flew virtually wing to wing for a short while, at which point they veered in opposite directions and began a systematic sweep.

"We're doomed!" Fagan wailed.

"Not hardly," Simmons said. The jets were concentrating their search in the wrong place and were almost out of range. He fed more power to the engines. Soon the blips blinked out and the screen stayed blank. "We did it, folks. We gave them the slip."

To be on the safe side, Simmons seldom took his eyes off the screen during the next ten minutes. He also ran an automatic scan of radio frequencies until he found the channel the Navy pilots were using. Judging by their conversation, they were completely in the dark.

One problem had been taken care of, Simmons reflected, but he still had a bigger, nastier problem to deal with, namely what to do about Green Rage. It would help if he knew beyond a shadow of a doubt that they planned to kill him once they reached the coast.

In order to find out, Simmons said, "See. This is a valuable lesson. Once we reach the drop-off site, we'll have to move fast unloading the sub. I hope you thought to have a few extra men on hand to help out."

"What you see is what you get," Creed replied. "We'll have to do it all by ourselves, but it shouldn't take long now that we know the ropes."

Simmons pretended to be interested in the screen to hide his anger. He had the answer he needed. The deal had been for Creed to pay a third of the money up front and the rest when the submersible was unloaded. Simmons had assumed someone would be there to pay him, but that wasn't going to be the case. Clearly neither the terrorist nor his cronies had the other seventy grand on them.

All of which pointed to bald-faced treachery.

Simmons made up his mind. He had to watch his back after they landed. Once he was shy of them, he was going straight to the Feds and telling them all he knew in exchange for immunity.

Maybe it was for the best, Simmons told himself. It was about time he traded in his pilot's chair for an easy chair. Immunity would let him do that without having to keep looking over his shoulder the rest of his life.

"What's so funny?" Creed asked.

Simmons hadn't realized he was grinning. "Nothing. I was just thinking about how we skunked those pilots." And, he thought to himself, how he was going to skunk Creed.

CHAPTER TWENTY

It was an hour or so before dawn when Mack Bolan heard the distant purr of aircraft engines far out over the turbulent Pacific Ocean. A storm front was moving in, and at first he thought the noise was the rumble of thunder. But as it grew in volume he recognized the sound for what it was and immediately sat up and laid his hands on the Weatherby Mark V Safari Grade big-game rifle at his side.

After studying the map in great detail and weighing the pros and cons, the Executioner had deduced that Simmons would land here. He was dressed in camouflage fatigues, with enough pouches and military webbing to hold all the ammo and tools of his trade that he needed.

Settling onto his stomach and propping his elbows on the green blanket under him, Bolan wedged the smooth stock to his shoulder. The feel of the superb rifle brought to mind his days as a sniper in Vietnam. During his tour and a half there, he had racked up one of the highest kill tallies of any serviceman.

Since then, the warrior had used his marksman skills time and again. The Mark V was one of his favorites. A bolt-action model, it could drop a charging elephant, if need be. And it was remarkably accurate at ranges where most rifles lost a lot of their stopping power.

Bolan glanced at the pair of scopes lying beside him. He had brought two because he didn't know what time of day or night the amphibian would arrive, if the smuggler showed up at all. So for daylight use he had a Zeiss telescopic sight, and for shooting at night, a second-generation Starlite scope that gave him crystal clarity in near total darkness.

With sunrise still so far off, it should have been an easy choice for Bolan to make. But the approaching storm complicated matters. Neither scope would be of help if it rained. A downpour would reduce his visibility to near zero, in which case he would be better off using none.

Bolan decided to hold off for a while. The plane was still a long way out. If it reached the bay before the storm, it wouldn't take him more than a few seconds to mount either scope and go into action.

But would Red Simmons try to land under such adverse conditions? That was the question Bolan pondered, and he concluded the wily smuggler might be using the storm as cover in order to slip in and out before anyone was the wiser.

Then again, the plane might belong to someone else, someone trying to outrun the roiling system so they could swing around to L.A., which lay to the south, and land before the tempest struck.

Farther up the coast was Santa Barbara. Almost due west of the bay were Santa Cruz and Santa Rosa islands. It occurred to Bolan that Simmons would most likely use the islands as landmarks to point him into the secluded bay.

A few light drops pattered down, and Bolan frowned. He strained to see into the clouds, but it was like trying to peer into pea soup. The engine noise wavered on the rising wind, and he couldn't be certain if the aircraft was still coming toward him or if it had veered off.

Snapping the Starlite scope to his eye, Bolan scanned the sea.

Then a vague gray shape appeared hundreds of yards out, flying so low that Bolan marveled it was still in the air. Waves were almost licking the undercarriage. The long wings stayed level, though, as the big plane zeroed in on the mouth of the inlet.

It was them. Bolan saw pontoons, the trademark of an amphibian. He was all set to attach the Starlite to the Weatherby when the scattered drops turned into a light but steady drizzle. In moments visibility was reduced to less than thirty feet.

The warrior quickly placed both scopes in their cases to protect them from the rain. Wrapping the blanket around the Weatherby, he rose and stepped sideways down the hill to where a shallow gully bisected the slope. Jumping in, he went prone on the seaward side and searched for the seaplane.

The rain increased even more. Bolan could barely see the bay, but he thought he heard a loud splash as the craft set down. The engines tapered off dramatically, cutting to a throaty purr. He knew the amphibian was coasting to a stop, but where? To the right, to the left or straight ahead?

The engines unexpectedly revved, as they would if the plane were about to take off again. Bolan realized that Red Simmons was turning the aircraft into the storm, pointing the nose at the ocean so he could take off at a moment's notice. The veteran smuggler knew all the tricks.

Thunder boomed overhead. The drizzle became a hard rain that kept Bolan from seeing whatever was taking place below him. Due to the storm, the Weatherby was now next to useless.

At close range Bolan would rather rely on the Desert Eagle and the Beretta. He wrapped the rifle carefully, slid it under a bush for protection from the elements and drew the big .44 Magnum pistol. Snaking to the top of the gully, he crawled on down toward the hissing waves below.

A shout registered faintly, then others. Bolan pressed his left hand to his brow to shield his eyes and discerned spectral figures moving out on the battered bay. He had to get much closer before he would be able to identify targets, a priority since there might be an innocent man on board.

The FBI was unsure whether the director of the National Oceanic Institute was a willing participant or had been forced to go along at gunpoint. Based on the Berkeley link, initially they believed that Fagan was a party to the theft of the bathyscaphe. But the fishermen off Oahu swore they had seen a man answering

Fagan's description, and from the look of things he had been badly roughed up. It was unlikely they were wrong since they had been using binoculars.

As a result, Hal Brognola had asked Bolan to retrieve the director alive, if possible. "He's a highly respected scientist with no criminal record whatsoever, not even a speeding ticket. We have to give him the benefit of the doubt."

Which was easy for Brognola to say, but difficult for Bolan to put into practice now that the storm had unleashed a downpour. The Weatherby would have given him the luxury of picking his targets with care. Conditions being what they were, he could only hope Fagan was bound and gagged, and somewhere out of the way in case a firefight erupted.

The warrior was soaked to the skin. The slope was rapidly turning into a mud slide, and he had to brace himself with his left hand to keep from sliding out of control. To the north, breakers crashed. To the south, lightning seared the heavens.

Bolan came to a strip of sand dotted with small stones. Crouching, he stalked slowly toward the blurred figures. Apparently they were attempting to unload the submersible, and it surprised him they would try in the storm. But, again, what better cover could anyone ask for than a temper tantrum courtesy of Nature herself? Not even the Coast Guard would be out in such weather unless an emergency arose. And as for aerial surveillance—it would be nonexistent.

Waves lapped the shore directly in front of him. He took another step, and the next wave rippled up across the beach and swirled around his shoes. He pressed on, the water rising to his ankles, then his knees, then his thighs.

"Attach another inflatable!"

The shout was so clear and loud that Bolan had the impression he was mere yards from the shouter, when actually the wind had died for a few seconds, enabling him to hear better.

Once the water rose above Bolan's waist, he pushed off and stroked toward the plane. The falling rain effectively hid him, and what little noise he made was drowned out by the drumming of the drops. He swam slowly, stopping every few feet to listen.

The amphibian was much farther out than the warrior had estimated. He was thirty or forty feet from shore when he saw the tail end of the aircraft. The Clipper was being buffeted by both the wind and the waves, and it was a minor miracle the plane held steady enough for the submersible to be unloaded.

The smuggler and the terrorists were hard at work. Bolan couldn't see them very well, but he could hear their shouts and curses. The cargo-bay door was down, buoyed by inflatable bags that cushioned it against the waves. A cable had been looped around the bathyscaphe at appropriate points and attached to a portable winch that hung from a small gantry-type crane welded to the reinforced ceiling. They were trying to hoist the sub through the opening.

But the storm made the chore next to impossible. Despite the inflatables, the rolling waves caused the door to rise and fall, and the sub kept swinging from side to side.

A rough voice bellowed, "Steady that guppy! Steady it, or we'll lose your precious sub and my bird!"

Bolan spotted three, possibly four figures. The rain made it hard to tell. Using a breaststroke, he swam closer. He could have shot two of them, but he held his fire. Either one might be Director Axel Fagan.

The warrior wasn't more than four feet from the bobbing cargo door, which doubled as a ramp when contraband was being taken on or off, when the unforeseen took place. He was in the act of reaching out to grab hold so he could pull himself out of the water at the very moment a tremendous wave rippled across the inlet, barreling toward the beach at twice the speed and height of all previous waves, catching the criminals off guard.

Bolan saw it coming. The door was supported ten to twelve inches above the surface by the six large bags. He happened to glance under it as he reached for the edge and beheld the mammoth swell surging to a height of four or five feet directly in front of the aircraft's nose. The next second the wave hit the Clipper and tilted the plane at a sharp angle even while pushing it landward—straight at Bolan.

The warrior barely had time to bend and dive. He kicked powerfully in a bid to get out of the way before the bay door or the plane itself smashed him to a pulp.

A blast of water slammed into him, propelling him end over end, disorienting him. He had no way of knowing which way was up, which way was down or where he was in relation to the aircraft.

Something hard gouged Bolan in the back but not deep enough to draw blood. He winced, in torment, and gritted his teeth, fighting the pain. The force of the wave gradually weakened. He tumbled less and less until finally he stopped himself and straightened, seeking some sign of the surface.

Bolan was surprised when his feet touched bottom and his head broke clear. He sucked in air and swiveled, taking stock. The monster wave had flung him almost onto the beach, only north of where he had entered the bay. There were no broken bones. Other than a few scrapes and bruises, he was fine.

The wave had also pushed the Clipper much closer to land. It was twenty feet out, in shallow water, the tail now pointing to the north instead of the east. Several men were cursing loudly.

"Is the door bent? Can you tell?" someone shouted.

"It looks okay to me," another answered. "But two of the bags are busted."

"No problem. I have plenty more. Hang on. I'll guide us back out so we can get this over with."

Bolan ran, his legs impeded by the water. After a few long strides he dived forward and swam smoothly, making for the cabin. The rain had slackened somewhat, enough for him to see more detail. Three men were over by the cargo door; none was looking in his direction.

The engines roared to life when Bolan was within a few strokes of the cabin door. He swam faster, but his hand missed its hold by inches as the Clipper jerked into motion and promptly began to turn, nose into the wind as before. The fuselage swung toward Bolan, so low to the water that he ran the risk of having his head smashed.

Taking a gamble he wouldn't be seen, Bolan tensed, then shot out of the water like a missile shooting from a sub's silo. His outflung left hand caught hold of a wing strut and he dangled, thudding against the fuselage, as the Clipper traveled back to about where it had been when the wave appeared. The pilot killed the engines.

Bolan let go and held his breath. He went under, but only a few feet. Surfacing, he moved close to the fuselage and worked his way toward the tail. The terrorists were trying to align the winch so the bathyscaphe would be centered over the cargo door, but the crane wasn't working properly.

"Damn this old crane all to hell! Garth, hand me up that hammer."

The sound of steel on steel rang against the background of cascading raindrops and tapering thunder. It was punctuated by a harsh cry.

"Stop that, you idiot! My equipment doesn't grow on trees. I know how to fix it."

"Then do so. We don't have all day to waste, Simmons!"

That had to be Jason Creed, Bolan reasoned, the one he wanted most of all. Without Creed, Green Rage would fall apart. The man was the twisted heart and perverted soul of Green Rage, the fount of evil genius whose personal war against humanity had to be brought to an end once and for all.

Coming to the huge door, Bolan slipped next to an inflatable and gripped it to steady himself against the bouncing motion of the waves. He couldn't see what was taking place above him, but he could hear clearly. Red Simmons was talking.

"I can't wait to be shy of you, mister. The trouble with you is that you have no respect for anyone but yourself."

Creed laughed. "Respect? Strange word for a smuggler to use."

"Trust a man like you to think so."

"Meaning what?"

"Nothing."

Bolan started to swim farther out from the fuselage so he could see into the cargo bay, but he stopped on hearing footsteps overhead. Craning his neck, he saw no one. Wary of being spotted, he gripped the door and began to pull himself up.

Abruptly a cry pierced the air. "Look out! The winch is giving! She's swinging wide!"

A huge shape materialized above Bolan. One glance showed him it was the submersible, swaying precariously at the end of the cable. He saw it lurch and drop a few inches toward him, and he realized the cable was on the verge of giving out. Should it, he'd be smashed flatter than a sheet of paper.

Bolan had to get out of there, but he couldn't go under the door because it would buckle if the sub landed on it and crush him. Nor could he swim out past the door because the terrorists were bound to spot him. The wisest move was to swim toward the fuselage and get under cover of the wing.

Like an Olympic swimmer going for the gold, Bolan shot toward the cabin. He cleared the bottom of the sub with feet to spare when there was a loud whirring and several shouts and the bathyscaphe smacked down into the bay, missing the door by a hair and throwing spray everywhere. The impact created a wash that caught the Executioner in its grasp and threw him against the Clipper.

The submersible bobbed and dipped but didn't flounder. Feet pounded on the ramp. Two men leapt onto the *Bio-Ark* and one dropped down a hatch too swiftly for Bolan to note his features. The other man, whom the warrior had never seen before, glanced down—and saw him.

Whoever he was, he wasn't the type to ask questions first and shoot later. In a practiced draw he whipped out a pistol, a Browning, and banged off two swift shots.

Bolan owed his life to the pitching of the bathyscaphe. It threw the terrorist's aim off, and the slugs struck the water next to him. Snapping off a shot of his own to pin the man down, he dived, coming up under the plane where there was barely enough room for him to raise his head out of the water. Confused shouts came from inside the aircraft and the deck of the submersible.

Swimming toward the nearest pontoon, Bolan watched the sub, thinking the gunner would likely climb down the outer ladder for a better shot. But no one appeared.

Then two shots boomed inside the plane.

The warrior paused, puzzled. The shots hadn't been meant for him. He heard people running, heard grating on the ramp and guessed that Creed and company were dashing to the bathyscaphe to take it out to sea. Evidently they had no intention of coming after him.

Reversing himself, Bolan swam toward the vessel. He was too late. The engine had already kicked over, and the sub was sailing slowly around the wing. He stroked out from under the Clipper and raised the Desert Eagle but had no one to shoot.

The rain was now a drizzle. Bolan shook water out of his eyes and headed for the ramp. There was still a chance he could stop Green Rage by ramming the sub with the plane. He located handholds and climbed, but as he did, the Clipper's propellers coughed, spit smoke and growled to life. The aircraft lunged into motion, nearly throwing the warrior from his perch. He had to jam the Desert Eagle under his belt and grab hold with both hands to keep from being pitched into the water.

The Clipper angled across the bay, swinging wildly from side to side as if the man at the controls didn't know what he was doing.

Bolan scrambled up onto the cargo-bay door, rose and leapt into the bay itself. A small door at the far end gave access to the cabin. He bounded toward it, then had to throw out his arms to maintain his balance when the plane swerved to the left. No sooner did it straighten out than it swerved to the right. The whole time it was gaining speed.

Staying close to the wall, Bolan made his way to the door. As his hand closed on the latch, the Clipper gave the sharpest pitch of all and he was flung a dozen feet. He had to brace himself against the side. Studying his legs, he tried again, throwing himself at the door and bursting through into the cabin. He drew the Desert Eagle and dropped into a combat crouch.

The sole occupant, a stocky man with red hair, was hunched over in the pilot's seat, desperately striving to work the control stick. A dark red stain marked the back of his shirt.

Bolan glanced through the windshield and saw the bathyscaphe. It dawned on him that the man was Red Simmons and that Simmons was trying to do the very thing he wanted to do—to ram the submersible. As he sprang forward, Simmons cried out and slipped from the chair. The control stick was wrenched, hard, and the amphibian swung at a ninety-degree angle to the left.

Staying upright was impossible. Bolan was hurled into the wall, jarring his shoulder. He bounced off and landed on his knees. Heaving up from the floor, he reached Simmons, who lay half across the control yoke and had wedged it in place.

Bolan attempted to lift the smuggler to get at the controls, but it was like trying to lift a wet two-hundred-pound sack of sand. Simmons groaned, his eyelids fluttered. Gripping the man under the shoulders, the warrior heaved and succeeded in pulling the smuggler partway off the stick. He straightened to get more leverage, then looked out the windshield.

The Clipper was racing straight toward the south shore, toward a ragged line of rocks.

Bolan threw all his weight into yanking Simmons clear. He did, but as he bent to take control he saw that the aircraft would run aground before he could do anything. Turning, he flattened at the very instant the Clipper hit.

With a tremendous grating din the plane plowed into the rocks. Torn metal screeched like a cat in torment, and Bolan was jolted every which way.

Suddenly all was still and quiet. The warrior rose and saw the cabin door ajar. He leaned out and discovered half of the fuselage had been sheared off as if it were made of matchsticks instead of nearly impervious monocoque stretched over steel bulkheads. In addition, one wing had been stripped off and lay half in the water.

A groan reminded Bolan of the smuggler. He knelt beside Simmons and frisked him for weapons. There was none. Undoing a button, he found two large bullet holes high in the man's chest. They were exit wounds. Simmons had been shot in the back.

The smuggler gasped and opened his eyes. He blinked a few times, then saw the warrior and tried to speak but coughed instead.

"I'd rest easy if I were you," Bolan cautioned. He saw no reason to add that the man didn't have much time left.

"Who—" Simmons croaked. "You're after them, aren't you?"

Bolan nodded.

"Did I get them? I tried to run them down."

"They got away."

Simmons broke into a racking cough. When it subsided, he spit, "Damn. Those back-shootin' bastards. I knew I couldn't trust them. Told Creed I wanted my money and his woman shot me from behind."

Bolan felt no sympathy for the smuggler. When a man swam with sharks, he had to expect to be bitten. He began to rise to see if the radio worked. Simmons grasped his wrist.

"Listen to me, son. I don't have much time. They're makin' that Fagan fella help them. Creed plans to sink a ship—"

"What ship?" Bolan asked, all interest now. He needed a clue to put him on the right trail or else all he had gone through would have been for nothing.

"Don't know the name." Simmons coughed longer and harder. "I was listenin' when they thought I wasn't." His voice was growing weaker with each word.

''Something about buyin' mines used for underwater demolition. That's all I know. Hope it helps.'' Simmons raised his head, his veins bulging from the effort. ''Get that bastard for me! Pay him—''

Red Simmons died with a plea for vengeance on his lips.

CHAPTER TWENTY-ONE

Hal Brognola's people did their best, but in this rare instance their best wasn't good enough. They had too little Intel to go on to be able to predict Jason Creed's next target. The port of Los Angeles had twenty-eight miles of sheltered harbor area. Passenger ships and freighters from all over the world stopped there.

So did military ships. The Long Beach Naval Shipyard was a bustling hub of U.S. naval power. Destroyers, battleships, submarines and aircraft carriers were all routinely serviced there. As a precaution, Brognola passed on word to the commander so extra security measures would be taken.

One possible target given serious attention was the *Queen Mary*, docked at Long Beach. Destroying so famous a ship was bound to garner worldwide attention. But no one could think of an environmental link that would qualify the luxury liner as a likely candidate.

Another angle was also pursued. The smuggler had mentioned mines for underwater use. Obtaining such devices was a lot harder than obtaining submachine guns or C-4 plastique. Few arms dealers, legitimate or otherwise, were expert enough to handle mines. Fewer still had sources that could supply them. Still, the Feds knew of a few. Brognola mentioned that he was sending agents to question them.

Mack Bolan offered to check one of the names on the list, determined to see the mission through to the end. Brognola gave him the name and last-known address of a man living on the waterfront.

It was shortly past six that evening when the warrior pulled up in front of a run-down brick dwelling that overlooked the Pacific. Fishing boats were sailing in from a hard day's work. Down the block, several rowdy fishermen were emerging from a bar.

Putting on a windbreaker, Bolan got out and locked the car. He didn't want the contents of his duffel falling into the wrong hands.

A rickety gate was all that barred him from a narrow walk that led to the house. He knocked twice and waited. Someone moved around inside, and he thought he heard a baby crying. The door opened a crack, permitting him a glimpse of a woman in a green shift.

"Yeah?"

"I'm looking for Jim Brewster."

"He ain't here. He's never here, unless he needs to sleep off a drunk."

"Do you know where I can find him?"

A bony finger slid out the crack and poked at the bar. "You might try the Surf and Suds. It's his home away from home."

The door slammed shut before Bolan could thank her. He caught her peeking out a blind at him as he closed the gate. Pulling up his collar against the chill breeze sweeping in off the glistening sea, he walked down the low hill toward the bar.

A black car suddenly wheeled to the curb in front of the bar. Out hopped two men, and on spotting them Bolan instantly dropped to one knee and pretended to be tying his shoe. He surreptitiously studied the pair, verifying they were who he thought they were.

One was tall and muscular and carried himself like a weight lifter. His hair had once been blond but now was black. It was Garth Hunter.

Bolan didn't know the second man, but he recognized him as the terrorist who had nearly blown his head off in the bay. The man laughed and clapped Hunter on the back as they strolled into the bar.

Bolan felt an unexpected sense of satisfaction. Unlike many of his missions, he was taking this one personally. He was going to see that Green Rage paid for its crimes—Creed, for all the innocents he had slaughtered, Hunter, for the unwarranted deaths of those two young women in Portland. He had the advantage now, and if he played his cards right, he'd have Jason Creed and the woman, too, before the night was through.

Returning to his car, Bolan drove to the corner and parked where he could watch the entrance to the bar in his mirror.

A few minutes later Hunter and his companion walked out with another man between them. From the description provided by Brognola, Bolan knew it was Jim Brewster, a former Navy mine man who had been drummed out of the service for dabbling on the black market while stationed overseas. Brewster resembled a bulldog in build and had a crew cut.

Hunter drove. The warrior let them travel a block before he started his car, backed into the intersection and followed. There was enough traffic to make shadowing them simple, but he had learned from experience not to take Garth Hunter lightly. The former Marine was a formidable adversary. When they finally clashed, Bolan intended to take the sadist down hard and fast.

The black car pulled onto Highway 1 and headed through Signal Hill, up past Torrance and Lawndale. El Segundo appeared up on the left and they slanted into the turn lane, but kept on going.

Bolan hung back, keeping cars between them. A passenger jet swooped down out of the sky, about to land at L.A. International Airport. Only when he saw the sedan's turn signal blink did he realize their destination.

But why the airport? the warrior wondered. It made more sense for Brewster to store his illegal ordnance somewhere far from prying eyes, not in the middle of one of the busiest airports in the world. But then, there was no explaining how the criminal mind worked. Logic seldom helped, since, as any FBI agent and beat cop could confirm, ninety percent of felons were so stupid or lax that they forgot to take the most simple of precautions when they committed crimes, such as wearing gloves.

The sedan turned onto a side road that followed the perimeter of the airport. There was less traffic, so Bolan dropped back farther than ever. Small hangars housing privately owned aircraft lined the road. One had the name of a big rock star painted on the side, and the star's personal jet was parked out front. Both had been painted bright pink.

Bolan watched as the sedan turned and pulled up in front of one of the smallest hangars. The three men walked to a padlocked door, which Brewster unlocked. Hunter was the last to enter, and he scanned the area first, as if he sensed he was being watched.

The warrior thought it prudent to drive past. Finding a spot to turn around took half a minute. Speeding back, Bolan drove to the hangar next door and braked beside it. He twisted to study the layout. Since the sun had yet to set, he would be a sitting duck when he crossed the open lot.

Biding his time was out of the question. If the mines were in there, Bolan had to prevent Green Rage from getting their hands on them. He slid out and quietly closed the car door. Circling toward the rear of the small hangar, he stuffed his hands in his pockets and tucked his chin to his chest in case Garth Hunter gazed outside. The killer had gotten a good look at him during the chase into Portland.

No shouts or shots rang out, and Bolan gained the cover of the back corner with ease. As he did, a loud grinding noise signaled the opening of the large hangar door. He flattened against the side and peeked out.

Brewster had one finger on the button that activated the door. He opened it only halfway, then walked to a tiny office along the far wall. Hunter and the other man were inside, waiting for him.

Bolan watched closely, and when none of the men was facing toward him, he ducked around the corner and sought shelter behind a row of metal drums. Nearby sat a single prop plane fitted with floats so it could land or take off on water. Crates of various sizes were stacked haphazardly here and there, and a sizable workbench littered with tools stood in one corner.

Peering between the drums, Bolan saw Brewster and Hunter talking. Brewster was relaxed and smiled a lot, especially when Hunter handed him an envelope thick with currency. Brewster riffled through the money, counting every dollar. Nodding in satisfaction, he motioned for the two terrorists to follow him.

A dolly leaned against the wall. Brewster wheeled it to a small, square crate, and the other men lifted an end so he could slide the dolly under.

Bolan guessed that the crate contained the mines. He drew the Beretta and inched to the left, seeking a clear shot. He was almost to the last drum when he heard brakes squeak out front. A delivery truck had just pulled up. Printed on the side were the words Bud's Aviation Supply, and an L.A. address. A chubby man in a starched brown uniform was at the wheel. For Bolan to try to hide would be a waste of time. The driver was looking right at him.

The truck's window was down. The man stabbed a finger at him and shouted an alarm. "Hey, Mr. Brewster! There's a guy behind those drums! He's holding a gun!"

Bolan shifted and trained the Beretta on the trio, but the damage had been done. All three had whirled. Hunter and the other terrorist had produced pistols, and they immediately cut loose. As the warrior flattened, he saw Brewster reach under his jacket, withdraw a mini-Uzi and fire a sustained burst.

A leaden firestorm swept toward the warrior. Slugs punched into the barrels or screamed off into space. Bolan scrambled on his belly toward the hangar door as bullets showered above him and bits of metal flew through the air.

The delivery-truck driver panicked. Madly spinning the steering wheel, he floored the gas and sped off.

Bolan snapped off a shot but missed. Brewster had stepped behind the tail of the plane and was firing short, steady bursts to keep him pinned down, buying time for Hunter and the other terrorist, who were rushing the dolly toward the small door. Taking aim at Hunter, Bolan was picking up the slack on the trigger when another burst from Brewster drove him to the floor.

The Executioner had to do something immediately or the terrorists were going to elude him yet again. He banged a shot at Brewster that clipped the edge of the tail as the man ducked back. Another burst from the mini-Uzi struck the barrels, then the weapon fell silent as the clip ran dry.

It would take Brewster two or three seconds to extract the spent magazine and ram home a new one.

Gathering himself, Bolan sprang into the open and rolled on his shoulder into a crouch. The upper half of Brewster's body was concealed by the vertical fin, but the lower half, from about the middle of his thighs down, was visible. The warrior sighted on the right knee and squeezed the trigger twice.

Brewster cried out as his leg buckled under him and he fell onto his wounded knee. Cursing in stark fury, he brought the Uzi to bear on his adversary.

Bolan stitched three bullet holes from the right side of Brewster's chest to the left. The man went down, but to the warrior's surprise he rose on an elbow and hammered off several rounds, which missed, but not by much. Bolan sprinted to the airplane, grabbed hold of a strut and swung up onto the wing. Moving to the cabin, he crouched and drew the Desert Eagle.

By this time Hunter and his friend had made it out the door with the crate.

The warrior hoped they would rush back in to try to finish him off so he could return the favor, but the growl of a car starter told him they had what they wanted. They weren't about to needlessly put their lives on the line.

A faint shuffling sound alerted Bolan to Brewster's latest tactic. The arms dealer was sneaking around to the off wing to flank him. He sought sign of a shadow or any other clue to the man's exact position but saw nothing.

It annoyed Bolan to realize that every moment of delay cost him dearly. By this time the terrorists were through the gate and heading for wherever the *Bio-Ark* was stashed.

Being careful not to scrape his clothing or feet, Bolan edged toward the opposite end of the wing. He passed over the cabin and saw the spot where Brewster had fallen. There should have been blood, at the very least a few drops, yet there wasn't.

Bolan figured the man was hiding under the wing, and he slid toward the edge to prove his hunch. Then Brewster jumped from cover and hobbled for the office door. Bolan got off a shot with the Desert Eagle before the arms dealer dived through the doorway, but the man didn't go down.

It seemed odd to Bolan that the arms dealer had made for the office instead of fleeing from the hangar. Brewster had to realize that the delivery driver would notify the police or airport security. In a few minutes the hangar would be crawling with officers. Anyone else in Brewster's position would be heading for parts unknown.

From Bolan's roost, he could see part of the office through a glass partition. A metal cabinet opened and a hand reached in. There was loud clattering, as if things were being tossed about. Bolan sighted on the cabinet, hoping Brewster would get careless, and he was still focused on the cabinet when a small object came sailing out of the office door and landed on the floor near the aircraft.

The warrior caught only a glimpse, but a glimpse was enough. Pushing to his feet, he whirled and ran the length of the wing. He took a flying leap and came down just short of the metal drums. As he landed, he coiled and jumped again, clearing the drums in a headlong dive. He hit the floor on his side, scraping his arm.

It was then that the hand grenade detonated.

The blast was deafening in the confines of the hangar. Fortunately for Bolan, the brunt of the explosion was borne by the plane, which hopped into the air, then crumpled, the far wing and most of the cabin ripped asunder. Simultaneously some of the drums were hurled against the warrior.

Bolan had raised his arms over his head to protect himself. One of the drums gouged him fiercely in the shoulder, but otherwise he was unhurt. He glanced up, and through a swirling haze of smoke and dust saw Brewster dart from the shattered office toward the hangar entrance. The man had swapped the Uzi for an M-2 carbine.

The Desert Eagle and the Beretta boomed in drumming cadence.

Brewster returned fire on the fly, shooting from the hip. He ran past the nose of the aircraft.

Compensating, Bolan aimed higher. He realized the man wore body armor, a Kevlar vest, perhaps. So he went for the head, three shots coring into the arms dealer's brain. In sheer reflex Brewster continued to squeeze off shots as he fell, the bullets whining off the concrete.

Bolan was speeding for the small door before the arms dealer smacked onto the floor. He squinted in the bright sunlight, seeking the black sedan, but it was long gone. The familiar refrain of sirens let him know the numbers had run down. People had appeared outside adjacent hangars and were staring at the smoke pouring from Brewster's.

Shoving his pistols in their holsters, Bolan jogged to his car. In order not to draw any more attention to himself than he already had, he held to the speed limit until the gate was a quarter mile behind him. From there on he pushed it, eventually blending into L.A.'s congested traffic.

A helicopter flew over the highway. Bolan tensed, thinking it might be a police helicopter searching for him. But it was a traffic chopper, bearing the call letters of a radio station on its side.

South of Culver City Bolan pulled into the huge lot of a shopping mall. He put in a call to Brognola and was informed that the big Fed had left for L.A. hours earlier to set up a temporary command center at the Federal Building. In another hour Bolan should be able to reach him there.

Another hour.

Bolan hoped they had that long before the terrorists struck again.

JASON CREED COULD HARDLY wait for the day to end. Each passing hour brought him that much closer to achieving a victory so sweet that he would savor it for the rest of his life.

By now it had become apparent to Creed that Envio Squad Two had failed. He'd bought a newspaper as soon as he reached Los Angeles and listened to hourly newscasts, but there had been no mention of his cleverly orchestrated disaster. And since there hadn't been any word from Packard, who had been all too eager to receive the rest of the promised payment, Creed had to assume the worst. Somehow the authorities had tumbled to the scheme and either eliminated Envio Squad Two or taken the members into custody.

Which made two failures in a row. First the presidential fiasco, now the New Jersey debacle. Creed needed to come out on top this time, or his credibility with his few remaining followers would be in jeopardy.

Not only that, Creed needed to have things work out for his own sake, as well. He was troubled by rare gnawing doubt. Despite his meticulous plotting, events weren't unfolding as he'd hoped. Was the fault his? Had he lost his touch?

No, Creed assured himself. In the attack on the President, no one was to blame. A lucky Fed had stumbled on the site and spoiled everything. As for New Jersey, until he knew the facts, he couldn't hazard a guess, even though he was inclined to blame Packard, who had never impressed him as being quite diligent enough.

In any event, this time would be different because Creed was handling every step of the operation personally. From start to finish, the L.A. affair had been his baby and his alone. If things went sour, he had to shoulder the blame.

But it wouldn't! Creed smacked his right fist against his left palm and inwardly vowed that come what may, he would carry his scheme through. Everyone would be made to see the nature of the nuclear evil that threatened to pollute the globe for ages to come unless humankind stopped its wicked ways.

Creed lowered his arms and looked about to see if anyone had noticed. It was dark, and few people were roaming the docks. Not far off was the busy Long Beach Marina, where many expensive yachts and sleek sailing craft were moored. In the other direction lay Long Beach, and the Long Beach Naval Shipyard.

After checking his watch, Creed scanned the street leading to the turnoff to the docks. He was finding it hard to control his impatience. So much rested on everything going smoothly. One little hitch would doom his master plan.

A horn honked. The black car Hunter had hot-wired on their arrival was coming down the turnoff. Creed folded his arms and waited for it, composing his features so his companions wouldn't know how upset he had been. A good leader, he mused, never let his followers see the chinks in his armor.

He was Jason Creed, the greatest eco-terrorist who had ever lived, the driving force behind Green Rage, a name that made corporate and government bigwigs tremble when they heard it. And he had to act the part.

Hunter and Dean strolled toward him, their cocky smiles verifying their success. "Got them," Hunter said.

"You're late," Creed growled. It wasn't enough for those who had enlisted in his cause to follow him blindly; they had to be punctual, as well.

Hunter's smile vanished. "We ran into a little problem." He went on to explain about the run-in at the hangar. "I only got a glimpse of the guy, but I'd swear it was the same one who nearly nailed me up in Portland."

"I've seen him before, too," Dean added. "He was the bozo who showed up at the bay."

The implications were disturbing. Creed studied the street and asked, "Are you positive no one followed you?"

"Why do you think we're so late?" Hunter retorted. "We've spent the last thirty minutes driving in circles to see if we had a tail. We didn't."

"Then let's go in. It's time you learned the next phase of the operation," Creed said. He had deliberately kept them in the dark, revealing only as much as they needed to know at any given point. It had been a natural precaution to take, in the event either or both of them had fallen into the clutches of the law.

Julie Constantine and Axel Fagan were inside the large boathouse at the end of the dock, both seated in folding chairs. She was reading a magazine. The director sat slumped over, his hands tied to the chair arms, his ankles to the legs.

"Join them," Creed told Hunter and Dean.

When he had their undivided attention, he cleared his throat and declared, "The time has come to fill you in. Tomorrow morning at ten a.m. we embark on an act of sabotage the likes of which no eco-warrior has ever attempted before."

Dean didn't act impressed. "No offense, Jason, but we've heard this line of yours before. Garth might buy into it, but I don't. You know there's only one reason I'm here, and that's for the money."

Creed held his temper by reminding himself that after tomorrow he would no longer need Dean's services. "You'll get what you have coming to you, never fear. Now pipe down and don't interrupt." Stepping to the window, he stared toward the shipyard.

"At the Long Beach Naval Shipyard, right this minute, is the USS *Liberty,* the newest of the Nimitz-class nuclear-powered aircraft carriers. She's the biggest and best the Navy has to offer, with two Westinghouse A4W nuclear reactors in her engine department."

Fagan glanced up, his haggard face seeming to shrivel. "Oh, my God!" he breathed.

Hunter looked around. "What's eating him?"

"For all his shortcomings, Axel is most perceptive at times," Creed said. "You see, the USS *Liberty* has spent the last six months being outfitted for her next tour. Tomorrow morning she will fire up her reactors and set out to sea."

"So?"

"So I've long wanted a dramatic means of showing the American public how dangerous nuclear reactors are." Creed turned, his eyes aglow with inner flames. "And can you think of a better way than breaching the carrier's reactors? In one fell swoop, we'll pollute San Pedro Bay for generations to come and force mass evacuations of those living within a ten-mile radius or so of the harbor."

Hunter nodded. "So that's why you wanted the sub and the mines so badly."

"The Navy will never expect an attack right outside their own shipyard. Thanks to the *Bio-Ark*, we can slip in, plant the mines and slip out again without them being the wiser. Then all we have to do is sit back and watch the fireworks!"

Creed laughed, a long, wavering cackle that made several gulls perched on the boathouse take wing with raucous cries.

CHAPTER TWENTY-TWO

The process of elimination could work wonders at times. Hal Brognola knew that Green Rage needed a waterfront facility to house the bathyscaphe. From his temporary base of operations at the Federal Building, he brought the full resources of the government to bear on pinpointing the location.

Marinas and docks from Santa Monica Bay to the Gulf of Santa Catalina were scoured. Photographs of the suspects were shown. Fingerprints lifted from a doorknob at the small hangar at L.A. International revealed the identity of the second man Bolan had seen— one George Dean.

Brognola had people contact marine-equipment suppliers, scuba shops and, on the off chance the terrorists might need to buy ammo, sporting-goods outlets.

For more than an hour Mack Bolan was left to his own devices. He changed into fresh clothes, shaved and had a quick bite. On his way back to the Federal Building he stopped and picked up a copy of the *Los Angeles Times*.

The big Fed was glued to the telephone, so Bolan made himself comfortable on a small couch and spread out the paper. He skimmed the contents, killing time until a new lead developed. Almost by accident he noticed a short article in the Local section.

The heading was more typical of the rags found at supermarket checkout lines than the prestigious *Times*: Sea Serpent Spotted off Long Beach. The story went on to relate how two early-morning joggers and a woman out walking her poodle had seen a long, dark hump cleaving the surface of Alamitos Bay. All three were adamant that it hadn't been a whale or some other aquatic creature. The lady with the dog thought it had a serpentlike neck, but she couldn't be sure because of lingering tendrils of fog.

Bolan folded the page and walked over to Brognola's desk. He set the paper down so his friend could read it, then stepped to the window and admired the sparkling skyline. The phone slapped its cradle.

Brognola glanced at the article, his brow knit, then at the warrior. Suddenly his eyes widened. "Well, I'll be damned. It could have been the submersible. And this story was right in front of our noses the whole time." His hand closed on the receiver and he punched in numbers. "Long Beach is where the shipyard is located."

Agents were advised to concentrate their activities in the vicinity of Long Beach. Hardly had the big Fed hung up than another phone buzzed. He motioned for Bolan as he listened to the caller and scribbled notes on a pad. When he hung up, he tore off the top sheet and handed it over.

"Bingo. I hope. The owner of a scuba store at Huntington Harbor claims that a man answering Dean's description arranged earlier today to pick up some gear shortly before closing time, which is in forty-five minutes." Brognola tapped the paper. "There's the address. Your call, Mack. I can have some agents handle this if you're tired of the cat and mouse."

"Need you ask?"

Bolan hastened to the elevator and out to his car. L.A. traffic being what it was, he needed all the time he had and then some to reach the shop in time. He knew the report might not pan out, that the owner might be mistaken. But his instincts told him to go with this one, so he did.

Why scuba gear, Bolan asked himself, when Green Rage had a submersible at their disposal? He remembered being told the bathyscaphe had mechanical arms that could be used to set and arm the mines. It would pay, though, for Creed to have scuba suits on hand in case something went wrong with the robot arms. And Creed did like to cover every contingency.

Rafe's Scuba World was situated along the waterfront, overlooking the beach. Twelve minutes remained until closing when Bolan drove down the street in front of the store and discovered he was almost too late.

George Dean, helped by another man, was loading tanks, masks and flippers into the trunk of the black car.

Bolan drove past, then parked. He saw Dean slam the trunk and pull out a wallet. The pair went into the store. Quickly sliding out, the warrior sprinted across the street. He paused next to the back door of the terrorist's vehicle, which was parked in shadows near a corner of the building.

As the Executioner saw it, he could try to take Dean alive and persuade him to talk, or he could take a chance and go for the gold. Pressing the handle, he crawled in, sank onto the floor and pulled the door shut.

Bolan felt confident the shadows would hide him, but he couldn't take it for granted. Drawing the Desert Eagle, he twisted so he could watch the driver's door without being seen.

It wasn't long before Dean appeared, whistling a pop tune to himself. The killer climbed inside and started the engine.

The short hairs at Bolan's nape pricked. He was certain Dean would sense his presence, turn and spot him, but the man drove off humming, as if he didn't have a care in the world.

At long last the end was in sight. Dean would take Bolan to Creed and the rest of Green Rage, and Bolan would put a permanent end to their murder spree. He listened as Dean sang to himself, the same words over and over.

" 'I'm in the money, I'm in the money....' "

Payoff time, Bolan mused, in more ways than one. Wind fanned his head when Dean rolled down the window. The glare of streetlights played over him. Never knowing if the terrorist would turn and spot him, he kept a finger curled around the trigger of his pistol.

Since the scuba store was so close to Long Beach, and everything pointed to Long Beach as being where Creed had gone to ground, Bolan counted on a short ride. But not two blocks. He tensed when Dean unexpectedly pulled up close to neon lights that lit up the inside of the car as brightly as day.

Whistling softly, the terrorist climbed out.

Bolan listened to footsteps, then heard a tiny bell tinkle. Rising on an elbow, he saw the terrorist entering a liquor store, which spoiled the warrior's plan. Dean was bound to see him on the way back. He had to get out of there.

Opening the door on the street side, the Executioner exited the vehicle. He was going to jump Dean as the man left the store, but he spied a cab parked catty-corner to the store. Holstering the Desert Eagle, he hurried over. The off-duty sign was lit, and the cabbie was munching on a hot dog while listening to the radio. Without ceremony, Bolan opened the rear door and slid in.

The startled driver glanced around. "Hey, what's the matter, pal? You can't read? I'm not in service."

Reaching into his pants pocket, Bolan pulled out a wad of bills and peeled off a fifty. "Maybe you'd like to change your mind."

The cabbie grinned. "Supper can always wait." Snatching the bill, he turned the engine over and said, "Where to, friend?"

Bolan pointed at the black sedan. "Follow that car when it takes off."

"Really?" The driver laughed. "Do you know something? In twelve years of cab work, this is the first time anyone has ever wanted me to do that."

"There's another fifty in it for you if you can do it without being spotted."

"Consider us invisible."

A minute later George Dean came out, a brown sack in hand. Once behind the wheel, he uncapped the bottle and tilted it to his lips. Then he slowly drove off.

"Doesn't that guy know it's not safe to drink and drive?" the cabbie mentioned. He let the sedan get a block head start before initiating pursuit.

The third time, as the old saying went, always worked like a charm, but Bolan had learned from hard experience never to take anything for granted.

A good soldier was one who knew how to adapt in the field, how to adjust to circumstances as they arose. Not taking advantage of a situation when it presented itself often meant the difference between success and failure. And Bolan had always been first and foremost a good soldier. He was acting as events dictated, but there was no guarantee it would be enough. If he lost Dean, that might be the ball game.

But the cabbie knew his stuff. He stayed two or three blocks back, and when the black car stopped for a red light, he contrived to veer to the curb until the light changed. They passed the U.S. Naval Weapons Station, then the Long Beach Marina.

The black car slowed and turned left onto a turnoff that took it toward the beach.

Bolan had the cabbie stop. He watched as Dean parked in a lot adjacent to some docks. "This will do," he said, and offered the second fifty. The taxi drove on, leaving him in gloom. Rather than use the sidewalk, he made straight for the lot, gliding past a closed seafood restaurant. Behind the building, a flight of steps led down to the sea. He descended two at a stride until he was in a circle of deep darkness at the bottom.

Dean had yet to get out of the car.

Moving to a line of shrubbery, the warrior crouched and bided his time. Several of the docks had enclosed boathouses, any one of which was big enough to house the stolen bathyscaphe. Lights were on in two of them.

Time dragged, but Dean failed to appear. Bolan wondered if the man could have gotten out without his noticing, and didn't see how it was possible. He'd only taken his eyes off the vehicle a few times while coming down the concrete steps.

Two other cars were parked near the sedan. Bolan made for the nearer one, doubled at the waist. From there he should be able to see the driver's side clearly and establish whether Dean was inside. He placed a hand on the Desert Eagle but didn't draw it. A passerby might come along and spot him, and the next thing he knew, cops would show up with their lights flashing and spook the terrorists into fleeing in the sub.

Bolan came to the front fender and squatted. Rising carefully until his eyes were above the hood, he studied the black sedan. George Dean was nowhere to be seen. Worse, the passenger-side door hung open.

The warrior was so focused on the vehicle that he almost missed the hint of movement to his right. Pivoting, he made a grab for the Desert Eagle but had to throw himself to the right before clearing leather to avoid the slashing Ka-bar that came within a hair of slicing his throat wide open.

Originally made for the Marine Corps during World War II, the Ka-bar model Dean held was an exact replica. The seven-inch gun blue blade had a deep blood groove and was razor sharp. Dean knew how to use it, too, as he demonstrated by closing in with the knife streaking in strokes as precise as those of a surgeon, going for the warrior's vitals.

Bolan twisted, ducked, shifted. Once the knife nicked his forearm, another time it ripped his jacket but spared his flesh. He was so hard-pressed that he had no chance to draw a pistol, which was exactly what the ecoterrorist wanted.

Dean's reason for resorting to the blade instead of a gun wasn't hard to fathom—gunfire would draw the police. And he was good with a knife, one of the best Bolan had ever faced. He skipped aside when Bolan flicked a kick or blow, promptly darting in, the steel blade constantly in motion.

Bolan backpedaled, drawing Dean after him toward the shadows. He pretended to trip and dropped into a crouch. Predictably Dean speared the knife at his shoulder. The warrior jerked to the left, seized his adversary's wrist in both hands, tucked the man's arm to his shoulder and heaved.

Dean did an ungainly somersault and tried to land upright, but he came down at the wrong angle. He landed on his left side instead, rolled and went to push off the asphalt.

Bolan reached him in three swift strides. He let loose a kick that caught Dean flush in the chest. Ribs cracked, and the terrorist was knocked onto his back. Snarling like a feral cat, Dean swung the Ka-bar at Bolan's legs. The warrior leapt straight up and the blade passed under his feet. He dropped, right on top of Dean's extended arm.

The terrorist's elbow snapped, and he cried out, more in rage than pain, then aimed a kick at Bolan's groin.

The Executioner blocked the blow, took a half step and slammed his knee into his adversary's face as the man tried to sit up. Dean's nose crunched, and blood spurted. Bolan bent, snatched the knife from the terrorist's limp fingers, reversed direction and lanced the seven-inch blade into the base of the man's throat.

Dean fell back, sputtering noisily, his good hand grasping at the polished leather handle that was so slippery he couldn't get a grip. He started to convulse, his teeth chattering as if he were cold, his eyes rolling in their sockets. Suddenly the dark eyes steadied on the warrior and for an instant radiated sheer hatred. Then he died.

Grabbing Dean by the ankles, Bolan dragged him to the black sedan and pushed the corpse into the front seat. He closed the door and moved around to the far side. Sooner or later one of the other terrorists would come out to see what was taking Dean so long. If he waited, he should be able to take down a second one with a minimum of fuss.

THE ECO-TERRORISTS WERE already aware of the Executioner's presence.

Garth Hunter had gone to the door of the boathouse several times during his friend's absence. He was eager to check the scuba gear, as Creed wanted, and to instruct Constantine in how to use it. She had no scuba experience at all.

Secretly Hunter liked Constantine, a lot. She was so damn beautiful, it took his breath away to look at her. Yet she was also as tough as any man who ever lived, and as cold-blooded a killer as he flattered himself that he was. Which made her a unique combination in his book, a woman he'd like for his own. It was too bad she had hooked up with Creed, because Hunter was sure they would make a dynamite couple.

This night, Hunter stole glances at her shapely long legs as she sat reading in the folding chair. He had to pass her to reach the door, which was another reason he looked out so often. About fifteen minutes had gone by since the last time when he rose from in front of the portable TV. Creed had insisted on having one so they could keep track of news reports in case stories were aired about Green Rage.

As Hunter went by Constantine, she idly glanced up and smiled, showing her white teeth and the pink tip of her tongue. He imagined what it would be like to have that tongue dancing with his, and sighed.

Hunter stiffened on seeing the black sedan. There was no sign of Dean, and he blurted, "Where the hell is George?"

Creed promptly walked over. "I don't like this. What could have happened to him?"

Both of them saw the commotion at the same moment. Two men were engaged in hand-to-hand combat on the far side of the parked cars. One was Dean. Hunter put his hand on the knob, anxious to go help, but Creed stopped him.

"Don't be a fool! Stay put. The place must be crawling with Feds."

Hunter didn't care. George Dean was one of the few friends he had, and if they went down together, that would be fitting. He started to open the door but froze when the cold tip of a pistol muzzle pressed against his neck.

"I wasn't asking you to stay," Creed said sternly. "I was ordering you." He pushed Hunter back a few steps and lowered the Astra Model A-90, a 9 mm pistol that boasted a 15-round magazine, but fixed the barrel on Hunter's midsection. "I won't stand for being thwarted this close to success."

Over Creed's shoulder, Hunter saw Dean and the other man swing and parry. It was too dark to be certain, but the big guy Dean fought looked a lot like the Fed who had chased him in Portland and inexplicably shown up at the bay. Who was that guy? Hunter wondered. The next moment they disappeared from view. Seconds later, only the big man straightened.

Creed had stepped to the right of the door so he couldn't be seen from outside. He glanced at Constantine, who had risen and drawn her own pistol. "There has been a change of plans, my dear. Get our friend Axel onto the bathyscaphe. We're going to fire it up and head out to sea. The Feds can't touch us if we sit off the coast until dawn."

"What about George?" Hunter tried one more time. Inwardly he seethed at being thwarted, but he wasn't mad enough to do anything stupid. He knew Creed well enough to know the man wasn't given to empty threats. One move toward that door, and Creed would gun him down.

"The incompetent fool is history," Creed declared, and smirked. "But seeing as how the two of you were so close, I'll give you a chance to avenge him." He nodded at the closet that held the weapons he had stashed there before leaving for Hawaii. "I want you to hold off the Feds as long as you can. When you judge the time is right, slip out the ocean end and swim underwater to one of the other docks. With a little luck, you can give the fascists the slip. We'll meet up again in Anchorage in one week."

Hunter was no dummy. He realized Creed was sacrificing him for the greater good of the holy eco-war, which was fine by him. He didn't think much of the idea of pitting their fancy sardine can against the biggest aircraft carrier in the U.S. fleet. It was certain suicide, in his book. "In one week," he said.

Constantine had cut the director loose and shoved him over to the submersible. They climbed onto the upper hull. Pausing to wait for Creed, she smiled at Hunter. "Wish us luck," she said.

"Luck," Hunter answered, when he really wanted to say, "You'll need it, gorgeous."

Creed went up the rungs quickly and gave a little wave. One by one they vanished into the belly of the submersible, then the hatch slammed shut. It wasn't long before there was a muted hum and the water was churned by the whirling prop. Ever so slowly, the bathyscaphe sank until only the control chamber remained above the water.

Hunter could see Fagan working the controls. Creed was studying a map. Lovely Julie Constantine sat behind the director, her pistol inches from his ear.

Then the entire vessel submerged and it sailed out of the boathouse, passing under the double doors on the seaward side. The only sign of its passing was bubbles left in its wake.

Hunter went to the closet. Creed had collected quite a variety of weapons from all sorts of underground sources. He had his pick of several subguns, assault rifles, pistols and miscellaneous weapons.

A MAC-10 caught Hunter's eye. He checked the magazine, slipped on the shoulder sling and removed a nearly new NVEC night-vision device from a small box. Shaped like binoculars, the device had a head strap and a neck lanyard and fitted snugly, leaving his hands free for the job he had to do. Finally Hunter palmed a Spye Knife shooting knife and slipped it into a pocket.

Stepping to the front of the building, he turned out the light and waited for his eyes to adjust to the gloom. He smiled in anticipation as he bent and cracked the door open so he could scan the parking area. No Feds were to be found, leading him to suspect he was up against one guy, the tough bastard who had caused them so much grief.

Perfect, Hunter mused. *Mano a mano* was just the way he liked it. He'd chop the meddler off at the knees and then treat himself by carving the scumbag into bits and pieces. Smiling at the thought, Garth Hunter slipped out into the night.

CHAPTER TWENTY-THREE

Mack Bolan saw the light go out in the boathouse and dropped to his stomach behind the black sedan. For several minutes shadows had been flitting about inside and he didn't know what to make of all the activity.

The light blinking off so abruptly spelled trouble. Bolan doubted the terrorists were turning in early, especially when they were waiting for Dean to deliver the scuba gear. He had a feeling that they knew he was out there, and if that was the case, he needed to prepare.

Moving behind the front tire, Bolan drew the Beretta and fitted it with a suppressor. Edging to the bumper, he peered around it and saw the boathouse door swing outward. A figure shot across the lot, making for a low wall across the way.

Bolan raised the Beretta, tracked the terrorist and squeezed off two rounds. But even as the 9 mm pistol chugged, the figure dived, half turned and brought a subgun into play. Slugs tore into the sedan, striking the hood and the windshield, which splintered and cracked.

A low burp revealed Bolan wasn't the only one to rely on a suppressor. Ducking, he darted to the next car and slid behind it. When he looked out, the figure was gone, having gained the cover of the wall. He moved to the third car, crawled to the rear tire and surveyed the wall from one end to the other.

The sounds of the metropolis seemed uncommonly loud. Mixed with the whisper of the surf was the snarl of traffic, the blare of distant horns and occasionally the whine of jets coming in for a landing at the airport.

Bolan listened for other noises, for the telltale rustle of clothes or the pad of feet. While he hadn't had a good look at the gunner, he suspected it was Garth Hunter, the former Marine, the psychopath who reveled in bloodshed and whose skills made him the deadliest of the eco-terrorists.

Hunter cut loose again. Rounds zinged off the ground close to the warrior. Bolan retreated to the rear of the car, puzzled as to how the terrorist had located him. A dark veil shrouded the three cars. For that matter, most of the parking lot lay in inky gloom. Had Hunter been guessing, he mused, or was there cause for concern?

Seconds later the killer opened fire again. This time the slugs slammed into the car above Bolan's head. He flipped to the left, snapped off two shots at a melon-shaped object that had appeared above the wall and sprinted back over to the black sedan.

There could be no doubt. Hunter had a night-vision scope or goggles. Bolan wasn't only outgunned, he was virtually fighting blind while the gunner could see his every move. To stay in the middle of the open parking lot invited death. It would be only a matter of time before Hunter picked him off.

The warrior turned toward the docks, where there were plenty of places to hide. All he had to do was reach them alive. He also studied the boathouse harboring the terrorists. Creed and Constantine were probably covering the parking area from the door or a window, he guessed, and would open fire the moment he appeared.

Unwilling to stay there and be a literal sitting duck, Bolan bunched his leg muscles and hurtled forward like a greyhound shooting from the starting gate. Weaving wildly to throw off their aim, he covered a dozen yards before the subgun chattered with a sound that resembled a muffled typewriter.

Garth Hunter rushed his shots and they fell shy, pockmarking the ground at Bolan's heels. The warrior veered right, saw the rounds do the same and angled left. To his surprise, no one in the boathouse opened up. He reached the next dock and ducked behind a piling.

The SMG went silent.

Bolan was safe, but only for a short while. Hunter would change position, pin him down and finish him off unless he came up with a strategy to neutralize the edge given Hunter by the night-vision device. He scanned the pier, noting several boats tied up for the night and another, smaller boathouse out over the ocean. He put a hand on the piling to rise and felt a rope under his palm.

Probing, Bolan confirmed the rope was looped around the piling and dangled from the dock. An unused mooring line, he reasoned, which he could put to excellent use. Slipping the Beretta under his belt, he grasped the rope and eased over the edge. The piling was as smooth as glass from being pounded relentlessly by the surf each time the tide rose. He went down hand over hand, seeking purchase for his feet, and brushed against a number of large nails that had been driven partway into the piling. They were almost too thin to stand on, but by bracing his knees against the piling he was able to bear the brunt of his weight with his thighs so the nails wouldn't bend under him.

Clasping the rope with his left hand, the warrior drew the Beretta. He was on the sea side of the piling, invisible from the parking lot. All he had to do was hold on tight and wait—and hope Hunter hadn't seen him climb down.

A salty, muggy breeze blew in off the Pacific. Somewhere a gull mewed. The tide was rising and would soon soak his feet.

How many minutes went by, Bolan couldn't say, but suddenly he sensed that he was no longer alone. Someone moved above him, but so quietly as to seem like a spectral wraith rather than flesh and blood. It was Hunter, hunting him. One of the planks creaked softly, giving him some idea of where the sadistic killer stood.

Bolan's head was below the dock. He straightened slowly, holding the rope tight so he wouldn't topple backward into the water. A shadow loomed between the piling on his side and the piling on the other.

Hunter had stopped, exactly as Bolan would have done, to scour the night. The warrior could tell he wore goggles, could tell that the man was scanning possible hiding places farther off when he should have been looking down at his very feet. Bringing up the Beretta slowly so the movement wouldn't give him away, the warrior sighted on the terrorist's chest.

At that exact second, acting as if he had sensed Bolan was there, Hunter spun and triggered a short burst that tore into the planks and would have cored Bolan's brain had the warrior not gotten off a shot of his own that staggered Hunter back into the other piling.

Righting himself, the terrorist raced southward toward the next pier.

A clear silhouette was Bolan's target. He aimed, but as he did, Hunter dropped from sight as if swallowed by a hole in the earth. Bolan wasn't fooled. The man had flattened, as he would have done, and would now jockey for position.

The Executioner was sure he had scored a hit but knew it wouldn't stop the former leatherneck. Marines were trained to absorb punishment that would drop lesser men in their tracks. And even though Hunter had been dishonorably discharged, enough of that training had been ingrained to render him next to unstoppable. Shots to the brain and the heart were Bolan's best bets.

First the warrior had to get somewhere else, fast. Hunter had his position pegged. He started to scale the rope, but as his head rose above the planks, Hunter cut loose with the subgun. Slivers rained down as the heavy-caliber deathstorm thudded into the piling, blasting the wood to bits—and the rope.

Bolan felt the rope start to give and tried to grab hold of the edge of the pier, but gravity took over and down he went. He managed to hold his body straight as he fell and braced himself, not knowing how deep it would be.

With a loud splash, the warrior hit. The cold water encased him like a glove, rising to just below his chest.

The sand underfoot was spongy and clung to his shoes as he turned toward shore.

Footsteps drummed on the pier. Bolan knew that Hunter had heard the splash, and he pumped his legs harder. The water impeded him, slowing him. A scraping sounded overhead and he looked up to see the figure of the killer poised above a wide crack. As he looked, the subgun, a MAC-10 apparently, spit lead. The water around him erupted in a patchwork of miniature geysers.

Bolan took a hasty bead and snapped off two shots of his own. Hunter stopped firing, and the warrior reached the strip of beach under the dock. He bore to the right and stopped in the shelter of a piling.

Cocking his head, he tried to detect his enemy. Hunter was either standing still or no longer on the pier. He studied the underside of the planks for as far as he could see, without result.

Bolan took a few steps, then froze. He was making too much noise. His shoes squished with every stride, and water dripped from his jacket. Sitting, he hastily stripped off the footwear and the windbreaker and left them behind as he rose and continued to the last piling.

A short slope led up to the dock, and Bolan crawled slowly forward. At the top he looked both ways. Hunter had blended into the night again and was no doubt waiting for him to show himself.

The warrior roved his left hand over the ground, seeking a stone or other small object. A piece of driftwood was all he found, but it would have to do. He threw it high, toward the shrubbery behind the restaurant. It fell short and made a sound like a rattle being shaken.

Hunter was too smart for him. No gunfire greeted the noise. Bolan eased onto the pier and lay flat not far from a bobbing boat. The lap of gentle waves was all he heard. He held himself still, senses probing the darkness but finding nothing. They were evenly matched, Hunter and him, two seasoned fighters who had learned the hard way that a single mistake could prove fatal.

Bolan registered movement off to the right. He lowered his head to the planks to better blend into the background. With his ear pressed flat on the musty wood, he felt rather than heard faint vibrations. Someone was moving along the dock to his left.

Slowly rotating his head, the Executioner saw an indistinct shape creep from behind a piling twenty feet distant. It was Hunter, staring toward the boathouse he had emerged from. Then the killer turned, and Bolan knew he had been spotted. The MAC-10 opened up. So did the warrior, stroking four swift shots, aiming high, going for the head.

Bullets smacked into the wood so close to Bolan's face that they nearly broke the skin. He fired twice more.

Hunter tottered. The muzzle of the subgun dipped, firing round after round into the pier. He reached the edge of the dock and let go of the trigger to clutch at the piling, his arms sluggish, weak.

Bolan raised the Beretta for one last shot. As he sighted, the terrorist arched over backward and disappeared. The splash reached the warrior's ears as he surged upright. Running to the spot, he looked down at the floating form of Garth Hunter.

There was no time to spare. Bolan replaced the clip in the Beretta and sprinted toward the boathouse. It bothered him that Creed hadn't appeared, that the lights in the boathouse were still out, that the door still hung open. It meant Creed and the woman weren't there. And if they weren't, neither was the submersible.

The warrior went in hard and low, kicking the door out of his way and vaulting inside with both pistols out and cocked. His eyes were accustomed enough to the dark to verify his suspicion. He noticed a pale rectangle beside the door and flicked on the light switch. The emptiness mocked him, showing that once again Creed had given him the slip.

Bolan moved to the far end of the boathouse. There was no evidence the bathyscaphe had been there, but logic told him it had to have been. And if so, if Creed had just fled, he had a chance of overtaking it. A slim chance, maybe, but not one he could ignore.

In swift order, Bolan raced to the black sedan, rummaged in Dean's pockets for the keys, unlocked the trunk and removed two tanks, a set of fins and the other gear he would need. He lugged them to the next dock, to a ten-foot outboard fitted with a large motor. Placing the equipment in the cramped cockpit, he tried to turn the motor over by pressing the starter button. But without the key needed to engage the starter, it was a lost cause.

Bolan reached under the cowling, pulled out several thin cables, then drew the knife strapped to his ankle.

Slicing through the plastic sheaths to expose the three wires in each cable, he experimented, touching them together, mixing and matching at random, not knowing which were the ground wires, which the neutral and which the hot wires.

Through trial and error, Bolan hit on the right combination. The one-hundred-horsepower outboard purred to life. He let it idle while he opened the fuel-tank cap and dipped a finger inside. The tank was nearly full.

After casting off the line, Bolan took a seat, gripped the steering arm and put out to sea, revving the motor for all it was worth. The craft was fitted with running lights, which he switched on so larger vessels would be able to see him.

A freezer for storing the catch sat in one corner. Lying on the bottom on the starboard side was an old fishing pole. To the left of the warrior was a bait well. Beside it, mounted on a bracket, was a portable depth sounder used by fishermen to locate schools of fish.

Bolan examined the small black box, then noticed a plastic packet attached to the side of the boat below the unit. In it he found a battered, water-stained instruction manual and a pocket flashlight, which worked.

Even with the aid of the sounder, Bolan realized his quest had the same hope of success as looking for a needle in a massive haystack. The *Bio-Ark* might be anywhere. He assumed Creed would head in the general direction of the Long Beach Naval Shipyard and cruised accordingly.

When Bolan had gone a sufficient distance, he stopped and idled the motor so he could devote himself to the fish finder. Using the flashlight, he skimmed the manual.

A press of the yellow power switch activated the small color screen, which was overlaid with a grid to indicate depth. According to the manual, the device had a depth rating of 240 feet, thanks to a 455-kilohertz high-definition sensor.

By military standards, the unit wasn't very powerful, but it was all Bolan had to work with and he intended to make the most of it.

The warrior hit the select bar and adjusted the device to suit him. Almost immediately fish showed on the monitor, outlined true to form, appearing as blue-green blips. He tilted the sounder so he could watch the screen, worked the clutch lever on the outboard motor and resumed his search.

Bolan checked his wristwatch. He would stay out for three hours, no more. If at the end of that time he hadn't found the bathyscaphe, he'd head in to contact Brognola. It would give the Feds time to deploy aircraft and a Navy submarine or two.

An endless parade of sea life passed under the boat. Big fish, little fish, they swam by singly or in schools. Once the sounder picked up a large creature at a depth of eighty feet. By its outline, Bolan judged it to be a shark, a whopper that would give most swimmers nightmares.

Each time something of any size came within range, the alarm sounded. Bolan adjusted the volume to suit him, never taking his eyes off the screen.

The alarm sounded yet again, and the biggest object so far materialized. The excellent resolution left no doubt as to its identity. Bolan had found the *Bio-Ark,* holding a stationary position at a depth of 210 feet.

Killing the outboard, the warrior turned to the pile of scuba gear. He donned the fins first, then the weight belt. As he strapped on one of the compressed-air tanks, he happened to glance at the depth sounder.

The submersible was rising.

And it was coming straight toward him.

ON BOARD the *Bio-Ark,* Jason Creed had been staring in amazement out the front viewport at the fantastic wealth of marine life caught in the glare of the bathy-scaphe's floodlights, when Constantine nudged his arm and pointed at the sonar.

"What do you make of that, lover?"

A small craft had appeared on the surface. It curved from east to west and back again as if conducting a search, and all the while it drew steadily nearer.

Axel Fagan looked and snorted. "Don't tell me the famous terrorists are afraid of a dinky outboard? It's just a fisherman out trolling."

Creed had never used a sonar unit before, so he couldn't say for certain what the blip represented. He wasn't about to take the director's word for anything, though, so a minute later when the small craft stopped almost directly above the bathyscaphe, he decided to act. "Take the *Bio-Ark* up. I want a closer look."

"You're the boss," Fagan said sarcastically, and angled the submersible up out of the depths.

Like a gigantic sturgeon, the *Bio-Ark* cleaved the water, scattering fish in its path. At Creed's command, Fagan turned off the running lights, plunging the vessel into gloom relieved only by the dim glow of bulbs and dials in the control panel.

Presently the bottom of a boat heaved into sight. "Slow down," Creed snapped, leaning forward. As the director had claimed, it was nothing more than a typical outboard. Yet it had followed the same heading they were on, and it had stopped above the bathyscaphe.

Since Creed wasn't a big believer in coincidence, he growled, "I want to see who is in that thing, but I don't want them to spot the *Ark*. Can you pull back to give us a good look?"

In response, Fagan deftly maneuvered the submersible around in a tight loop that took the *Bio-Ark* fifty feet farther out and brought it to within eight feet of the surface. From there they had a fish-eye view of the entire outboard. It was distorted by the intervening water and the darkness, but they could still see clearly enough to make a puzzling observation.

"There's no one in the boat," Constantine remarked.

"What the hell is going on?" Creed said, his unease growing. First the Feds had nearly foiled his purchase of the mines. Then they had shown up at the boathouse. It seemed as if they knew every move he made, as if he were at the center of a constricting federal net that might close around him at any moment. He couldn't stand the thought of being thwarted when he was so close to achieving the greatest deed of his whole career.

Constantine had stepped forward between the chairs. "Maybe we should get the hell out of here, Jason," she said. "I don't like this one bit."

"That makes two of us." Creed swiveled and stared at the magnetic mines, which had been fitted with radio-controlled detonators. His original plan called for the submersible to lurk outside the shipyard until the aircraft carrier appeared sometime around noon, then to move in close to the hull and attach the mines before anyone was the wiser. The carrier would be moving so slowly, the task would be child's play. But maybe waiting was unwise, he decided. "I believe another change in plans is in order," he announced.

"What now?" Fagan asked.

"Now you sneak us into the shipyard so we can deliver our surprise packages tonight," Creed said.

"Tonight? Are you insane? We have to use the robot arms to attach the mines, and we won't be able to see what we're doing unless we turn on the floods. Someone is bound to spot us and sound the alarm. Then what?"

"You let me worry about the mines. Just move it." Creed glared at his former friend until Fagan obeyed. Smirking, he sat back and stretched. If the Feds thought they could stop him at this stage of the game, they had another think coming.

MACK BOLAN WAITED until the depth sounder revealed the submersible was close off the port side before he slipped over the starboard side and clung to the boat by an arm and a leg. The spare air tank was draped over his right shoulder.

The warrior watched the blip on the screen slow to a crawl. He could guess why. Creed had come up to check him out. The bathyscaphe started to loop around, passing within a dozen feet of the outboard.

Instantly Bolan let go, pushed off and knifed toward the vessel. The extra tank was a burden, but he had no way of knowing how long the *Bio-Ark* would stay under. He might need a lot of air before the night was over.

Kicking and stroking with his free arm, the warrior drew alongside the sub and grabbed at its side, hoping to find purchase. But the hull was as smooth as glass; his grasping hand slipped off. Lunging, he tried again. His fingers closed on a metal rung, part of a ladder leading to the upper hatch. He clung fast, wincing as the tendons and muscles of his shoulder were taxed to their limit.

Thankfully the vessel wasn't moving at its top speed or Bolan would have lost his grip. Pulling himself closer, he looped his other hand under the rung and held his body loose against the hull.

The submersible glided in a circle and coasted to a stop about fifty feet from the outboard. Bolan glanced to stern, his mask taking in a little water. He had another use for the spare tank, given the chance. By ramming it into the propeller, he might cripple the craft and force it to the surface. He started to let go, to swim aft, when the sub suddenly picked up speed.

Clinging tight, Bolan clenched his mouthpiece firmly to keep it from being torn loose. He had no problem guessing their destination—the Long Beach Naval Shipyard lay only three to four miles northwest of their current position.

The *Bio-Ark* cut the water as smoothly as a sleek torpedo. Bolan spotted a small port a few feet off and was glad no one bothered to look outside. Every thirty seconds or so he checked the depth gauge strapped to his wrist. If the submersible dived deep, he would be in trouble, but for the longest time it held steady at a mere ten feet.

Bolan's arms ached terribly by the time bright lights flared off the port bow. It was the shipyard, bustling with activity. He wondered why until he remembered reading an article in the newspaper about the USS *Liberty*. Sailors and shore personnel were preparing for its impending departure.

Suddenly Bolan knew which ship Creed planned to strike. He felt the sub slow and relaxed his hands to relieve some of the pain in his knuckles. Without warning, the bathyscaphe dived at a steep angle and he nearly lost hold.

The luminous dial of the depth gauge let Bolan know when they passed the fifty-foot mark, then the hundred-foot level. The water darkened, the temperature fell. Bolan wished he had a wet suit. All he could do was hold on and hope they leveled off soon.

They did. At 120 feet the *Bio-Ark* pulled out of the dive and veered into the heart of the shipyard, passing a destroyer, a cruiser and a submarine.

An immense surface craft loomed above them, blotting out most of the shore lights. There could be no question it was the nuclear-powered carrier, since no other vessel in the U.S. fleet was so enormous. The *Liberty* even dwarfed Iowa-class battleships.

Creed was clever. He had the submersible brought in close to the carrier's keel on the seaward side, which was shrouded in shadow and not visible from the shore.

Bolan braced his knees against the hull to ease the drag on his arms as the bathyscaphe crawled upward, rising as might a balloon, blowing ballast in short spurts to reduce the noise and the surface disturbance.

With scarcely a ripple, the control chamber reared out of the water. Bolan promptly climbed, his arms and legs half-numb from his frigid ordeal. The spare tank slipped and would have banged against the hull had he not caught it in time. Hiking the strap higher on his shoulder, he ascended the rungs one by one, having to go slow on account of his fins, which made his footing treacherous.

The warrior's head broke through. He spit out the mouthpiece and gratefully gulped in fresh air. Then he fell silent as the upper hatch creaked open. Someone whispered, but he couldn't catch the words. An exceptionally tall man armed with a pistol rose up onto the deck.

At long last Bolan set eyes on Jason Creed. He saw the terrorist stoop, heard him speak softly.

"Hand up the first mine. And don't try any tricks, Axel. You'll die if you do."

Bolan proceeded with caution. He wanted to spare Fagan from harm, if at all possible. Raising his right leg, he reached down and slipped off the flipper so he could climb unhindered. He did the same with the other fin. Holding them in his left hand, he slowly rose onto the next rung.

Creed had wedged the pistol under his belt and leaned down to grab the mine being passed up. He set it on the deck, then bent to get a second one.

Taking advantage, the warrior scaled three more rungs. He was so close to the deck that he could reach up and touch it. Creed reappeared, however, so Bolan pressed his chest against the hull, waiting for just the right moment.

The eco-terrorist turned to the carrier and stood gazing up at the flight deck.

Bolan saw his chance. Rising up and over the side, he put down the fins and the spare tank and stalked toward his prey, his naked feet making no sound on the steel surface. The Beretta had been jostled during the underwater journey but hadn't fallen out. He wrapped his palm around the butt.

"I wouldn't, if I were you!"

The voice was a woman's but as icy as a glacier. Julie Constantine's head and shoulders were framed in the hatch. She held a pistol, pointed at the warrior.

Jason Creed whirled, drawing his own weapon. He recoiled in shock, then grated, "Who the hell are you? Where did you come from?"

Bolan made no comment. He was going to take them both down, even if it cost him his own life in the bargain. Glancing from one to the other, it occurred to him that they wouldn't shoot unless they absolutely had to. Shots would draw attention, the last thing they wanted.

The woman climbed higher, exposing her chest. "He was about to draw on you, lover."

The founder of Green Rage halted, his features twisted in baffled confusion and rage. He extended the 9 mm pistol while giving Bolan the once-over. "You're him, aren't you? The one who has been dogging us every step of the way. The one Hunter told us about."

Bolan remained silent. He could tell Creed had a short fuse, so he was ready when the man suddenly took another stride and made a move to smash the pistol against the Executioner's skull. With that last step, Creed had blundered between the woman and the warrior.

As the terrorist swung, Bolan ducked, drew the Beretta and planted a slug in the taller man's shoulder. Creed dropped like a rock, giving Julie Constantine a clear shot. She fired twice, but she was too slow. Bolan had thrown himself onto the deck. He took aim and drilled her cranium from front to back. Her arms flew into the air, her pistol fell and she plummeted down the hatch.

Bolan's attention shifted to Jason Creed, who was scrambling madly toward the far side of the submersible. He fired just as Creed slipped from sight, then he heard a splash.

The warrior began to give chase, darting to the hatch. Lying in a twisted heap at the bottom was the woman. A terrified man stood beside her. "Axel Fagan?"

The director nodded, then said, "I'm saved! Oh, thank God!"

"Take the submersible in. Explain the situation. Tell them I'm going after Creed."

Fagan gasped and gripped the ladder for support. "He's still alive?"

"Yeah. But I'll find him."

Three bounds brought Bolan to the front of the vessel. His nemesis was swimming strongly, making for shore. He jammed the pistol under his shoulder, placed his legs close together, sucked in a breath and dived. The water tingled his skin. He crested smoothly and stroked in somber pursuit, guided by the pale blond thatch of Creed's bleached hair.

Bolan was a good swimmer, but he was handicapped by fatigue. Clinging to the *Bio-Ark* for so long had sapped his strength. He gritted his teeth and pushed on, unwilling to give up. It wasn't in his nature.

Several hundred yards from the carrier was a ship under construction. Based on its size, it had to be a minesweeper or a destroyer. The keel had been laid, the hull built and parts of the superstructure added. The berth was only one of two or three showing no activity at all, with no lights anywhere. So Jason Creed headed right for it.

A cramp speared the warrior's right leg, but he forged on, spurred by the thought of how many more innocents would be sacrificed on Creed's holy green altar if the fanatic got away. He wasn't able to close the gap but he didn't fall behind, either.

Creed reached shore and staggered out of the water, a hand pressed to his wounded shoulder. He glanced back, then lumbered into the shadows.

Forty seconds later Bolan hauled himself out of the ocean and sought cover behind a heavy crane used in the construction of the ship. More large equipment lined the berth on both sides, and somewhere among it was the terrorist.

The warrior didn't know if Creed still had a gun, but he acted on the assumption the man did. Drawing the Beretta, he crept around the crane and paused under the gantry. Twenty feet off, a wide gangplank linked the berth to the superstructure. He would have liked to rest, to catch his breath, but the stakes were too high. Sprinting to the gangplank, he dropped to his knees underneath it and scanned the vicinity.

All was quiet, other than the lapping of the waves. Bolan could have heard a pin drop. That he heard nothing proved nothing. Creed was out there. The challenge was to find him.

The Executioner rose and started to skirt the gangplank. He drew up short on seeing a string of fresh prints left by soaked shoes, leading up into the ship. Keeping low, Bolan paralleled the tracks, squatting at the top.

Creed had crossed the main deck, which was only partially completed, to the bridge, which was even less so. Like a mountain lion brought to bay, he was going for the highest spot he could find and luring Bolan after him so he could pick him off when the warrior least expected it.

Bolan sprinted to the right and dropped behind a half-completed gun mount. From there he crept to a row of crates. A short ladder gave him the means of gaining the next deck, but he delayed, studying every square foot of the bridge, the mack tower, and the mast.

Expecting a shot to ring out at any moment, Bolan left cover and raced to the ladder. He climbed swiftly, jumped to one side and went prone, ready to shoot any target that presented itself. But none did.

The wind moaned through the steel spiderweb above him. Over at the aircraft carrier, someone bellowed through a bullhorn.

Bolan warily stepped to the mack and worked his way around it. The signal bridge rose in front of him, and beyond that were the bridge and the flying bridge, all in a state of construction, heavy equipment everywhere. He walked onto the signal bridge, alert for sounds, checking the deck for footprints. Rounding a welder, he spotted them, pointing his way toward the bow.

Holding the Beretta at shoulder height, Bolan stepped onto the bridge and abruptly stopped. Sections hadn't yet been laid down, which left a gaping hole criss-crossed by beams. The tracks led onto one of the girders. Evidently Creed had crossed onto the flying bridge and hidden there.

The Executioner had the man dead to rights, but he hesitated. He didn't like the idea of crossing that beam. He'd be too vulnerable, exposed, helpless if Creed was waiting on the other side to blow him away. He looked in vain for another way across.

Turning sideways, Bolan edged out onto the beam. His toes and an inch of heel hung over the edge. Sliding his lead foot forward, he placed the other behind it. In this manner he eased across the gaping dark maw. He couldn't see the bottom, which he guessed to be thirty or forty feet below.

Just then the wind gusted, blowing hard enough to make him sway. He steadied himself by bending at the knees. When the wind died, he inched onward. The girder was only twenty feet long, yet it seemed as if he took an eternity to draw within a few steps of the far side.

A metal housing for radar flanked the hole. Bolan glanced at it, then glanced down at the beam. He almost missed the rush of movement as the founder of Green Rage leapt from behind the housing with a long length of pipe raised on high.

"Bastard!"

The warrior leveled the Beretta, but at the instant he squeezed the trigger the pipe smashed into his wrist, deflecting the shot and knocking the 9 mm pistol from his hand. It tumbled into the black hole. He saw Creed draw back the pipe to swing again and quickly slid backward out of range. Almost too quickly. He came close to following his pistol and had to flail his arms to keep his balance.

Creed smiled triumphantly and straightened. "Well, what do you know. The mighty Fed is helpless." He stepped to the edge of the beam. "All I have to do is knock you off and you're history, pal."

Bolan didn't need the obvious pointed out to him. He held himself as still as a statue, awaiting the fanatic's next move. Something told him Creed would be a talker, and he was right.

"How does it feel to have the tables turned, fascist pig?" the eco-terrorist ranted. "What will your superiors say when they find out you blew it? You're the best they've sent against me so far, yet look at you now." He smacked the pipe against his hand. "Do you know what I'm going to do?"

"Bore me to death?" Bolan suggested, taking a calculated gamble. He wanted the man to come after him, and he got his wish.

Hissing like a viper, Creed put one foot on the beam, leaned out and swung with all his strength.

The pipe swished above Bolan's head as he ducked. In a blur, he lunged and caught hold of the end. He was nearly torn from his perch but he managed to keep his footing, twisted and yanked.

Taken unawares, Creed was pulled off-balance and stumbled forward. He would have fallen into the hole had he not hopped onto the span and then stood grasping one end of the pipe while the warrior held the other. "I'll finish you!" he growled, and shoved.

Bolan had figured he would. Snapping his body to the right, he tore the pipe loose from the other man's hold, reversed his grip and drove it around and in.

Creed's knee shattered with a loud crack. He cried out and fell onto his good knee, his hands gripping the girder. Sputtering and trembling, he glanced up, the veins in his temples bulging. "You miserable son of a bitch!"

The warrior slammed the makeshift staff on top of the terrorist's left hand. Creed howled like a wolf in torment.

The warrior struck a second time, driving the tip of the pipe into the terrorist's right hand.

Creed roared and held both shattered hands to his chest. His knee was all that kept him from pitching from his precarious perch. Quaking, beaded with sweat, he stared blankly at the warrior as Bolan drew the Desert Eagle. "You had a gun all along? Then why—" The leader of Green Rage moved forward abruptly, intending to take Bolan with him in a suicide play.

"You figure it out," the Executioner growled as he snapped up the muzzle and fired a round into the terrorist's brain. Creed flew backward, into oblivion.

Mack Bolan carefully made his way back to solid ground, thankful that Jason Creed's madness had been stopped in time. A battle had been won, but the war against the predators would rage on.